# Selling the Lite of Heaven

# Selling the Life of Heaven

◆◆◆

Suzanne Strempek Shea

POCKET BOOKS
New York London Toronto Sydney Tokyo Singapore

POCKET BOOKS, a division of Simon & Schuster Inc.
1230 Avenue of the Americas, New York, NY 10020



Library of Congress Cataloging-in-Publication Data

Shea, Suzanne Strempek.
Selling the lite of heaven / Suzanne Strempek Shea.
p. cm.
ISBN: 0-671-79864-2 (hardcover)
I. Title.
PS3569.H39126S4 1994
813'.54—dc20 93-49359
CIP

First Pocket Books hardcover printing July 1994

10 9 8 7 6 5 4 3 2 1



Printed in the U.S.A.

In loving and thankful memory of my dear father,
Edward Frank Strempek,
the angel beside me.

# Acknowledgments

This story is seeing lite of day because my dear husband, Tommy Shea, bragged about me to the author Elinor Lipman, who was kind enough to read this stranger's overgrown short story and become its full-time fairy godmother. I thank them both from the bottom of my heart for helping this dream come true.

Through Ellie I have come to know and work with four special people to whom I am indebted: my agent, Ann Rittenberg; Mary Anne Sacco, formerly of Pocket Books; my editor Jane Rosenman; and her associate, Donna Ng, who rooted for the book from its earliest stages and have been unfailingly warm and helpful.

I also am appreciative of the encouragement from friends and relatives, and of the intercession of Saint Jude.

Finally, I am ever grateful to my mother, Julia (Milewski) Strempek, who placed in every room pencils and crayons and paper, and in my heart the need to create. I cannot thank her enough for starting me on this wonderful ride.

# Selling the Life of Heaven

EVEN THOUGH WHEN HE TOLD ME I WRENCHED IT OFF MY FINGER and pitched it at him so hard it stuck with a *thock* right into the cloth of his green down vest, he still said I should keep the ring.

"I want you to have it—it's yours," he mumbled hollowly, looking at me, then away, as he picked the thing from the vest very carefully, like it was a shard of glass in a wound.

I remember seeing some small pieces of feathers escape from the slit the point of the pear-shaped stone had made in the fabric. One bit of fluff stuck beneath a prong in the setting, and he extracted it quickly and rolled it between his fingers, then gently placed the ring on a stack of magazines on the coffee table.

Saying he would pray for me, he opened the front door and that was it.

I can say I was stunned, I can say I felt darkly empty. But I cannot say that I mourned—at least not just then. There was too much to do.

Because, my mother said, of what people might think, dozens of rules of etiquette would keep me busy for the next few months, right up to and through the day I was to have switched the engagement ring to my right hand during the ceremony, to allow my wedding band to take its rightful and permanent place on the base of the fourth finger of my left hand.

Because, my mother said, there was a chance she could get some of her deposits back if I acted quickly enough, there were telephone calls to make: to the hall and to the caterer and to the band and to the travel agent, plans canceled and refunds politely granted without so much as a cluck of sympathy from the clerks and secretaries and representatives at the other end of the line—like this sort of nightmare was something they dealt with every day.

Because, my mother said, people had to be told, there were telephone calls to make and expressions of shock and grief to hear from uncles and aunts and cousins who had just arrived at the point where they actually believed someone would want to marry me, and had gone beyond that even to spend good money on new shoes to wear to the event.

Because, my mother said, now none of them were mine even though they had been given to me, there were gifts to return, and weeks to spend repacking and sending back what seemed like a hundred boxes. There must have been that many, because there were about that many ladies at my shower that day in the banquet room of Saint Casimir's Hall, where I sat beneath a painting of a smiling Pope John Paul II and tore open the packages that held the vital ingredients of my new life.

With each serving spoon and dish towel and toaster tong I saw it materializing in the same detailed clarity and lush Technicolor in which I dream each night, and in the same posed perfection I had found on each and every one of the 802 pages of *Today's Bride;* I not only had bought the telephone book-size February-March issue but also eagerly had bought into its every vision of the perfect marriage: each page of laughing, intense, communicating couples was one more tiny reinforcement of my suspicion and hope that, despite the silent and bland marriage I witnessed daily in my own home, love could be a joyous and living thing.

And these, emerging from their layers of tissue paper and nests of foam pieces, would be the finishing touches: a sterling candle extinguisher, so we would not spray wax onto our new cut-work linens when we blew out our color-coordinated candles; sets of matching cornflower-patterned Corning Ware, for those make-ahead dinners to be frozen for the days I would be late coming home from work; a bedside clock set into a square of crystal, to wake us on those many mornings we would oversleep after nights of passion that would start out with us wearing that matching pajama set—scarlet silk-look top for me, scarlet silk-look boxer shorts for him—the only thing in the haul that was remotely racy, but hot enough to make my mother redden and turn away in her seat at the head table and reach for the balled-up Kleenex that is always somewhere up her left sleeve.

There were accessories for the bathroom: shell-shaped white porcelain soap dishes and toothbrush holders, and a catchall for hairpins. There were glass vases to hold the flowers that would grow in our backyard garden. Heavy ceramic nested mixing bowls for the peanut butter cookies he would beg me to make. Rolls of film and a photo album for our honeymoon photographs. Trays and platters and sets of towels. And a picnic basket stocked with two plates, two sets of silverware, two white linen napkins, two fluted glasses, and a split of asti spumante. We would eat from that basket every night, I had imagined, dipping strawberries into cream, lounging on a blanket on the top of some hill, maybe in our matching pajamas, watching the sun set on one perfect day after another.

But there would be none of that now.

I was a woman who had been left for God.

I'M CALLING ABOUT THE RING," HE SAID. "IS IT A GOOD ONE?"

Though I was not the one who had purchased it, I felt kind of insulted. But I tried to be polite: "Well, yes, it is. It's a 2.75 karat stone. All fourteen-karat gold—two colors: yellow and rose."

"It's not one of those fake ones, is it?"

"No. If you'd care to see it, we could meet."

Even as I spoke those words I realized I was making a mistake. I didn't want to talk to this person, much less meet him face-to-face.

But it was too late. I had said it, and he was saying back to me "OK, where do you live?"

My mother did not like one bit the idea of a strange man, who, she pointed out, possibly could be a murderer, coming to our house, where we lived, to see a ring that he would know was stored right there in that house when it was not being shown off to potential buyers.

She said I should tell the people who answered the advertisement that I would have it at my house just for our meeting, and that after they left I would be returning it to a safe-deposit box at the bank. Even if it was nighttime, I was supposed to say that. I was to point out that I had made arrangements with the bank president to bring it back there after-hours. Better yet, she suggested, just meet him at Friendly's.

But I was not interested in bringing the ring to a neutral place, where there would be people I knew, eating their Jim Dandies and Big Beefs while watching me, making a buck from my misery, looking, I imagined, so pathetic and at the edge. Anyhow, at this point in all this, I figured how bad would it be to be killed in my own home by a murderer posing as somebody's idea of Mr. Right?

I told the caller to come on over, and hung up shaking. I was nervous not so much because I was meeting my first prospective customer, but because I was doing this, the last act in a string of bizarre scenes I had starred in since the prospect of a new life for me screeched to a halt. And this was, I was beginning to realize, the most daring one.

While gifts could be returned to senders by setting the boxes on their back steps when I knew they were at work, and while the reservation for that long white cloth you can rent to roll down the church aisle on your wedding day could be canceled over the telephone, selling the engagement ring would have to be done in a face-to-face manner. In person. And so, the living room was vacuumed, some refreshments were set out, and the velvet box was placed on the stack of magazines, in just about the same spot the ring had been deposited that afternoon.

I had made an effort to look halfway decent for the meeting. I wasn't sure how I was going to answer the question of why was I selling the ring, and didn't want this person to take one look at me and, from the unremarkable looks of me, figure out why: It would have been bad enough to tell people I had been left at the altar, but I would have to say I had been left for it—if I chose to say anything at all.

I tried to tame my hair before just getting it out of the way with the tight fake tortoiseshell headband that, if I leave it on for a while, makes me dizzy and gets me pale and sick-looking enough to be excused from whatever it is I've put the thing on to get out of. Despite thirty-two years of baking it in the sun every summer, the hair never has gotten brighter than my mother's color—ash, a great and fittingly devastated name for a color of hair—but it is my father's hair: wavy and thick, something you could use to restrain an animal. It is this way because, he has told me, as a young man he spent hours standing beneath Chicopee Falls, letting all the millions of gallons of water and nutrients wash over him, headfirst. "It won't last," my mother laughs when she sees me struggling to detangle after a shampoo. "Soon you will be like this," she adds, then comes at me, head down, fingers digging into the crown of her head, where so many strands have fallen out that a goldfish-shaped patch has to be rubbed with SPF 15 even when she wears a hat. If during all this my father is in the background, where he usually is during anything, he'll just smile at me from beneath his still-thriving Conway Twitty flip, his hazel eyes meeting the set that matches his, and he'll shake his head to say never—not in a million years.

I applied the lipstick I'd never worn before Eddie came along, and touched two dots of it to the spaces that would be beneath my cheekbones, if I had any. I stuck my one pair of small sterling hoops through the holes I got punched into my earlobes at Marlena's Beauty Castle the day after Eddie told me I looked striking (that was exactly the word) when I wore a little jewelry. I pulled on the squirrel-and-acorn-patterned cardigan I'd knitted way in advance to present to his mother for the birthday I'd never made it to as her daughter-in-law, and I was ready.

Over the phone, the guy had told me his name was Dick—though he really was a Richard—and that I could call him that. So "Hi, Dick," I said when I pulled open the door and unlatched the storm.

He extended his hand for a shake. It was meaty and big, kind of like the rest of him. His was a Humpty-Dumpty kind of body that Hula Hooped out at the beltline, then angled in both above and below. He was dressed in pressed jeans and an ample white oxford shirt, over which he wore a black quilted fake-fleece-lined vest and a huge navy denim jacket. His fingers frequently pushed back his dark hair, which was either freshly washed and still wet, or had been greased this morning for the day's wear.

"Just got out of the gym—hair's still wet," he told me, answering that one.

"Figured I'd start getting ready for the big day now. Dropped three pounds already. By the time we get married, she won't recognize me."

"When is that—the wedding?" I motioned for Dick to take a seat on the couch.

"A year from now—sometime in ninety-five, we're hoping, but we're not sure," he said as he eased back into the cushions. "We have to wait until her mother croaks, so we can just move right in and gut the whole house and fix it up the way we want to. No sense moving in twice. I'm in wallpaper, so we're going to be able to fix it up pretty cheap."

Dick pushed back the hair again, then rummaged in his vest pocket. He produced a business card with his name—Richard Wilkins—and his place of business, Nu Design.

Striding across the top of the lines stating the address and phone number was a drawing of a man wearing overalls and carrying an armload of wallpaper rolls. His pockets were jammed with brushes, rollers, and rulers, and one arm was looped through the handle of a glue bucket.

"Just had them made up. Nice, ha?"

I looked at the card and watched the little man wait for the little hearse to pull away from the little house. He wasted no time putting a little steamer to the little faded cabbage rose print in the little front hall.

"Is she supposed to die, or are you just, hoping?"

"Oh, no, no, no," Dick set me straight, his face falling serious. "She's bad off. Some kind of blood thing. She'll be lucky if she sees Christmas."

"I'm sorry," I said honestly. Dick stared at something on the toe of his big black work shoe and then looked up at me and shrugged. "It's OK. I'm not sure she likes me anyway. So it'll be less of a problem. Where's the ring?"

He worked into his front pants pocket and unfolded a copy of the ad, the one I had placed in last week's *Penny Saver*.

"It's time, Ma, I want to get rid of it," I said one night last week, almost six months since Eddie had left. It had taken me just about all that time to unarrange all the arrangements and details except that one, the one that sat on my bookshelf in what once seemed a holy vessel of a box, something that now was more like a kind of a fuzzy maroon coffin that needed to be interred.

My mother, however, thought I should keep the ring. She said it was a fine piece of jewelry that really should hold no meaning for me now. She knew well that no one before Eddie had wanted to marry me, and felt certain that no one would want to again. Always a shy, unquestioning daughter who did what she was told, I had followed my mother's order to stay away from boys until I was eighteen. Actually, her exact words on the day I turned twelve—about two seconds after my Cioci Julia had hugged me, given me a pearl strung on a silver chain because she always said I was the pearl of her life, and told my mother she'd soon have to put up a fence to keep the boys away from such a beautiful young woman—were "God knows there are no decent people left in this world and not that anybody would want you, but if you dare go near a boy before you're eighteen, you'll be out on the street so fast it'll make your head spin."

Though he wasn't sure of the exact wording, my father later confided that the same instruction had been given my mother by another mother in another place and time, an edict he said was tradition in her own hometown far away in the middle of Poland somewhere. In my hometown right here, however, it put me in the category of social oddity—especially when, in a moment of false sisterhood created during my best friend Anna Jarosz's thirteenth birthday party by a round of I'd Never Tell Anyone Else, I was moved to tell my secret by the trust of Diane Pikol, who had just shared the amount she spied listed in her father's bankbook, and Louise Sliski, who told how someone who says he is a Gallup Poll researcher regularly telephones and asks the size of her mother's brassieres—and how she each time without delay or question runs to the dresser then back to the line to relay the information.

Anna was still squinting in an effort to come up with something no one else knew about her when I rose and said, "I'd Never Tell Anyone Else that I'm not allowed to date until I'm eighteen."

But somebody ended up telling somebody else, and in a world very different from that in which my mother grew up, the wait labeled me. I sought solace in Anna, who needed only her meek nature to ban her from occasions that included boys. Together we rode our bicycles and went for ice cream and watched the Movie of the Week. Who needs a date, she would ask me when we'd see boys and girls doing those things together. I'd smile in agreement when she looked at me for my answer.

Though she had brought it upon me, my lack of male companions eventually caused my mother great concern once I did turn eighteen and just about the only person I continued to go out with was Anna. My mother feared for my future, that I might forever live by myself in our house after she and my father passed away. "How can I die knowing you will always be alone?" she would ask me. I never could think of an answer.

I jokingly asked Anna for one the night she turned twenty-one, which she chose to celebrate by getting a pizza and watching the Miss USA pageant. "You're an adult now," I pointed out with reverence, "what's your advice?"

"Tell her something like that will keep her alive. She might even break some kind of age record," Anna replied crisply. Because the comment was so unlike her, I turned from the parade of states to make sure it was really she who was sitting there, as she had been for every televised pageant that I could recall. In my fascination, I missed seeing a good portion of the representatives from the southwestern states, though I knew Miss Arizona probably once again had been dressed like a phoenix.

"She should just leave you alone—you go out once in a while, don't you?" Anna added this with an edge in her voice, with her eyes focused on the TV screen, on Miss New Mexico, who wore a huge mountain over her head and torso and whose nervously smiling face appeared in a space carved out to look like the entrance to the home of cliff dwellers. The show being televised from Santa Fe, the crowd went nuts as the geological formation wobbled across the stage.

I'd been trying to lift her spirits by seeking her advice, but Anna, busy consuming half a double cheese with green peppers and onions, and her share of a two-pound bag of peanut M&M's, only got reminded that I was her date. Not Dave from maintenance or Eugene from radiology or Dr. Young or any of the other people who could repair her air-conditioning unit and take pictures of her gallbladder and go probing around in her brain but who apparently couldn't read her mind.

Maybe she got jealous once in a while, but Anna really

cared about me. She cried the night I phoned and told her I was going to finally sell the ring, the night I flipped to the classifieds of the weekly paper, the night something told me that was the place people like me went, and the night I found plenty of myself in there.

I guess I could have gone to a store and sold it, but one look at Jewelry and Gems, also known as category number 509, and I felt it my destiny. There were far more of the cast aside than I would have guessed—hearts broken in ad after ad, little maroon box after little maroon box left on coffee table after coffee table, girl after girl seeing the room spin around her as each tried to take in what had just happened to her life while well-meaning mother after well-meaning mother wrung her hands and decided it must have been something you said.

The first one read: PURPLE PASSION—2K amethyst heart-shaped pendant surrounded by 1½K diamonds. Was $4,500, will take $1,500. Also, gold shrimp ring to match, size 6, $450 firm. Beautiful. Call today.

BELLS ARE RINGING. Bridal set. Half K diamond ring size 5 w/ 4 .25 pt. diamonds. 14K gold band. Paid $2,800. Now $1,100. Have receipts.

SHE'LL SAY YES when you take your pick from my collection: Small ruby engagement ring with diamond accents, $75, size 7. Dbl marquis simulated emerald ring, $100, size 7. 14K gold earrings, opal dinner ring, more. Call anytime.

ON YOUR HAND, 14K BAND with pave diamond accents. Make an offer.

The leftovers continued to be served in the following column, Wedding Apparel, category number 510, where somebody was trying to rid herself of this year's edition of the Eve of Romance dress in size eight, which supposedly had retailed for $649 but was selling there "for only $150." There were matching shoes, size seven, and a handbag, both for $85. "All new never worn. Have receipts." There were numbers for both day and night.

It was some sort of sick consolation that maybe I was not the only one to whom something like this had happened. Bolstered by the courage of the former wearer of the small ruby engagement ring, and the one who was in effect telling the world that she never got to have her Eve of Romance, I took out a sheet of looseleaf and wrote down my own sad details.

I sat at the desk in my room, the box open for inspiration, though I did not need any to write a fitting description. Even under my small lamp, the stone seemed to glow magically. I took the thing from its box and examined it closely, but I did not make myself put it on. I placed it to the side and picked up the pen.

Not interested in echoing the style of the other ads, in which bold capital letters were meant to catch your eye, I simply wrote "Engagement ring, 14K yellow and rose gold, Tiffany setting, 2.5K pear-shaped perfect diamond, .75K diamonds on each side, size 8." That said it all, including the K numbers a drooling jewelry collector who happened to come into my shop one day hadn't hesitated to calculate for me. All that was missing was the price. Working without a receipt wasn't easy, and I couldn't go back to the store, because I never knew where he got the ring. There was no name inside the box lid, and Eddie had never mentioned shopping. I only know that when he first slid it onto my finger, the ring fit like it had been there forever, and would stay on for at least that long. I had taken that as an omen.

"$5,000," I scratched into the paper. I glared at the ring, and added "Firm."

I counted out the words and read the fine print rules. For $8.25, this could become one of the *Penny Saver*'s guaranteed classifieds, running until the ring sold or the paper went out of business. I dropped the description and the check in the mailbox the next morning.

The following Thursday, the ad appeared and I tore into

the last section to see what place I had among the other sorry stories. I saw nothing that looked familiar. Then I spotted it—with a title:

"THE LITE OF HEAVEN isn't as brite as this engagement ring . . ."

The rest of the copy was intact, right up to what now hit me as was a shocking amount of money to ask for something I actually owned. I checked it again. Except for *lite* and *brite,* it was acceptable. And, somehow, it stood out among the others, with their introductions of ONE OF A KIND and YOU'RE NOT DREAMING. Maybe because it wasn't an exaggeration.

I imagined the classified ad clerk, a frustrated former reporter who had begun her career on the obituary desk, but who never got past that point because of the one incident in which the newspaper had been sued because, in the interest of sensationalism, she had inserted the word *suicide* into the obituary of someone who had not taken his own life. Demoted to the classifieds, she vented her creativity there by adding six or seven free words to the beginning of otherwise unimaginative advertisements. Like mine.

I also imagined that even in the mind's eye of a stranger, this ring was shining rays of its odd light, and that she could pick that up even from unfolding a piece of looseleaf that once had shared the same table with the stone.

Whatever the reason, the ad already had attracted one potential buyer. And now Dick Wilkins, future homeowner and leader of a deathwatch squad, was planted on my couch, gripping a roughly ripped-out copy of my ad, waiting to see the ring.

I suddenly wanted to say that I had lost it, or that it had been sold, or that he had the wrong house. I did not want my ring to become part of Dick Wilkins's life. I imagined his fiancée at the office, her left hand arched into the faces of co-workers, wearing the stone like a validation, saying how the date would be set "pretty soon," maybe winking after that, because everyone in the office knew the domino lineup that would bring her to the altar.

But it was too late to say anything: Dick had spotted the box, set on a neatly fanned display of last month's issues of *People,* and he snapped it up eagerly. "This must be it. Let's see!"

He clicked the lid and there it was, sure enough.

"Weh-hell," Dick singsonged. "It's a beauty all right. How much'd he pay for it?"

I began to get that feeling you do when something tells you to run. I even think one of my ankles jerked forward. Dick was not the one I wanted to start this with. I wanted a customer who would be kind, who would be considerate, who would know how hard this was for me. Someone, well, like Eddie. But because Eddie already had been a customer, somewhere, here I was, doing this. Thinking about him probably chanting and lighting candles right at the same time I was sitting across from Dick Wilkins, I got a little mad. The anger surprised me—my mother's post-Eddie worklist of canceling and returning and apologizing had left me little time to think about how I really was feeling about what had happened to my life.

Now some kind of emotion was demanding my time, and it didn't care that I was conducting business right then.

"How much did he pay?" I asked him back, suddenly fuming, knowing that I was locking my jaw forward in the same way my mother does when crossed, and realizing that I had no choice in what those muscles were doing. "Not enough, in my opinion. But on the ring he paid a lot."

Dick looked confused. "You say you want four thousand dollars for it? Well, it's nice, but I don't know. Could you come down a few thou?"

"That's five thousand and I don't think so," I said, jaw still stiff, manner firm, just like the ad said. "Take it or leave it."

Dick had wedged the ring onto the first joint of his bulbous pinky, and he wagged that under the lampshade, as if to more professionally make an assessment of the piece. "It's a lot of money—"

"You're getting a house for free—splurge a little," I broke in. He was really getting on my nerves.

"Hey—that's none of your business," Dick snorted.

"I'm sorry. This isn't easy. But think about it—if you were in a store, you wouldn't be asking for a break."

Dick gave a little chuckle. "Why'd you think I was looking in the paper? You want to unload it, and I'm your man."

"You'll have to leave," I said, scrambling for an excuse to get him out of my house. "Somebody else is on their way to look at it. Soon. I have your card, if I need to call you."

Dick rose from the couch and we both stood there like we didn't know what to do, because I don't think either of us did.

He moved toward the door. "Well give me a call if you change your mind—I like it and I'd take it . . . for a little less," he said, half to me, half to a slightly gaping seam he was examining in the knockoff Laura Ashley with which my mother had covered the living room about ten years ago.

I was shaking when I closed the door after him. My mother's fresh lemon cookies, refreshments meant to seal the deal, were untouched, and the pot of tea stood tepid. Moving aside the shade I watched Dick climb into a van with the smiling little wallpaper waving from the side. I saw him check his hair in the rearview mirror before turning his key.

We met in church. In the vestibule, to be exact. I had been hearing about him for a long time, as my mother had made it her mission to keep telling me that Mrs. Balicki's son was moving back to town. I think she was getting nervous: fourteen years into the date-eligible portion of my life, there were few signs she would be allowed to spend her eternal rest free from tossing and turning over the welfare of a daughter so far headed to the altar only for communion.

I had spared her any false hopes by keeping from her the details of that day two summers ago when she pushed me into giving, in my car and in my shaky Polish, a tour of western Massachusetts to Tczup's thirty-four-year-old nephew, who was visiting from Poland and who, suddenly seeing his permanent ticket here, proposed to me in front of a llama at a petting zoo on the Mohawk Trail.

My first real proposal, however, she knew all about.

It happened when I had just turned fourteen, when

sixteen-year-old Andrew Ligawiec asked to come over one night before Christmas. I thought maybe my parents would say it was OK. They knew his parents from church, plus he attended Confraternity of Christian Doctrine classes, had two sisters who were nuns and two brothers who were priests. How evil could he be?

"What does he want?" my father asked me after I had collected the courage to say Andy wanted to visit.

"I don't know."

Then my mother broke in: "Stashu, it's Zyg and Wanda's boy. I made a pie for his brother's ordination reception. Maybe he's returning the plate. I hope so—it's Pyrex."

My father said "Oh," and went to his room. I took that as permission and was relieved at not having to call Andy and tell him something like sorry, we're moving.

Our house was all decorated for Christmas. The tree lights were on, glowing mutedly through a swath of fiberglass angel hair. The small orange bulb that illuminated the manger scene set on top of the TV was glowing over the empty manger scene into which a tiny Baby Jesus figure would be placed after we returned from midnight mass. The plastic candelabra were plugged in and placed on the front windowsill. Except for the stuffed Uncle-Sam-dressed-as-Santa Claus doll my Cioci Wanda had made for us in commemoration of this Christmas in this, the Bicentennial year, the room looked pretty nice. I hoped I did, too. Then, all of a sudden, I hoped I didn't—if I looked so good that Andy got interested, I would only have to fend him off for four years. It just seemed easier to avoid all that. I stood up and looked in the mirror over the sofa as I pulled the wooden pin from the piece of leather that had been holding my hair back. I checked the result and could hear my mother telling me I looked like a witch, as she had before I reluctantly pulled my hair away from my face after dinner. I was pretty sure no guy would want a witch. I was safe.

The doorbell rang. I yelled that I would get it, and raced, then slowed, to the door. Andy was standing there wearing one of those green air force jackets, with the fake fur around the hood edge. Now I recall him as looking goofy—shaggy black hair, a pointy and crooked nose, a row of top teeth that were crowding into a space long ago vacated by one that had been knocked out. I knew he liked sports—maybe that had happened in a game.

Andy was smiling, and maybe it was the lighting, but he suddenly looked to me a lot more attractive than he actually was in real life. I smiled back. He extended his hand and, like a messenger, offered a small box.

"Please come in," I invited, but I still stood there and looked at what he was holding. It was not a piece of Pyrex.

I hadn't expected a present. As he walked to the couch, I quickly thought about what we might have hanging around—was there some canned ham in the kitchen, an unused guest soap in the bathroom, something I could quickly wrap and give to him in return?

"Nice digs," he said, walking in past me and giving the room the once-over. "So. Where's the Mr. and Mrs.?"

"They're here somewhere," I said. "Sit down."

Andy unzipped his jacket but kept it on. He flopped onto the couch in the same manner that, if I used it, I would get yelled at. "Real nice digs. Real nice. Always wondered what your house would look like."

"Soda?" I asked. Why had he wondered? Our only connection, other than the pie donation, was attending the parish school two grades apart, his giving me a couple of rides home from CCD on two rainy Sundays, and our being among the handful of kids who heeded the priest's request to attend the funeral of one of our own, Stefan Busa, a disheveled loner a couple of years older than us who, for no reason the cops were ever able to figure out, slammed his car into a telephone pole on the same afternoon he would have been receiving his diploma over at the high school—had he ever enrolled.

"No soda, no thanks—trying to cut down," Andy said, putting his hand up as a stop sign.

"So," I began, not knowing what other conversation to make, even though right then my mind was full of my few memories of Stefan Busa, the strongest being the way he could reproduce perfectly—freehand and by heart—the far-out lines and colors of a Peter Max print. "How have you been?"

"Since you saw me at fourth period? Just peachy. Had a test with Dunn. Aced it, I think. At least I aced it if Polly did. She talks a lot, but she knows history—and she writes real big, too."

Andy grinned, one angled tooth shining in the light of the tree. He was proud of cheating. I felt a little sick. I didn't want him in my house for a visit. I didn't like this at all.

"Well," he said, the tooth glinting again, "don't you want your present?"

"I didn't get you anything," I said quickly. "I didn't know we were doing this."

"What did you think I was coming over for? My health? Come on—it's just a little something. Open it."

Andy motioned to the box, which he had set on the stack of *People*s arranged in a fan shape on the coffee table.

The box from Andy had been wrapped in Christmas paper, brown and gold pinecones on a snowy background, all creased and used before. A shiny yellow ribbon topped the package. Its color clashed with that of the paper.

"Go ahead—take it," he ordered impatiently, though he still appeared very happy to be in my house. I found myself wishing that my father had said something other than "oh."

It was a small block of a box, the size that fits into your palm. I shook it—something hard was loose inside. I slowly ripped open the paper, smiling up at Andy so he could see I looked happy. I felt he needed to see such an expression. All of what was going on seemed to be very important to him.

I opened the lid of the white cardboard box. Then I gasped: "What's this?" It was a sincere gasp—there was no doubt that the fuzzy black box inside the shiny white one contained some kind of jewelry. I had seen containers like this before—not in my own home, but I had seen them given on TV, and I knew.

"Well, go on," instructed Andy. "You'll see."

The small black box had a goldish edge. I grasped it and the thing flipped open. My mouth did the same, but I did not make a sound. It was not so much amazement as it was here I was, fourteen years old, not allowed to date for four more years, getting a ring, and my parents were going to kill me.

"Do you like it?" Andy leaned forward, brown eyes wide, waiting for an answer.

"I can't believe it," I mumbled. Mostly due to the above reasons, but more because the ring was plain ugly. It was gold—or gold tone, at least—and was made up of the word *LOVE*. Inside the fat letter *O* was a diamond, or a diamondish-looking sparkly thing.

I was in a daze, but somewhere coming into my ears was his voice: "Try it on. Go ahead, try it on. I want to see you wear it."

I slid the ring onto my right hand ring finger. It stopped just beyond the first joint. I was saved. It did not fit. Andy punched his knee and called himself such a retard.

"I should have looked at your hand first," he moaned in exasperation. "This was supposed to fit a girl."

"You know," I said, trying to sound pleasant and pleased, "I really don't have a girl's hands. I have my father's hands."

I was saying something that was actually the case. Looking down, I saw my hands transform—and only a slight bit of imagination was necessary—into those of my father. A little more huge and a little more hairy and wearing the *LOVE* ring on the first joint of his ring finger as he held the plank he as about to feed into his table saw.

"Try it on another finger," Andy suggested. He was frazzled, and played with a zipper on one of the many pockets sewn into the sleeve of the coat I had forgotten to offer to take from him. I didn't want him to be mad so I tried the ring on my pinky. With a little forcing at the knuckle, it settled on, though kind of tightly.

He took my hand and yanked it toward the lamp for illumination of his gift. "Not bad, eh?"

In reality, it looked stupid. Like a tiny pinky ring jammed onto a large pinky would. But I just nodded and managed to say, "Nice."

"I want you to wear it all the time," he instructed. And in the same breath, hopping to his feet and hooking the start of his jacket zipper, he added "Gotta go—confession starts in fifteen minutes and I gotta drive the old lady over there."

He was a boy who called his mother his old lady. I felt sick.

Andy took my hand again and pulled me to my feet. I got him to the door as quickly as I could, and, opening it, tried to appear grateful, even though I felt collared and choiceless.

"Thank you," I said, then added what I knew was a wan smile.

For a you're welcome, Andy moved right up to me and shoved his lips onto my face, sort of covering up most of my mouth, sliding across it like it was greased. He pulled away and pushed aside a length of my hair and told me he loved it loose like that. Then he turned and left.

I closed the door slowly, still in shock and a bit disgusted. With the back of my ringless hand, I wiped off half my dampened face. Then I turned. Both my parents were standing in the hall doorway.

"What did he want?" asked my father, apparently still hooked into our last conversation.

"Where's my pie plate?" my mother wanted to know.

I don't know why I didn't just lie. Instead, I approached them happily, like I actually believed they might think this was a good thing that had happened to me, something I knew well would only be the case with parents on a television show. I extended the ringed hand and lifted it in front of their faces.

"*Matka Boska,* Stanislaus! He gave the kid a ring!" cried my mother intoning the mother of God and crossing herself with great speed. She put her hand to the side of her face, like people do when they are totally distraught.

To answer, my father began chewing the inside of his cheek, just as he does in most stressful situations. He said nothing, only looked at me and shook his head from side to side.

"Who gives a fourteen-year-old a ring?" my mother asked in a sarcastic tone. "What? Are you engaged?"

I wanted to cry, and I began to.

"It's just a ring," I sobbed so hard I could only get a few words out at a time. "It was a present. It . . . it doesn't mean anything. Really. Did you want me to, to hurt his feelings and give it back?"

My mother's eyes were steel. "Rings do not mean anything," she said, grabbing my hand and dragging me over to the lamp for a better look. "*LOVE*. Oh, that's so sweet. Very nice for a fourteen-year-old. *LOVE*."

My father turned to leave, looking at me in confusion just before he disappeared into the hallway. My mother took over the situation as he knew she would. "You have to give it back," she told me. "We'll go right now, before he gets the wrong idea. Taking a ring from a boy! Hurt his feelings? More than that needs hurting. What—do you want to get married, are you in such a rush to get out of here?"

I wasn't even sure if I ever wanted to look at Andy Ligawiec again, with his sloppy clothes and mannerisms and a first kiss that had left me feeling like I needed to be disinfected. I just wanted to wash my hair, to be by myself, without my mother or the stupid ring.

"It's just a present. I don't know, he must like me. What's wrong with that?"

I must have said that rather loudly, because my mother said, "Don't you yell at me—I never yelled at my mother!" She squinted and shook her finger in my direction, quickly, like she was trying to get something off the end of it. "Get your coat. We're going to his house."

"He's not there," I shot. "He's going to confession with his mother."

I thought maybe she'd think what a nice thing that was of him to do, that maybe this kid wasn't so bad, going to church, at night, when it wasn't even Sunday. Taking his mother, who probably never ever did one bad thing, to a special confession that would get her soul all clean and ready for Christmas morning.

But my mother was unimpressed. She just said, "Then we'll go there."

My father would remain at home, and out of this, flat on his back on his bed, a Bruins game on the television the only light in the room. I passed his doorway on the way to get my sweater, but he didn't look up.

In the living room, I scooped the boxes off the couch and tried to pull the ring from my finger. After I wrestled with it for a while, it popped off and rolled onto the carpet. I sat on the floor and tucked the thing back into its black velvet box after checking to see that the word hadn't been inserted upside down. Then I placed the container into its white carton.

The ride to church was a quiet one. From crying, I was

occasionally sniffling, the kind that makes you catch your breath by sucking it in with sounds that you don't really want other people to hear you making. I couldn't tell what my mother was or wasn't hearing. She just was looking straight ahead and the only time she spoke was when we neared the church: "His car here?"

I spotted it near the crosswalk—a faded blue Valiant with two large living room stereo speakers bolted to the back window shelf. It was the same car in which I had heard "Why Must I Be a Teenager in Love?" playing on an oldies station as Andy had driven me home from CCD that first time, and he had groaned, in a painful tone after the song came on the radio, "Oh, man," and snapped it off halfway through the first chorus. Somehow, that he had been injured by love gave him an air I had curiously found appealing, not having any connection at all to the experience at that point in my life. I remember thinking that I would be like that someday—shaking my head and biting my lip when reminded of some heartbreak I had endured. Someday, I would have a history about which people could only wonder and speculate.

Me. An enigma.

Imagine.

"There," I, the still-open book, said and pointed my shaking mitten in the direction of his empty and dark car.

"At least he's still here," my mother said angrily, jerking us into the first available parking spot.

She snapped off the ignition and we sat there in the dark, in the cold, the vinyl seats crackling as any heat that had accumulated in the ride over leaked from the car's interior.

I began to shiver. I wanted some sympathy. We both wanted to get this over with.

"Let's go," she said suddenly and sharply. "Let's wait in the vestibule. I'm not going to freeze to death for this kid."

I got out and slammed my door shut, maybe just a little harder than I had to. My mother glared at me and chugged ahead up the front walk, her feet making harsh crunching noises on the icy surface.

Both of us had our heads down into the fronts of our coats. It was like a Siberia, and I had this vision that we really were there, and, because I had disgraced my family by accepting a pinky ring, I was being led to a desolate new home, one far, far away from the few who knew and loved me.

Just then, a hinge creaked and I looked up. There was Andy, leaving the church, lit from above by a fixture over the front door, sliding a pack of Camels from the pocket of his parka. Seeing us approaching, he pushed it back just as swiftly and smoothly.

"Hey—what a surprise! How nice to see you ladies," he called in our direction. His smile was broad.

My mother went straight for him, like the TV nature show shark that sees what it wants and gets right down to business. Like the shark, my mother's eyes were bugged out and direct, and her mouth was ajar. That second row of teeth almost was visible.

In an instant she was upon him, taking his elbow, whispering something in a surprisingly kind voice. "She's too young to accept a ring," I was hearing. "It was nice of you, but no, she can't keep it."

I was staring at the little holes that had been made in the sidewalk by salt pellets. They were many and deep, and I wished I could fit into one of them right now and hide out until the spring thaw. But, instead, there I was, and there was my mother, sticking into Andy's hand a small white box. And he was staring at her like he couldn't believe what was happening—that his *LOVE* was being returned by a mother who was telling him that she was sure that even if he didn't have the receipt, that he could get a full refund if he only told the clerk "the situation."

Then she said it: "Take it back. Go and buy yourself something nice."

That was all. She turned and brushed past me and, never wanting to see Andy again, I turned and followed her, looking only at the scuffed heels of her black rubber boots, down being the only place I could bring myself to look.

I lived through that humiliation and through the next four years to make it to my first real date, with Buddy Kent, who had my workplace, Fast Foto, on his UPS route the first fall I worked full-time. Every few days or so he'd come in with a shipment of some ammunition we'd need for a successful holiday season. The owner, Mr. Herrman, prides himself on preparation and wanted to make up gift boxes of camera, film, instruction booklet, frame, Fast Foto gift certificate, all to have ready and waiting and wrapped on the counter for when people started thinking Christmas. How about this, he would be ready to ask. All set for you. Look—with a bow. One less thing you'll have to think about.

So, in advance of all that, there was Buddy, again and again.

I knew who he was because he'd been a year ahead of me in high school, and a member of the varsity cross country team that had Anna and me as regular spectators. It wasn't a very exciting sport to watch—see them line up, see them take off up the street when the gun went off, then an hour or so later see them staggering over the finish line, sweating and gagging and throwing up—but because of that fact there weren't that many people to cheer and we figured we'd stand out. Certainly at some point they had to realize we were showing up at every meet and at least one of them would have to come over and say how much they all appreciated our being there, and, maybe, would tell us how thinking of our waiting for them was just what they needed to make it to the top of Thorndike Street. What we would have done with such attention and gratitude I'm not sure. But, applauding and yelling and watching them wheeze past, we waited patiently to be noticed and thanked in some way. Call it our version of playing with fire.

I remember that Buddy always did quite well at the meets, and that he never once looked at us. As a UPS guy, though, he was pretty friendly. Some weather, ha? How about them Red Sox? You're gonna carry that by yourself? I'm impressed!

Then one day it was hey, think you'd want to do something sometime?

He said this as I was signing for a couple boxes of baby-size Santa hats Mr. Herrman wanted to have on hand for those who came into the shop. He loved to give things like that away, and I didn't care as long as he didn't make me wear one.

I looked up at Buddy and answered "do something like what?" though I knew he meant something like a date and I knew this was it. I'd been gathering dust for the two months since my mother stuck twelve pink-and-white candles in a pineapple upside-down cake (they come in packs of twelve and, if she'd bought two, what was she to do with the extra six, she asked me). I wished for blessings in my new life as an available person, and blew out the flames in a single breath. The candle in the far upper left-hand-corner pineapple ring sparked and reignited.

"Like a date," Buddy said, taking back his pen. "You know, go somewhere or something."

"Sure," I replied maybe too fast and maybe with too much of a grin.

So that Friday I came downstairs at seven-thirty, but not to settle down with my parents and watch "The Inside Word's" main feature on celebrities who eat only root crops. I came down to tell them I had a date.

"Where's the obituaries?" my mother asked, rifling the paper.

"I said I have a date," I repeated, a little louder. "I'll be back later."

My mother looked at me with disgust, like I had chosen a see-through blouse and a micromini rather than the green corduroy pants and the yellow cardigan it had taken me three days to decide on. "Who is this, this date?" she wanted to know, for the both of them.

"A guy from high school. He was a grade ahead of me. Anna knows him." I said all this as I got out my coat and I added the last part to, I don't know, give him some more of a connection.

"Does he have a name?" They both were looking at me now.

"Buddy. Kent."

My mother shook her had. "What's his last name?"

"Kent. His name is Buddy Kent."

My father came to life. "There's a Frank Kent at the lumber yard. Boy he can lift—"

"What kind of people name a baby Buddy?" my mother interrupted, apparently not interested in what Frank Kent was able to hoist.

I shrugged. A car horn sounded. I grabbed the front door handle. I said good-bye.

At the curb stood a mustard Chevelle. From inside, Buddy, his blond shag golden under the dome light, stretched across the passenger seat and pushed open my door. "Ready?"

Where he took me, as he would every Friday night for the next eight weeks, was seven minutes away—to the home of his brother and sister-in-law, Doug and Kathy, where we mostly played Yahtzee and made sundaes and watched the 11 P.M. news. After the news, Buddy would get my coat and bag, drive me home, and kiss me on my left temple just before I let myself out of the car.

My mother couldn't have directed a more benign outing. There was that one touch per date, and very little intimate conversation—very little conversation of any kind, when you think about it. The whole time, except when it was their turns at the game, Buddy and Doug complained to each other about their parents, with whom Buddy still lived and away from whom Doug had moved after his marriage that summer.

I was a captive audience for Kathy, who missed the family she'd left half an hour away in Springfield, and I nodded sympathetically at the stories she told with great sadness of how she and Doug had no car to get to the city and how her parents were afraid to come out and see her because there were woods to drive through. But mostly I eavesdropped on Buddy and Doug, on the latest stories of their father's obsession with the *Titanic,* the time he spends in the basement playing with a scale model of the ship cut on an angle and glued to a mirror to make it appear sinking and reflected in the North Atlantic, and how his mother isn't kidding when she screams from the top of the cellar stairs how that wreck is gonna wreck their marriage.

"They think there are bears out here," Kathy confided to me and to a letter cube, then, over the *h,* looked up with tear-filled eyes. "Are there?"

"What, are you going steady with this guy?" my mother asked gruffly when she saw me drying my hair in preparation for the eighth Friday.

I hadn't thought about it, but when I did, I decided I was. Why not? Eight in a row without anybody else in between was eight in a row without anybody else. I could tell people that, yes, it's pretty steady, or, I've been seeing him steadily. I liked the way it sounded. I was wanted around on a regular basis, and Buddy would stop into Fast Foto several times a week—delivery or no delivery—to remind me of that. Don't forget Friday, he would tell me with a smile, shaking a finger like there would be consequences. Don't forget.

"I'd say it's steady," I told my mother, shaking my head to agree with myself.

She narrowed her eyes for a minute then slowly and

seriously repeated what she'd been telling me since the first night out with Buddy and Doug and Kathy, the warning that translated into I'll break your neck if you ever so much as touch him or let him touch you: "Remember who you are."

On that eighth Friday night, I ended up going so far as to let Kathy hold my hand while she shook and recounted her telephone conversation that afternoon with a little sister who cried about wanting to see Kath-Kath and her new big home in da woods. This is what you do for your boyfriend's family, I guessed, feeling pretty good about having such a responsibility to shoulder, even if it cost me hearing the entire story about how Mr. Kent has begun to build a lifeboat in the garage. And at the end of the evening, right after the car came to rest and right before he head for my face, Buddy Kent told me we wouldn't again be going out.

"I'm uh, uh," he started. I thought he was going to say moving or sick or helping his father. Who would know at such a time? But what he said was "bored."

He was bored. With me.

"Well not really with you, maybe it's just that you're not the right girl for me. I need somebody, uh . . ."

I don't know why but I helped him. "Not boring?"

Without missing a beat, Buddy answered "What can I say? Sorry."

He twirled the pine tree air freshener that hung from the rearview mirror. I looked at my hands, the ones that maybe tonight would have pulled my steady boyfriend a little closer, as a steady girlfriend might. Those hands grabbed the door handle. I said good-bye.

Whatever he had been all about, Buddy Kent was the feast that led to a famine broken in nine years mostly by being pushed to do the chicken dance with embarrassed out-of-towners attending mutual friends' weddings, and one time by a scary makeout session to which I felt obliged, the offer being made by Anna's grabby cousin, Mitch, during a ride home from the 1984 parish picnic. I finally got to see part of the famous town water tank I'd always heard about in high school—as in "he never wants to go up to the water tank" or "he doesn't want to do anything but go up to the water tank." And after a couple minutes there, I also could have had my chance to see the part of Mitch he told me was famous, too.

"Yeah, baby, how about it, right here?" he slurred into the Polish flag on the front of my T-shirt, crawling his spidery hands up the legs of my red shorts. His greasy hair was in my face and into it I said no, thank you, and slid back into the door of the van he had told me, explaining the mattress that filled the back, he used mostly for camping. There was only so much I was going to do for Anna, whom I thanked when she called the next day for a full report. Nice guy, was all I said, skipping how I ended up running home from the tank, Mitch screaming dirty words into my back as I escaped him.

Had I gone to college, I suppose I would have met more young men, but I really wasn't interested in going to school for longer than I had to. I viewed Mr. Herrman's offer of a full-time job—I'd learned all the machines in the two years in high school that I'd worked at the counter—the way my classmates were looking at the letter of acceptance from college. I had something somebody wanted and they were saving a place for me.

So I stayed in my town and in my little life and everything was going along pretty much the same until Eddie Balicki rolled a U-Haul up to his parents' house and I began hearing the details: how he hadn't lived here since he left for college years ago. How he was sick of city life, the rush of things there—or at least it was some reason like that, she said. Maybe he'd join his mother at her real estate office. He was smart, my mother said. He could do anything, really. Mainly, she said, he was "a nice boy. He even goes to church."

And that's where I first saw him. I was waiting for mass to begin, and noticed a tall young man in a long gray dress coat genuflect very deeply, then politely nod to a couple of old ladies to move on over in the pew so he could have some room.

The first thing you think in my church when you see somebody like that—somebody young, good-looking, alone—is that he isn't from around here. The church is always filled with people you already know—either your family or your friends or their families and friends. These are the same backs of heads you've been staring at Sunday after Sunday for your whole entire life. The heads are taller or shorter, hairier or less so now, or maybe they have gained or have lost a few other heads in their particular pews, but they're here, just as you are, just as I am.

In front of me that particular Sunday was the blond home-cut bowl-style hairdo of Stevie Przyzyla, who had suffered severe public humiliation twenty or so years ago when the nuns secretly collected, then presented to him before his entire seventh-grade classmates, an envelope full of the fingernail pieces he used to chew off and spit out around the altar while serving mass.

To his left were the overprocessed carrot-colored strands of the balding Stella Wilczak, an unpleasant old maid with an illness that made her head shake back and forth like she was disagreeing with everything, which she probably was.

There are few strangers in our church, except when somebody dies and the entire family from out of town shows up the following Sunday for a special memorial mass. So when I first saw Eddie Balicki, I figured he was some dead person's long-lost relative, somebody like that, in town this week because he hadn't been able to get away for the funeral. I watched him as he adjusted the kneeler then bowed his head low as he said his first prayer. His hands were folded in a way you only see in First Communion photos or in portraits of the pope—fingers meeting exactly and pointing toward heaven, thumbs crossed and locked. Dark hair and features stood out from his paper-white skin. With his eyes closed, he looked like he should have been a statue up on the altar, reeling in the ecstasy of what he already knew about heaven.

It was then I knew I was in love.

After mass, throughout which I took in his perfect movements—the way he unashamedly sang aloud, how he extended the sign of peace to anyone within the reach of his long arms, how he bowed deeply when the Host was raised—I headed toward the exit at the end of his aisle. But I beat him to the door. He had remained in his pew in the nearly empty church, his head down, his soul earnestly engaged in some silent dialogue I right then would have given my life to have been able to hear.

I took a spot next to the holy water dispenser and tried to appear engrossed in the church bulletin. They wanted people to attend a retreat, they wanted more donations in the poor people's food basket, they wanted everybody to join in the singing and not to leave the church before the end of the first chorus of the recessional. Who left the new leather gloves in the choir loft, they wanted to know. And if your car is leaking oil, they asked would you please put a newspaper beneath it while you are in church as the newly tarred pavement is getting stained already.

I watched a nun water the poinsettia plants near the communion rail. She genuflected each time she passed the center of the altar, and, because something was wrong with her knee, a cracking sound echoed through space each time she crouched low.

Finally Eddie stood, but he walked to the front of the church, where he stopped in front of the Saint Mary statue and stared at it for what seemed like a long time. Then all of a sudden he was coming back my way. I wasn't sure what I was going to say to him, so I turned my back as he approached.

"Any left?"

It was his voice. Deep. Sort of scratchy, like he had a cold, but soft at the same time.

I tried to appear surprised that somebody had come up next to me.

"Oh!" I said, and raised my eyebrows to help with the looking startled. "Am I in your way?"

"No, not at all. I was late and didn't get a chance to pick up a bulletin. I need a mass schedule."

"Are you just joining the parish?" I asked, like he was going to tell me something I didn't already know.

"Not really—I've belonged since I was born. But I moved away, been away. I'm back now. This used to be the most popular mass—is that still the case?"

I jumped at the chance to be helpful, to say something that might make him grateful. "To be honest," I confided, "the four o'clock on Saturdays is your best bet. We can't afford an organist for two Saturday masses, so there's no singing at that one, without the music. It takes only about twenty-five minutes—great if you have somewhere to get to."

"I sort of like the singing part," he said, shrugging and smiling, looking like a shrugging and smiling statue on an altar.

I felt crass for suggesting an abbreviated spiritual experience. "Then stay with this one," I told him. "The junior chair has just organized and the little kids are pretty good."

"You must be a regular," he said, looking right at me, and I could see he had eyes that looked like new pennies—golden copper, without the picture of Lincoln, and maybe just a little more sparkling.

"I'm here every week," I said.

"Then I'll be seeing you," he told me and smiled again.

I just nodded and gripped the edge of the literature rack, where a folder offered devout teenage girls the opportunity to take a trip to Rome led by the solemn-looking guy in the picture, Father Walter Gonet, a priest who had organized so many trips to various shrines he was known, the paper said, in bold letters, as "The Pilgrim's Choice."

There was a good chance that anyone who went to my church would see me again—that they would have seen me there from just about the third or fourth week of my life. I was born on a Sunday, and my mother would have brought me to church on the next one had Tricia Plattner from down the street not coughed on me and given me pneumonia on my first day home. In some people's opinion, I got the next best thing to going to church at age seven days, though, when I got so sick I had to get the Last Rites four days after I was born—even before I got around to being formally baptized.

When I got older and learned the map of the great beyond—how the top layer of heaven rests on the middle layer of purgatory, which sits on the thin layer of limbo, which is kept warm atop hell—I realized how close I had come to being an unbaptized baby dead of pneumonia and doing the limbo forever.

But I lived and left the hospital not for the faux-brick-faced Wazocha's Funeral Home but for the white clapboard farmhouse in which I would lead a very protected life as the sickly child of Edna and Stanislaus, two Polish immigrants who loved polka music and, I sometimes suspected, though to the naked eye there was no way of being absolutely sure, each other.

They met in 1953, then both recent immigrants brought by their respective relatives to the Friday night dance in the Polish Home in Chicopee. Tall, skinny, and fair Stanislaus asked short, plump and ashen-haired Edna to dance to *"Jak Szybko Mijają Chwile"*—"How Quickly Time Flies," which my mother since has held as her favorite song—one of her few bows to romanticism. I once took her on a bus trip to a dinner theater, where she asked a wandering violinist if he knew the tune.

"I love it so much I want it played at my funeral," she told him.

"Why don't I play it now," he suggested, raising his bow, "while you can still hear it?"

Because of my early brush with death, I received what my Uncle Louie once said were more innoculations than you'd get if you were headed to a Third World country. I was shielded with more than the usual amount of tender handling given the typical porcelain only child, and, especially after a few kids told me how lucky I was not to have an older brother to beat up on me or a younger sister to spit up on me, I came to pretty much like my life. It was just Vicks-slathered me, and passive Stanislaus, and vociferous Edna. Many times while in church as a child, I would look to the ceiling, at the huge painting of the Holy Family: Jesus between his folks, his arms extended at an angle, rays beaming from them and all around. And I would do the same in our pew, tucking my left hand behind my father's old brown suit and my right hand into the worn tweed of my mother's coat. There we were, some kind of Holy Family incarnate. I could see the pieces of light flying out of our heads.

I attended grammar school along with another 150 or so children who were one or two trans-Atlantic crossings removed from a life in which you could get an ice cream cone for less than a penny but had to live under the rule of Godless Communists. Right next door to the church, in the parish school, we prayed a lot, including at the beginning of the school day, before and after the 10 A.M. recess break, before lunch, after lunch, before we all got in line for the toilet, and after we returned. That last prayer, I had suspected, was in case we never came back from our stalls. If so, it worked.

We studied and played at the school, but we just about lived at church. All eight grades attended mass each morning, twice on Holy Days, and marched next door for every funeral that was held, including those of people we didn't even know.

We sang in a choir, and practice for that took up several afternoons a week. There were rehearsals for Holy Day processions and for the receiving of new sacraments. And there were day-long cleaning sessions in which we polished pew after pew after pew. It made no sense to me that we didn't just head right for the church when we stepped off the bus.

But now, now that I was in love, I went to church just to sit. And kneel and stand up. And start the whole sequence over again. For the next couple of weekends after I first spoke with Eddie, I attended every mass until I learned which he had chosen. I stayed in my usual pew, which was across the aisle from where he was sitting each week. I carefully selected my place in the communion line so I'd be walking up while he was already back in his seat, which I felt would give him an opportunity to take a good look at me passing by. That turned out to be not so great an idea, though, because once he returned from receiving, he put his hands to the sides of his face and stared down into the seat in front of him, into the wood grain, praying in that position until the priest began the final part of the mass.

Eddie was not one of those churchgoers who rest their heads on their hands and, sideways, examine people's fashions, who is there, who isn't, who is with whom. And even when he did look up, I wasn't so sure he noticed anything that was going on around him. His eyes were straight forward, seeming to be focused on some far-off thing nobody else even knew was there. Unless he had great peripheral vision, I was sunk.

So I resorted to becoming one of the ones who linger

after the mass to get in one more plea or promise or word of thanks. There was a regular group that did this: Miss Truda Zalicki, the aged lifelong elementary school English teacher who knelt at each Station of the Cross in the silence of the quickly emptied church. The Koza family, who had arrived in town from Poland more than a decade ago and who prayed long after mass, as if they still couldn't believe they had made it here. And Mr. and Mrs. Chapel—I am not making this name up—a devout woman and her equally devout husband who parked themselves in the front pew half an hour before mass and remained there until I can't say how long because I don't know anyone who ever outlasted them.

It wasn't long before Eddie began the habit of holding the door for people until I came through, and he would walk a ways with me outside, until we got to my car or his. Our conversations focused on the sermon, on the new song, whether or not the priest would get the increases he was asking for in the weekly envelopes.

There was no way I could bring myself to mention anything outside our immediate world. As it was, any Sunday now, I was expecting him to say how he hoped his girlfriend could drive up from Bridgeport and make it to mass here someday. Or that any day now his wife would get over her terrible illness and the kids could come back from her mother's and they would all be living together again. But Eddie said nothing of the sort. I knew only his name, that he was a good boy, that he went to church each Sunday at 9:30 A.M., and that I was in love with him.

According to my mother, who knew—save for the love part—a little more about him than did I, Eddie had always been nice, and a fine student, Lottie and Michael's only child. His mother once had grand plans for him to join her in the business, but Eddie had wanted something else. My mother said he hadn't been exactly sure what that was, but that he had been smart enough to win a scholarship to Holy Cross, where he studied accounting, graduated in 1976, moved to somewhere near Boston, and only rarely came back. Until a couple of months ago.

As far as my mother knew, Eddie wasn't living at the family home, a fact I had verified by calling directory assistance and learning he had his own telephone number, a listing on a side street at the other end of town.

I had no courage to drive up that street—or even the one his mother lived on—just knowing my car would stall and there I'd be, waiting for the AAA right in front of his house.

But my mother didn't think like I did. Come with me, she said one Saturday morning. Help me bring these cake pans over to Mrs. Balicki's so the ladies can use them for the bake sale.

It sounded innocent enough, so I said, "Oh, all right," trying to sound unenthusiastic. Then I ran, well, actually, I walked very fast, to change my clothes and arrange my hair for any chance meeting.

At the Balickis' front door, my mother rang the doorbell, pushing it with an index finger of a hand extended through the tube of a bundt pan.

"I hope she's home. I'd hate to leave these on the porch," she said, imagining, I was sure, the ring of pan thieves that would materialize the minute we got back into our car.

Suddenly there was a pulling sound from inside the house. The storm door sucked in and Mrs. Balicki appeared. "This always sticks in the winter," she told us apologetically. "Come right in, please."

Mr. and Mrs. Balicki lived on the second floor of a duplex. While Mrs. Balicki, owner of the only realty company around, was about as successful a businesswoman as you could get and still be located in dinky little town, there was no evidence of affluence in her home.

There wasn't even a sign of the latter half of the twentieth century there, where 1940s chrome appliances and accessories—toaster, mixer, bread box, waxed paper dispenser—stood sentry, shining on the counter. The kitchen set was of chrome accents and white Formica decorated in a design that looked like hairpins had been strewn over the top of it. Sunlight streamed through bright green-and-yellow floral-print sheers. Something cabbagey boiled on the stove. Polka music rang out from a big boxy wooden radio on a metal tea cart that stood on polished chrome legs. Above it, in a round brass cage, a lime green parakeet bobbed its head to "Julida, Julida, you are my honey. You only love me 'cause I got money . . ."

The room was overly warm, like the home contained a baby or some sick old person. As we walked over the vintage linoleum, our feet made that curious sticking sound like something had not entirely been cleaned off the surface—though there was no doubt Mrs. Balicki had been over it on her hands and knees every Saturday morning since it had been installed.

I noticed all this because I was thinking that here is where Eddie grew up. There was no doubt that the kitchen set had been there forever, and he had his first real meals there, drawn up to the table in a heavy polished chrome highchair, Lottie and Michael beaming at each other over the top of his one dark brown curl. He probably learned the Connecticut hop right in front of that radio, "Freddie Brozek's Sunday Morning Polka Explosion" providing the music to which, once he got the hang of it, Eddie circled the kitchen table with his mother. That tap was where he went for water when he came in from playing ball at the park. And the phone—he had to have dialed it for all his calls, important and less so, and it had to have been the one that rang and told his mother her precious child was coming back home.

Right then, though, Mrs. Balicki, whom Eddie had to have looked at every day for many years, probably from the first day of his life, was going on about something and I struggled to catch up.

"Will you be helping us bake for the sale?"

I hate to bake. I hate to spend my free time with a bunch of ladies forty years my senior, to hear nothing but how terrible the world is now and how promising it had been when they were my age. It is depressing to me to be the only young woman who ever helps out at these things. But I do because I think about how when they die who else will do it?

For the first time, however, I will be doing this for myself. "Of course!" was what I answered with great enthusiasm, knowing both that it would make her—and me—happy. "Just let me know when it is."

"What a nice young girl," Mrs. Balicki almost sang, touching the top of my head and smiling at my mother. "You can always count on her to help out. Not at all like the other kids of today. She's like we were—cooperative, kind, respectful. Can you believe how things have changed, Edna?"

My mother shook her head no, that she couldn't, and collected her handbag off the counter.

"Wait," Mrs. Balicki said, putting her hand up. "You can't leave before you see all the wonderful donations—monetary, even—that I've collected for the raffle we'll have when we sell all these things. Come, come, let me show you."

This was it! We were going down the hall! There had to be a bedroom—Eddie's bedroom—down there somewhere. I would see it. Maybe even stand in it. Maybe even lean against the chest of drawers that once held his clothing. Maybe, just maybe, even touch the same exact bed he had slept on for so many years. And maybe he was still there—maybe his mother forgot he was visiting and had decided to take a nap after a filling lunch enjoyed at the hairpin table and we would walk in on him, his clothing disheveled, shoes off, shirt unbuttoned and probably pulled from his jeans. Maybe he even had taken off his jeans. And there

I would be, walking in on my first in-person nearly naked man, and, I know, my mother would start shrieking and would slam her hands across my eyes the same way she slaps her right one across my front to keep me from flying through the windshield when she is forced to make a quick stop in the car. She would be dragging me into the hall and would be yelling how Mrs. Balicki ought to be ashamed of herself, leading us in there on the premise of seeing a savings bond.

I got ready for all this, even held my face muscles tight so when my mother blinded me it wouldn't come as so much of a shock. But rounding the corner over the oak threshold, I saw through squinting eyes only a heap of cardboard boxes that Mrs. Balicki apologized for in advance as she waved us in. "We have no attic, you see," she told us. "So Eddie's room became one when he left for school."

I relaxed my face and inventoried the rest of the room's contents as if I were a game show contestant who would be asked upon leaving how many items I could name. And I would answer that, other than the boxes, there was a pine dresser and a mirror hinged on a stand, and a small white doily—probably put there after his departure—and a silver-plated man's brush and comb set, neither piece bearing a stray strand. There was a small pine desk, and, on it, a leather-edged blotter, blank notepad, and a glass cup containing a bunch of pens. Above the desk were a couple of framed certificates—a letter award for track, a certificate for his Scout troop's 1969 essay contest, and brass-toned plaques naming Edward Balicki the Jesus' Helper Best Altar Boy for four years straight beginning in 1965.

There was a floor lamp, probably something Mrs. Balicki had moved from the living room, with a huge glass shade painted with a scene of what looked like a bayou. There were a couple of hockey sticks in one corner, and the end of an Easy Money game box could be seen just under the dresser. And there was the bed. I felt kind of warm just looking at it, as I could see Eddie as a big-eyed smooth-faced kid maybe holding a model airplane as he slept and dreamed. Then, instantly, I could see him maybe just a month ago, much older, when he returned to town and needed a place to stay until he found his own. He had to have slept here. I felt warmer yet, and saw him holding me as he slept and dreamed, his parents not in the next room as they conveniently had moved to Florida.

We would live here. We would keep it warm as it was. We would have lots of shiny appliances and a lime green parakeet.

"I don't think that would be such a good idea," his mother was saying. "If everyone just donates something without a minimum dollar value, we're going to have just a lot of junk. Look—Mrs. Barakomski gave us this beautiful comforter she bought at the K Mart. It must have cost her twenty dollars. But she's an exception. Mrs.—well I won't tell you who—brought me this letter opener. I give something like this out to new homeowners. I know how much this kind of thing costs, and let's just say she didn't put herself out. Who's going to buy a raffle ticket to win junk?"

She was looking at me. I was still looking at the bed, which was covered with the donated comforter, the aluminum letter opener, a set of cheap cocktail glasses, a seafood cookbook, and, up on the pillow, a trio of boxed cutlery assortment. Next to the knives, Eddie's face was settled into the pillow, and he was smiling at me.

"Would you?" she asked me.

I was staring at her eyes. Copper-colored and familiar. I recovered quickly and answered, "I just like to give a donation. If I win anything, I think it's a premium."

"Well you're a nice girl, like I said already," my future relation beamed. "But most of the rest of us are buying a ticket because we want to win a hutch or a riding lawn mower or some cash. We don't want junk. And if we don't set a minimum prize value, that's what we'll get. Junk."

"We'll have to think of that next time," my mother said quickly, moving toward the door.

"All the good ideas come too late," Mrs. Balicki sighed, shepherding us into the hall. I turned back to the empty room. Surrounded by years of fronds from years of Palm Sundays, God stared at me from his crucifix above the bed. He had seen it all.

We passed the living room, which held a plain and cozy collection of old, lumpy furniture arranged in a semicircle around a wood stove fitted into a blocked-up fireplace.

"We spend all our time around that thing," she said to us, and began to calculate how much they saved in heating oil by keeping the woodstove blasting all winter. Mr. Balicki, as she called her husband, even had cut a series of vents through the walls, and now all rooms were warmed from that one stove.

I was listening to this, but my attention was elsewhere, on that group of photographs across the room—one of those framed montage things with cutout spaces for Eddie's baby picture, his first day of school, a Confirmation portrait. I could only guess all that as they were too far away, but I could sort of make out the different outfits he might wear on such days, and the eyes.

"Come on, we have to go," my mother was saying, tying her babushka beneath her chin. A professional at body language, she was flexing the energizing material of the driving gloves she selected at Wojcik's when she returned the flannel sheets I got her for Christmas, the ones she told me, after sliding only half the present from the wrapping paper, would make her sweat like a hog.

Mrs. Balicki thanked us for bringing the pans over, and reminded me she would call when the baking was to begin.

I said I would be looking forward to it.

"Oh, to have such a daughter—Edna, you are blessed."

My mother, already halfway down the stairs, did not answer.

JOSEPH PHONED ME AFTER DINNER ONE NIGHT. "YOUR PRICE IS very reasonable for a ring that size. Is there something wrong with it?"

"No," I said quickly. I wondered if everyone was going to ask that.

"I just meant, is it chipped or scratched?"

I recalled the way the ring had plunged itself into Eddie's vest. It was a tough ring. It had been through a lot and had endured beautifully. I wished the same could be said for me.

"There's nothing wrong with it," I answered. "I'm just trying to sell it.'

"May I ask why?"

"I just don't want it anymore."

"Didn't work out, ha?"

"Not for me."

"Well could I come on over, maybe take a look for myself—at the ring?"

"Sure," I said. "I'm free."

I didn't bother with cookies and drink. Joseph already was lukewarm, so, I figured, why go out of my way?

I sat on the couch and clicked on the TV. My father came in, settled into his La-Z-Boy, unfolded the evening paper, and began calling for his eyeglasses. My mother and I began the routine search—in the bedroom, on the coffee table, near the phone, in his pocket. They were at his side, on the lampstand. He put them on and leafed to the obituaries.

Joseph arrived a little after seven-thirty. The "Inside Word" had just come on and was promising a revealing exposé on stars who had made it big and never ever go back home to see their loving parents.

There was a clip of one father, in some muggy southern town, watering his front lawn, in a sorry pair of Bermudas and a dirty, sleeveless T-shirt.

" 'Cept for on TV, we ain't seem him since he packed his bag that day," the man drawled, an turned to spit out something. The camera zoomed to the front door of the tired ranch house, where his wife was watching the interview from behind a pushed-in screen window.

I love this kind of stuff and grumbled as I thought of missing the story. Then I realized I could leave the set on, with the volume lowered, and it would look like my father was the one watching it. So that's what I did, right before the bell rang.

Joseph was in a shiny, black suit covered by a khaki raincoat. He was short and neat, with small blue eyes and a thin growth of dishwater brown hair combed precisely over a large white bald spot at the top of his flat, otherwise pink head. We shook hands and I noticed an oval blue star sapphire set into a brushed gold pinky ring.

He sat on the couch. "This is my father," I said, and my father lowered the newspaper and extended a hand.

"How are you?" he asked Joseph, and Joseph nodded that he was pleased to meet him.

"Now," Joseph began, turning to me, "let's see the ring."

I reached for the box and handed it to him. He opened it slowly, as if savoring all those things I had once enjoyed about the same act. Then he pursed his lips and let out a little whistle.

"It's a beauty, for sure," he said, reaching into his coat and taking out one of those little spyglass things you see jewelers sticking into their eyes when they go to examine something.

"No flaws—nearly," he announced, peering into the stone.

"Nearly," I agreed. "How do you know how to use one of those?"

"Part-time job," he said. "I'm a bank teller by day. At night I go through the classifieds and look for all the available gems, then I go and see them. Then I buy them and bring them to the jewelers and they buy them off me. It's a long process. For this one, I could get a great price. Very unusual. Very. Very nice."

"I'm sorry," I said, grabbing the box from its spot on his knee and opening my hand so he could drop the ring into it. "I want it to go to a person—you know—someone who actually is going to wear it."

"Why be sentimental—the guy dumped you, right?"

Joseph had a good question. I saw my father lower his paper, and look over at me. I looked away. On TV, the neglected parent still watered. Over the spray I could hear him recalling how happy his son had been growing up there. No one thought he ever would leave, but when he did leave, they were sure he'd be back. To bring souvenirs, at least.

I didn't know what to say to Joseph, so I decided on, "He had to go away. It's really none of your business." I took the ring from his hand and stood up.

Joseph, who got the message, told my father again that it was a pleasure.

The father on TV was rolling up his garden hose. "Where did he get the idea he could just forget us? Go to Hollywood and ask him, will ya?"

The interviewer put a sad look on her face and shook her head like she knew how the man felt.

F**UNNY HOW SHE DIDN'T MENTION HER SON,"** **M**Y MOTHER NOTED as she gunned her engine outside Mrs. Balicki's, where we sat and watched the woman slam the storm door five or six times to get it to shut correctly. Mrs. Balicki is one of those ladies who gets her dull brown hair styled every Saturday morning into a big pouf that lasts almost all week. Except for the dangerous eyes her son inherited, she is nothing to notice. Sitting there, my mother made a point of this, how Mrs. Balicki was "a big shot," but if she didn't have her business, no one would take a second look at her. She gunned the gas pedal on the words *no one,* as if to underline them in fumes.

My mother is a big believer in warming a car before asking it to go forward. Though we have a two-stall garage, it is never used for automobiles. It contains lawn furniture and tires and wheelbarrows and the barbecue, sacks of lawn food and lengths of pipes and pieces of lumber. But never a car. My mother prefers to have that parked just outside her kitchen window, where she can look out and watch it. When she has to go somewhere in the winter, she dresses early just so she can start the car and leave it running for about ten minutes. Then, while drinking her coffee back inside the house, she stands at the window so she can see if anybody passing by jumps in and drives off in it.

She was toeing the gas pedal again. It sounded ready to me, but there was a chance we would be there for a while.

"Mrs. Balicki mentioned Eddie," I defended. "We were in his room. She said it was his."

"Yes, but you would think, here's what she calls a nice young woman—how many times did she say that about you—in her own house, and you think she would take the opportunity to say a few words about her son. How maybe he's new again to the area, and would like some young people to go around with."

"Maybe he told her to mind her own business," I said, annoyed by the way she used Mrs. Balicki's compliments like needles. My mother is stingy with kind words, yet it bothers her when anybody beats her to saying one.

Putting on this little stone face, my mother became silent.

"What?" I wanted to know, but I could read her mind. I was good at it. "What's the matter—I didn't mean you minding your business about me. I meant Mrs. Balicki minding hers about Eddie."

"You meant me," she snipped. "That I should mind my own business."

"No," I said, enunciating the one syllable clearly, in case there was a question about which word I was using. "I meant maybe he said 'I'm back, but I'm an adult. I don't mind living in the same town as you, but you have to stay out of my life.' "

"Is that how you feel?" my mother asked in her best

shocked tone, her eyes bugging out. "I told you that you can move out any time you like."

"I like living at home," I said, because I felt that was mostly the truth—though I have to admit I did not often stop and really think about it. "I was talking about Mrs. Balicki. Don't be so sensitive."

My mother exhaled sharply through her nose and fished in her pocket for her Lifesavers. "Want one?"

I reached over and picked the pineapple one that was at the top of the roll, then sat as the car continued to rumble. I would be crazy not to like living at home. I have it made. I do not pay groceries and I do not pay rent. "I never paid my parents for food or rent, so you never will," my mother told me sternly when I began working forty hours a week at the Fast Foto.

I had brought home my first pay, in cash, folded into an envelope I'd taken off the bank counter. I had seen something similar in a movie once—somebody, maybe Jimmy Stewart, had done that, had paid his parents the first money he ever made. His parents protested, but they ended up taking what he was giving. It was the Great Depression, and Jimmy's $7 was going to be a big help. I was offering $165, and in pretty good times. Imagine what my parents could have done with it. How many Stanky and the Coalminers records they could have bought, or how many times in a row they could have gone to Symphony Hall for the Jimmy Sturr Christmas Show.

But the money only offended them.

"I never paid my parents for food or rent, so you never will," Edna told me and she added a little short nod at the end of the information. Behind her, Stanislaus scratched his head and put his hand on her shoulder. He winked at me, as he usually does, but said nothing, as he also usually does.

"Don't argue, don't argue," Mr. Herrman warned me

after I told him this story. "You don't know how you kids in America have it made."

That was one of the few times he alluded to having been a kid in another country, a kid who struggled for years to make it to this one, where he could live in freedom and in a place where he could make a lot of money off his talent for hand coloring photographs.

Mr. Herrman worked for decades applying rouge to the cheeks of coeds who, if they ordered a dozen five-by-sevens, usually wanted their angora sweaters to be a different color in each of the twelve. And he did that, dipping the cotton-wrapped tip of a toothpick into a blob of aqua or cerise or vermillion and applying the color to the sienna-toned surface of the paper, blending the color with larger pieces of cotton and making the lines sharp with a kneaded eraser.

He once told me he had felt in those days like a kind of god, with abilities to be revered. He said people were astounded by the talents that made a name for him throughout the state. "Have Herrman color it," photographers as far away as Boston were ordered by their clients.

Then the color developing process became refined enough to make Henry Herrman's skill obsolete, and it was either go out of business or step into the mainstream, which he did, and soon was selling cartons of film, and flimsy tripods and the entire Time-Life Library of Photography to enthusiastic amateurs whose results he found saddening.

Fast Foto guarantees your pictures will be ready in twenty-four hours. It is located in a small shopping plaza, between a day-old bread store and a sixty-minute dry cleaner. We all are working against the clock in one way or another.

I sit at a big machine that automatically develops the photographs. All I have to do is view the negative as it passes by me under a little piece of glass, decide from the density of the film which of three exposure levels of light it calls for, and press the correct button. Two minutes after I complete the roll of negatives, a length of photographs is cranked from the end of the machine, gets sliced up automatically and lands in a pile. My job is not too technical, and not at all artistic, but it allows me to say I work in photography, which, I find, most people view as exciting.

Anna is one of those people, but that is not saying much. Nothing personal about Anna, but I think any other job would seem fascinating to someone who folds towels in the hospital basement all day. She never sees anybody, she never talks to anybody and she has to wear a hairnet.

"You still live here?" Some people say this to us at reunions. "Somebody has to," we tell them and we usually add a laugh. Then they tell us how great it is that they work right in New York City, but they add wistfully that it's too expensive to live there so they have an apartment in Connecticut, and that means they have to spend hours on the train each day, just to get to jobs they only hold in hopes of advancement to the point where they will be making enough money to live in the same city in which they work. Halfway through the story, I can already smell the diesel fumes of the train or the bus or whatever it is they have to board and I have to interrupt and say something like wow is that Teddy Dudek over there?

I am here as I always have been. Sometimes I think that if everybody left after high school, who would live here? Then I think that maybe people who left other towns after high school would have moved here, and when their kids graduate, those kids will leave for somewhere else. Sometimes I think like this and I get a headache.

Very soon I might get one from the carbon monoxide I fear might be leaking in as my mother and I continue to idle outside Mrs. Balicki's. The engine sounded warm to me, but my mother had her own time clock and it hadn't rung yet. Suddenly, an old green Datsun swerved into the space in front of us. The same old green Datsun I have seen so many times at church. I slide down in my seat.

"Who's that—why that's Eddie Balicki," my mother announces, like I actually needed an announcement. "See him?"

"Yup," I answer, and sneak a look over the dashboard as Eddie flips his front seat forward and retrieves a wicker laundry basket containing clothes that once had been right next to his skin.

I can see the bold stripes of some athletic socks, and a few of the thin blue and yellow lines I know are found on the waistbands of some men's briefs. Eddie has on a green down vest, fashionably large, and a gray sweat suit—the type of outfit you wear when you have nothing clean left. He climbs the snowbank in his sneakers and bounds up the back stairs of the duplex. Familiar with his own home, he rams the door with a hip after turning the handle. Then he is inside and out of sight.

"A boy who brings his laundry home is not yet an adult, you know," my mother quotes from something.

"Maybe he doesn't have a washer."

My mother just harrumphs, then engages the transmission and turns the car into the street.

THEY BOTH WANTED TO SEE IT. SHE WAS THE ONE WHO MADE the call.

"Would it be all right if we both came by? It's a big decision and I'd like to be in on it."

I told her it would be no problem.

I was getting pretty good at this. Because I was selling something of quality, there was great interest. I received about three or four calls a week, and I made at least one appointment from those. So far, all had been men. And, except for Joseph, they all were about to become engaged, or were engaged but needed a ring so she would know he really meant it. All of them said they were out to save money, which explained why they had been going through the classifieds. Most of them looked at me with some degree of what I saw as a cross between pity and curiosity. They'd really like to know my story, but I have not felt up to that yet. I usually just work around it, getting them to talk about how they met or what her family is like or what was that exact point when he knew she was the one, or what they plan to say when they hand this box over to her. It is a morbid curiosity, but these people come into my house and I almost have no choice. Here, someone is saying to me: hold this handbook on embalming and I'll be back in an hour. Who would not want to take even a quick peek?

Sharlene and Bill were the first couple. He repaired copy machines for a living, and looked like he spent the rest of his time in the gym. Veins stood out on his tree trunk of a neck like interstates on a road map, and either his muscles were getting too big for his sports logo clothes or he was just buying them smaller for that effect. She was short and petite and left no mysteries about her wardrobe, many times working into the conversation the great difficulty she experienced when trying to purchase business suits tailored for her small frame. She was employed as a travel agent, which, she pointed out, was great for their free time.

For a price of fifty dollars, the two of them one week ago had flown to Florida, where they toured Disney World for three days and two nights, then took a chartered motor coach to Fort Lauderdale and boarded a cruise ship headed to Paradise Island, where they enjoyed two days and one night. They flew home from there, and the only extra fee was for tips.

Sharlene was breathless as she described EPCOT Center, the deals on oranges in the gift shops along Highway 1, the endless buffets on the cruise ship, and the island straw market where she paid a woman to braid a section of her hair.

"I had them do it way over here," she said, flipping aside the back of her shoulder-length blond hair to reveal a tiny braiding that ended in a turquoise-colored plastic bead. "This way, it's kind of hidden, so I still look proper at the office!"

I smiled. Sharlene continued. Bill smiled, too, and remained silent. He looked like he had become good at that through many experiences such as this one right here.

Sharlene told me how both she and Bill had attended American International College, but never had met until they were graduated and he carded her at the door of the dance club where he worked part-time as a bouncer.

"People tell me I look so young, that I have so much energy—I always get carded, even when they lower the drinking age," she beamed.

"Anyway, I went back there a few nights in a row, and we finally got a chance to talk. That was that, two years ago last week—the trip was an anniversary thing, you see. We've been waiting to set a date—we have some strict financial goals—and now we're ready. The wedding will be a year from next March twentieth—the first day of spring! It'll be sea foam and cream, the dresses, the decorations and the cake and everything. We just love that color combination."

Bill smiled. I could tell it was a favorite of his.

"So, anyway, we're really trying to get the best for our money. So I said to Bill, let's see what kind of bargain we can get. And we went around to stores and did some research, and you wouldn't believe what they want for a ring this size! I told Bill I had to have something at least this big—I always have wanted a large diamond, even though my hands are so tiny, you know. So when I saw your ad, I said what a steal! You know, in that diamond ad, the one with the guy giving the girl a ring in some romantic place, a rowboat or something, it says 'is two months' salary too much to spend on something that lasts forever?' Now I'm not saying we make that much, but it is more than two months, so at least we're kind of following the rule."

Bill smiled. I smiled, too, but my face was beginning to feel like it felt that day at the bridal shower, where, though elated, I thought that if I had to follow my mother's orders to look cheerful for one more photograph, something was going to crack.

"Anyway," Sharlene continued, "we are sooo excited to be making plans. You can't imagine."

If there hadn't been a chance I could make $5,000 off this woman, I would have stood up and told her that I could imagine. I could imagine very well. I would have told her that I once had been right where she was. That the dress was awaiting the final fitting. That I had the tickets to Cancun tucked safely in the back of my underwear drawer. That our color scheme was to have been a kind of salmony pink, like the very edges of the poppies I once ordered through the mail and had no hope for when I planted the seeds as small as sand. But they grew and they blossomed, and those flowers, so beautiful, would fall apart if you looked at them the wrong way.

I would have told Sharlene that I hadn't seen this coming. Everything had been happening the way I thought it was supposed to. And on many occasions, it looked like we, too, were walking across a page in that fat magazine, with the *B*-monogrammed place setting all we needed to reach a state of perfection. I would have told her really to look at what is happening in her life, to peer closely into that beautiful advertisement, to sit up and open her eyes and make very sure that life actually was headed to the place she wanted it to be going.

Like I really wish someone had told me to do.

But I didn't think Sharlene could see her life if it came rolling over her on eighteen wheels—even with the driver laying on the horn for about a mile before he got to her and the pedestrians waving their arms and screaming look oouuut! She just seemed to look ahead and see the open road, places to go and things to buy, and while that seemed exciting enough to make me a little envious, I also somehow got the feeling that she was a lonely girl who was hoping the trips and the stuff and the copy repairman and his deltoids and his acquiescence could fill in some of the spots nothing else seemed to. Supposing that, at least, made me a little less jealous.

Bill, smiling at her, added a laugh when Sharlene's stories—like the one about their two-day "Cruise to Nowhere," which she initially had believed was the name of an island—neared being funny.

"I don't want to seem like I'm not enjoying this," Sharlene said, for the first time not talking about herself, "but could we see the ring?"

I tapped myself on the side of the head, as if to say I'm so silly, of course, that's what you're here for, and slid the box over to her on the coffee table.

Sharlene let out a little squeal and petted the container like she never had seen flocking. Then she flipped it open.

"Bill"—she choked, grabbing his knee—"I . . . it's so gorgeous . . ."

Sharlene emoted for what had to be several minutes. The ring was the most amazing thing she ever had seen. She never could have imagined one like it. She never knew anything could sparkle so. She went on and on, and hadn't yet touched it.

Somehow, though she was turning my stomach with her effusions, I knew exactly what she meant. The ring did have a quality that reminded me of something in mythology—like it was a stone with power, that wearing it could get you past the beasts at the edge of the cave, through the pass with the jagged rocks sticking from the water, out of the land of where your worth is invisible. Those few days in December, that whole January, February, and March, and that tiny bit of April during which I had worn it had been the happiest days of my life. In each and every one I knew without a doubt that one person in this world thought and actually said I was the absolute most wonderful thing. And though it hurt at first to look at it off my finger and back in the box, I most of the time could stand seeing the ring, the last physical reminder (since I dumped at the Salvation Army the once-a-date trinkets—brightly colored ankle socks, a tiny wooden box containing a jumping bean, a Bible measuring an inch square) that I once had been loved like something you read about in a book.

Sharlene was slipping the ring onto her finger, and I realized I felt like jumping at her. But it was on, and she was sticking her hand into Bill's face.

"Wow," Bill said, honestly sounding impressed, his brow lifting and, somehow, his entire head of shiny black hair jerking back at the same time then returning to its place.

Sharlene ooohed and aaahed. She went around to every lamp in the room and then admired her reflection in the mirror by the door. I have to say the ring did look good on her, though I could see from how she held it secure with her thumb the back of her finger that it would need to be sized. She had the kind of hands you see on the television shopping programs: long fingers, just enough lines at the joints to allow the bones to flex, and long, oval fingernails painted meticulously in a deep red that matched the lipstick striking against her powdered skin. She spread out the fingers over the front of her blouse and stared into the mirror for a long time. I looked over at Bill, who was looking at her, obviously admiring the whole picture. Then he looked at his watch.

"Uh, Babe?"

Sharlene was in her own little world, which I knew consisted of all the Teflon pans and cordless appliances and coordinated pillow shams I had spent countless days returning and apologizing for.

"I have to get to the club."

Bill's words snatched Sharlene from her orbit, and she looked somewhat embarrassed.

"Pardon me—I just can't stop looking at it . . . but we should go—Bill still works the job as a bouncer. It'll help us reach our goals sooner."

"Good for you."

Sharlene returned the ring to its box, and pushed it over to me so I could see she was not making off with it. There was no talk of money or deals. They just went to their coats, which I had piled on an armchair.

"We're only looking right now," Sharlene said, and she flipped her hair to the side so she could arrange her collar. The bead dangled, a frivolity in all her order.

"We have your number—we'll let you know when we've made our choice. It was so nice to meet you. You have a lovely home."

Bill smiled and shook my hand with the clench I expected.

He held the front door for Sharlene and did the same when they got to the car, a small red import that even under the dim streetlight showed the results of religious polishing and of scrubbing in small places with an old toothbrush.

I hoped I would never see them again.

"One."

Anna was breathing hard and grabbing onto the door frame.

"Did you hear me? I said 'one.' 'All that time and I only met one woman who really meant anything to me.' One!"

She was still on the doormat, and I was considering leaving her there to rave about the one woman in her life within earshot of Mrs. Podgorski, who, at 7:10 A.M., was bow-tying plastic eggs to the dormant flowering crab in her front yard across from ours.

I was tired, having worked late the night before—Mr. Herrman was running a triple-print special—and didn't appreciate being roused by Anna's banging on the front door. Anna, I figured, should be beat, too, having just ended the double shift she was forced to work when the night folder decided two nights ago she needed a job with less stress. I guessed it was the long shifts that had pushed Anna over some edge, and onto my porch.

I took her by the arm, pulled her inside, and shut the door, glad this was the morning my parents had picked for their trip to Hadley, for cabbage. Once a month they drive to warehouses all over the farm country, haggle for the best price, and come home with dozens of bags full. They spend the rest of the day boiling it or cutting it up or mixing it into something. What they make out of it gets locked into plastic containers that are then arranged in the basement freezer purchased long ago just for such occurrences as a real find on cabbage, specials on roasts, or the grocery store's freezer compressor shorting out, as it did last summer, when they hurriedly drove down there and bought several carts full of rapidly softening sherbet marked at a ridiculous price just to get it out of there.

"One. Only one. I don't know what you think—I know none would be the best, but one, hey, in all those years, that's pretty good—for you, I mean."

Anna said all this very quickly, then crumbled onto the La-Z-Boy and scratched slowly at the Toni home permanent we tried last month to add some zing to her tired and dated Dorothy Hamill bob. It didn't come out half-bad, I noticed. "I am so tired, but I just had to come and tell you this. I couldn't wait . . ."

I settled onto the couch. "Start over. Slowly. I have no idea what you're talking about."

"Eddie!" Anna said, like, what was I, stupid? "Eddie Balicki—he said he's only had one real serious attraction."

She smiled and leaned back and brushed the front of her baggy white coveralls, embroidered over the left breast pocket with her name, and the stylized Blessed Virgin shape that was the logo of Our Lady of Hope Hospital. She crossed her stick legs over the armrest and jiggled one dingy white sneaker. She was very pleased with herself, but I still didn't know why.

"What would you know about Eddie Balicki?"

"A lot more than you do," she said, very satisfied with this situation. "Ask me anything. I know it all."

I was half-annoyed and half-entertained. It was kind of nice to have an opportunity to discuss Eddie, even just to say his name over and over in all these questions. But my fogginess made aggravation win out.

"Come on, Anna, I just got up. Tell me what you're talking about."

Anna rolled her eyes, disappointed, I guess, that I wasn't in the mood to play. "Fine. Be that way. I could be home, sleeping, too. But I decided to come here because I knew this would be important to you to know"—she stopped here, well aware I was hanging on the little dots that made up the silence before she said, real fast—"that I went for a snack last night because I didn't bring enough food with me and who did I end up in line next to in the coffee shop but Eddie Balicki, who was going for coffee with Chet Banas, whose sister was in having a baby and just from what I heard them talking about while they waited to pay I decided I would sit near them and try to hear more—for you—after all, he doesn't know me, so how would he know I was going to tell you?"

I hugged a pillow to me and leaned forward slowly.

"Tell me everything."

Anna said there was a lot to tell. Did I have the time, she asked, toying with me, enjoying being for once in the driver's seat. I whipped the pillow at her. She caught it and turned it into the hospital cafeteria—pointing at the corner pompon to show the door she entered, the braid along the edge was the line she got into. Halfway up the seam was where her progress stalled, behind two guys who were just beginning to catch up after not seeing each other for a whole long time.

I could see Eddie, dressed, as she said, in jeans and sneakers, and some kind of turtleneck and a slouchy brown corduroy sport coat, picking through the foil packets of tea before deciding on a carton of orange juice to go with his pumpernickel bagel. Anna was good—she even said how he read the side of the juice carton before putting it on his tray. And, though I didn't care about Chet, she was able to recall that he had on a green ski jacket and wore a Band-Aid halfway down the second finger of his right hand.

"Eddie's charge was a dollar sixty. Nearly a dollar for that juice! That's why I eat downstairs, my own food. From home. Cheaper and what I can save over a month—"

"Eddie! Eddie! Eddie!"

"Right. Well, Chet got his coffee and some kind of sweet roll and they went over here," Anna said, pointing across the pillow, to the button in the center. She showed me how, the cafeteria being pretty empty that time of evening, she had her pick, and sat on the other side of the button, at a table one down and one over from them, Eddie facing her.

"Eddie told Chet how happy he was to see him again. He said he'd hoped to run into him—he was there to deliver a present to Vera, his mother told him about the baby and since he'd had so much fun with Chet and Vera and some other brother when he was a kid, well, why not bring a gift, since he was in town now? Chet told him what a nice guy he was, what a nice guy he'd always been, and he remembered how Eddie used to stand up for him when they first started high school and got picked on by the public school kids who looked at them—Chet, especially, from the sounds of it—as geeks. He told Eddie how he would never forget that, defending him in front of everybody. Of course I couldn't look at him for long periods, but I did right at that time, and Eddie looked like he was blushing, you know?"

Spellbound is not too dramatic a word to use to describe how I sat and listened to Anna, who, and I realized it that morning, can tell a pretty good story when she's got something to tell. She talked about how Eddie and Chet reminisced a lot about growing up on Gabriel Street. She said she missed some of this when she went up and got another order of nachos—she had to look like she was there to eat, after all—but assured me most of it was pretty boring. They played ball in the park, they served mass together, they once, after seeing something similar in a cowboy movie, used a magnifying glass to set a fire in a small pile of leaves. "They were laughing and cracking up about that one, on and on, like that was the craziest thing two kids ever could do." Anna shook her head and looked at me. "You sure about this guy?"

I wanted to ask Anna what were the craziest things she ever did, but I knew them all. And I had to admit that even Anna had stories that could top burning a couple of leaves. So maybe Eddie wasn't the most daring guy. He still was Eddie, and that was enough.

"The good stuff, Anna—get to that."

"Well, Chet said that he never much comes back to town. His wife has custody of their kids and she lives near where they lived when they were married—somewhere north of Portland—so he's stayed around there to get his regular time with them. A girl, Kayla, nine, and three boys, Travis, Jared—"

"I don't care about Chet!" Anna sort of jumped when I shouted this across the room. The La-Z-Boy jerked.

"And Brandon. Eleven, seven, and four and a half, respectively." Anna gave me a dirty look and continued slowly. "So then. Chet says 'You ever have kids?' "

She stopped, knowing it was killing me. "You are doing such a wonderful job," I said sincerely. She sent the pillow back to me, the row of vending machines knocking against my forehead, Eddie landing sprawled on my nose, the bagel and juice flying past.

"So Eddie says 'No. I've never had kids—never been married, never had kids.' And Chet has a big grin and says

'Not that you know of,' and leans and punches Eddie and Eddie says 'None. That's one thing I'm sure of.' Chet tells him that he must have a girlfriend. And Eddie says he doesn't." Anna is using great expressiveness here, knowing this is her shining moment. "He tells Chet that he has not had that much luck with dating. He says he finds many people not his type. He says he wonders if it's just him or if it's the world. So Chet says there are chicks out there for every kind of guy. He uses that word. *Chicks.* What century is he from? Anyway, Eddie says something like 'I guess if I gave more people a chance. I've just been so busy with my work. Too busy.' He says that when he lived in Boston he dated, sure, but in ten years, he says exactly this, 'all that time and I only met one woman who really meant anything to me.' "

"Yeah, yeah then what? Who was she? Where is she?"

Anna told me that's what Chet wanted to know, too. He leaned into the table and stopped chewing on his plastic spoon and listened as Eddie said this woman was an actuary, someone he met through a mutual friend. "Sweet, a very sweet woman with a wonderful, big heart," was how he remembered this one woman. Her idea of a fun evening was to go out and buy a dozen blankets and ride around and cover up a dozen sleeping homeless people. A few times a week she made at least one more serving of some fancy food than she needed and would bring it, steaming hot and garnished, to some old person on the first floor of her building with the excuse that she never learned how to measure. Whenever she was out walking she'd casually drop at least one quarter so somebody else could have a little piece of good luck in their day when they came across it. But for Eddie, her heart was just a tad too big, something he found out on the eight-month anniversary of what he described as "some pretty intense dating." That night, over what was left of homemade garlic and walnut tortellini, she asked Eddie to move in.

"So?" Chet asked.

"Well"—here, Anna noted, Eddie paused and dug at the floor with his sneakers—"I didn't want to."

Chet looked at Eddie's face. "Ugly, ha?"

Eddie looked at Chet's.

"She was ugly, right?"

Eddie laughed, Anna said, as hard as he had over the burning leaves. "Far from it, Chet." He took a breath after that, she said, as if the thought of her made him need more oxygen. "She was gorgeous. The whole thing. She was smart, funny, great-looking, outgoing, did all those things for people, most of them she didn't even know."

"You're the one that got all those scholarships, right?" Chet asked. "What, did you get dumb once you left school?"

Eddie laughed again. "I don't know, Chet. Maybe it's hard for you to understand, but I suddenly realized I didn't believe in that. It might sound crazy, but it's what I think. There needs to be some lasting commitment—like marriage—before a step like that. And she didn't want that."

Anna said Chet just sat there, like he was entering all this into his data bank—new information he'd never considered personally. Then he spoke and he was kind of smiling. "I hope you don't believe in marriage before everything . . ."

"I do now," Eddie told him. "I admit I didn't always—there were lots of nights those blankets never made it out the door, if you know what I mean—but I believe in a different kind of relationship now. One that will last, forever is what I'm saying."

Anna said Chet seemed relieved, like Eddie wasn't that much of a freak, having at least gotten some action before such a sad end. I don't know if she read Chet correctly here, but she was right on target with me.

"Now don't go feeling jealous—she's history," Anna assured me. "Just be glad he didn't have five wives by now. Got anything to eat?"

In the kitchen, Anna poked through the refrigerator. I sat at the table and started to process all the new facts that only underlined Eddie's eligibility, and virility, and a desire for a life with someone in which both parties would promise never to part.

Eddie just got better and better, as far as I was concerned.

"I'm gonna pay you for this," I told Anna as she set down a bowl of cling peaches, five cents at Fruit Fair's dynamic dent sale. Damaged cans for next to nothing. The kind of event that drove my mother wild.

"Well how much is this worth to you?" Anna asked, slowly passing me a piece of paper she had found on her side of the table.

I studied it as if there were something I had missed in the two short sentences written in my mother's rounded old-country handwriting. "Call Mrs. Balicki. Gone for Cabbage." I saw nothing more.

Straightening the lapels on my housecoat, as if Mrs. Balicki owned one of those picture phones we are supposed to all have sometime in the future, I dialed. The number was inscribed inside my head—the exchange inside the left eyelid, the remaining four numbers inside the right one.

"Sorry to give you such short notice—I didn't remember to call until last night," she said to me, "but I wanted to start the pierogi today for the sale. We're not ready to do the pastry. Can you make it today—even for a little while?"

My heart did that little flipping thing: I had an invitation to Eddie's mother's home. "I do have some time today," I said, trying to sound like I had fit her in. "I'll be over after lunch." Not that I expected to be able to eat—I just needed time to prepare myself.

"That's wonderful. It'll be just us, and Harriet and Frances. I couldn't seem to get ahold of anyone else this week. How can I ever thank you?"

"You don't have to do a thing," I said, and I meant it.

I hung up the phone and dragged Anna and her bowl upstairs to agonize over what to wear. I would be going somewhere that Eddie might be going, too—I said a prayer that, at this very moment, he was discovering he was out of clean socks. So I would have to look good, just in case, but not so fancy that I would stand out. However, I knew that anything I chose would make me stand out from the crowd I suddenly for the first time honestly hoped I'd be spending every Saturday with: my neighbor Harriet Bukowski, who had been the town librarian I think since they invented type. Frances Piela, a widowed retiree who decorated the church altar the one week a year the nuns left for wherever it was they spent their vacation. And Lottie, grandmother to my offspring.

After a frustrating search for something flattering in a wardrobe bought for a job that centers around caustic chemicals, we decided on my better pair of jeans, and the red hooded sweatshirt Mr. Herrman had bought for me when he went to visit his son at Stanford. I figured it would make Mrs. Balicki happy, as it contained the colors of the Polish flag. Once while wearing the shirt, I was walking into the bank and a well-dressed older man stopped and pointed at the letters on my chest and asked "alumna?" I figured out what he meant and I surprised myself by how it didn't take much to smile and say yes, you're right. He shook my hand vigorously and said, "Class of 'thirty-nine. Made me what I am today." I remarked wasn't that something—it had done the same for me.

When I got to Mrs. Balicki's, I saw that the three of them, as I knew they would be, were wearing gaudy housedresses protected by pinafore aprons. When Mrs. Balicki took my coat, she assured me that she had one more apron just for me. "You don't want to get that nice shirt dirty," she told me.

"It's a sweatshirt. That's what it's for," I assured her in what I hoped would be taken as sounding kindly rather than snotty. But I knew I was going to have no choice but to put on what she was holding out to me the next second: a red and yellow daisy print apron with red ruffles around the neck, the tie, and the edges of the two generously sized pockets.

"Really. I don't need it."

"I would feel so badly if you ruined that beautiful shirt. Here, all the ladies are wearing them."

I relented and put my head through the top. I let the ties hang, but Mrs. Balicki was behind me all of a sudden, securing me in.

I noticed the other three also were wearing chiffon scarves over their hairdos, so I quickly pulled my hair back into an elastic, before Mrs. Balicki got any other ideas.

The hairpin table was covered by a large plastic cloth—red and white checks like you bring to a picnic. On top of that were sacks of flour, cartons of eggs, a container of salt, and a bowl of water. Harriet and Frances regularly dipped into all these things, filling individual mixing bowls with just the right ratio for a good dough.

Several large aluminum bowls sat on the shining counter, the mixture inside them resting before being rolled out.

"You've been busy," I said.

Mrs. Balicki smiled and nodded: "Yes, but we'll get so much done now that we have a pair of good, strong, young hands."

She loved to talk like that.

Mrs. Balicki swung open the door of a metal utility cabinet and removed something from a pincushion inside. She held it out in her hand as she came toward me. "Here," she offered.

It was a large safety pin. "Thanks," I said, and pushed it into my pocket. This had to be one of the few old country customs I'd yet to run into.

"No, no, dear," Mrs. Balicki said, waving her hands and pointing to my pocket. "It's for your rings."

She pointed above her left breast, where, secured to her apron by the same kind of very large pin, was her diamond engagement ring and a silver band with three colored stones set in a row.

"Keep them near your heart when they're not on your hand," she told me. "That way you won't get dough in your settings."

"I don't have any settings—any rings, I mean," I told her, and I took the pin from my pocket and handed it to her.

"Pardon me. I just assumed you wore a ring—so many young people do," she said, reaching for the pin. "It's just something I do each time I'm working in the kitchen. Then I know just where they are. Like these—I would be frantic without them, my beautiful engagement ring from Mike, and my mother's ring."

Now this I had heard of: a ring holding stones that represent the birth month of each child. I saw three different colors. "You have three children?"

"No," said Mrs. Balicki, pulling forward the pinned-on ring so I could get a better look. "The aquamarine is for December, for me. The ruby is July, for my Mike. The emerald is for my Eddie—in May. I have my whole family, right here."

"This was *my* mother's," Harriet spoke up from over at the table, in a voice that more than anything else was an offer of would I like to hear about her jewelry. I gave her an interested look so she continued.

"Freddie couldn't afford an engagement ring so I always had just the band. Then, on my mother's deathbed, she pulled me close and told me, she said, 'Harriet. Don't let me rot in the grave wearing this good stuff. You take it.'"

Harriet pulled a wadded-up Kleenex from the pocket of her pinafore, pushed once at each eye, and continued.

"So, after the funeral, I began to wear it. I put it on. It looks nice, and, you know, I kind of feel closer to her, having it on all the time."

She looked down at the solitaire. A tear fell onto her flour-covered wrist and got soaked up by the powder.

"I just have junk, but it's my junk," Frances said, then cracked an egg. "It's all cubic zirconium, but it looks real. I always wanted a nice ring—Walter wanted to give me one, too. But I always said no, we have bills to pay. Why do I need a real ring?"

She glanced at her pin, which was shining with three or four big, huge, rectangular diamondlike stones, and Frances looked sad for a minute, like she knew the answer to that question but didn't have the words to use to say it.

"Some day," Mrs. Balicki told me as she steered me by the shoulders over to a floured rolling pin and board, "you'll come in here with something to pin on."

She sent the safety pin back into my pocket. "Keep it until then."

RANDY SAID HE WAS TOO DIRTY TO SIT DOWN.

"I just had a game," he told me, but he didn't have to. He was wearing the baseball uniform of the Hadley Homers—a red-and-white striped polyester V-necked jersey and tight matching knickers. Red stockings extended down into a pair of taupe suede Hush Puppies at which Randy caught me staring.

"My cleats are in the car," he said quickly, realizing someone had seen his real shoes. "These are for work—I have to dress up there before a game."

There, he told me, was the Quick Stop, and suddenly I knew why he looked familiar. I don't often go in there, but a couple days ago I was driving by it and noticed a tall, skinny blond guy in dressy-looking clothes lowering one of those huge sticks into a hole in the ground, to check, I figured, for the amount of gasoline left in some storage tank down there. The day was hot and I was in a slow line of traffic behind a funeral procession. I had time to notice how little tails of his hair were sticking to the back of his neck as he stood out there, all dressed up, on the convenience store's tar parking lot, in the hot sun.

"You're the guy with the stick, the gasoline stick—do you check for gasoline with a stick?" I realized I was sounding like an idiot.

Randy smiled and his face brightened. "That's one of my jobs, can you believe it? I'm supposed to make the Frostees and put the hot dogs in the cooker and, with the same hands, I'm supposed to work with deadly substances. That's not my idea of what a real store should be—they just don't pay me enough to poison people's nachos and still sleep at night, I can tell you that."

From the mention of his pay, I sensed the approach of a story that would detail for me why he needed a break on the price. Most people who came to me seemed to get to that sooner or later. I figured I would spare him the trouble: "I should tell you up front that the price is firm," I said, and Randy looked at me like where did that come from—I was talking about fumes.

I knew I had lost him, so I said "You were talking about how little you make. I just wanted to say the price in the paper is what I want. I'm sorry. I can't give you a break."

"Oh, I don't want one—I mean that would be nice, but my father's paying for this," Randy said, looking as happy as you would expect to look if this were your circumstance. "It's not something I'm that crazy about, but it's something his father did for him, and he's big on tradition. It's what he wants . . ."

"That's nice," I said, and I felt right then that this could be the end of all this. Randy looked easy to please and he had no problem with the money. I offered him a drink, maybe a snack?

"Could I just have plain water? I'm in training, you know."

I went into the kitchen. My mother was making what

she calls schnitzels. She had the counter cleared and had mounded pounds and pounds of hamburger right onto the surface of it, a huge volcano of ground beef, the crater of which she was filling with eggs, onions, spices, and the crusts from some bread that was so old you really would be better off not knowing it was being mixed in there.

For something this much, she didn't bother with a bowl or pot. It was just slap it onto the counter. She got this idea from my father, who had been a cook in the Polish Army during World War II. He came back home without having had to kill anybody and with a recipe book full of instructions for things like jelly roll for six hundred. My mother has tried to downscale the directions, but most of them still yield great amounts of food, and keep the freezer in use.

"He wants water," I said, reaching for a glass. My mother didn't respond, only made gushing sounds as she squished her fingers through the mass. She wore a housedress and a pinafore to which, I noticed, she had pinned her diamond engagement ring. The part of the band that stays in the back of the finger, I could see, was very thin from years and years of wear. That got me a little sad.

She spoke: "Let's just hope he wants the ring. I'm getting sick of this—people in and out, in and out. For eight months already—I'm counting, you know—in case you forget and say to me one day 'do you know how much time I have wasted with this nonsense?' And I'll be able to say yes I do. Really—how much of this do you want to put yourself through? Go to a store. Get rid of the thing. Go on with your life."

I twisted an ice tray and half the cubes fell out, some into the glass, some crashed onto the counter, where they skidded into the hamburger. With one greasy hand, my mother picked those up and flung them into the sink.

The way I saw it, I was indeed going on with my life. Before I began selling the ring, before Eddie, I only went to work and came home and talked on the phone with

Anna and knitted. I made sweaters for myself, for presents, some I even sold to the owner of a little yarn shop that opened in my shopping plaza. She was so taken by my work that she hung them in the display window, to show people what they could do with their spare time if they just tried. I love the Norwegian knits—no cables or fancy stuff like that, just flat knitting made interesting by colors and patterns: deer and pine trees, lines of snowflakes, sailboats racing, people holding hands. I turned them out at a steady rate, using the finest number one and two needles, carrying the colored yarn in back with every stitch rather than the more common every three, something I had seen done on a television documentary of Norway.

So, to me, having people come to the house and look at the ring—even just having people come to the house—was a change I didn't find too disruptive. I could use the telephone and knit before and after appointments. It was sort of interesting to have some new people to talk to. I didn't see what the problem was.

So I asked her: "Exactly what am I supposed to be doing? What would you want me to go on and do? I go to work every day, I'm no trouble. What's the problem?"

All I got back was the soft squishing sound, and that hard concrete look on her face. I filled the glass from the faucet and left the room.

Randy had perched himself on the arm of a chair, on top of which he first had placed the newspaper, so his dusty pants wouldn't harm the fabric. I thought there was something nice about that.

"Sorry it took so long," I said. "The ice was stuck."

He accepted the glass and drank it all, his Adam's apple riding up and down like a piece of machinery. He made a satisfied *aaah* sound and handed it back to me. He told me there was nothing like cold water, and I agreed.

"Did you win the game?"

Randy shook his head from side to side. "No, but I don't

care. I just love to play. There's nothing like it. I know someday I'll be too old, I'll be too out of shape to run and I'll look like a jerk in this uniform. So I enjoy it now, whatever happens . . . though it is nice to win."

He smiled at me, sweetly, and my heart twinged as I saw for a split second a piece of what somebody else must see in him. That made me remember why he was here, so I asked him when he would be getting married.

"I don't know," he answered. "I mean, I haven't even asked her yet. This will be a total surprise—I'm hoping, at least. You don't know Roseanne Malachowski, do you? I'm asking because she went to school here—I'm from Hadley—and wouldn't it be something if you did know her and you'd say to her one day, 'Hey I met this guy Randy and he wants to buy my ring?' And then it would be no surprise."

I thought for a moment, then assured him the only Malachowskis I knew were dead, except for the one living in a retirement home in Alabama. Alice was her first name, and she used to make donuts in her kitchen for my mother when my mother first came here. Somehow she had always been in my life—sending me cards of congratulations and a hanky edged with hand crocheting whenever she heard I had done well in school, showing up on Christmas Eve with a plate of homemade cookies just for me, making my mother disgusted over the effort somebody had chosen to make for "only a kid" but making me suspect I had something somebody could appreciate.

Alice's daughter, Tonya, a lean and sullen woman who never put aside styling her hair in the Shirley Temple curls she had fallen in love with in the Sunday afternoon reruns, passed on to me her outgrown clothes and killed my only cat by backing over it in her Plymouth Fury III on the one time she baby-sat for me, the one time I had a baby-sitter, the one time during my childhood that I can remember my parents going out for fun. Returning from the game dinner at the Adams Gun Club, stuffed with the bear and the raccoon and the rabbit and the other creatures Rudy had promised them would be so tasty when he sold them the tickets, they spotted a flattened Humphrey beneath Tonya's back left tire. Rather than tell me the cat had to be scooped into a grocery bag and taken for one last ride up the street, where his body was pitched down a wooded embankment, my parents decided to say he was lost. I searched the neighborhood for weeks, hanging up Magic Markered reward signs that bled in the rain. A couple of years ago, one of us mentioned Humphrey and my mother scowled something about how Tonya really never had said she was sorry. I asked about what, and my mother told me, adding with a surprised look that she thought she had ages ago.

I never had cared for Tonya, but I liked her mother a whole lot. When Tonya married some kind of account executive and had to move down south for his work, Alice Malachowski used to come and visit us and would always end up crying, How could she have a life without her family around her? And my mother would sit on the arm of the couch, just like Randy was doing, but without the newspaper, and she would put her arm around Alice's shoulders and pull her close. She would tell her we were like her family, having known her for so long, and that we were always there to help her.

She should realize that, my mother said.

I rarely witnessed my mother getting mushy, so that was something to watch. I do remember another time, back when I was very small, when she found out her friend Betty's sister had died. My mother dialed the phone and spent a long time sitting in the corner chair with her face to the wall. She was very silent most of the time, except for every once in a while she would just say, "Betty, oh, Betty."

She kind of cooed it. I still remember that call, even though I just heard those couple of words. I wonder does Betty?

"No, I don't think she has relatives in Alabama," Randy was saying.

"This is an old lady—she moved there a few years ago to be with her daughter and her family."

"No, no old ladies that I know of," he said and he smiled a smile that made her eyes crinkle up. "I guess we're safe. You're not telling anybody about who comes here, are you?"

"Believe me," I said plain and simple. "Sometimes I don't even like to tell myself."

What I said just sat there. I thought Randy looked insulted, so I went to clarify myself. "What I mean is it's all so strange. I really want to sell it, but I can't just sell it. Do you know what I'm talking about?"

"No," said Randy, "but somebody must have done something bad or you wouldn't be sitting here with this." He pointed to the box on the coffee table. "I'm thinking how I'm coming in here all happy and you're at the other end of it. That's too bad."

"Thank you. It's nice of you to say something like that—because it's really got nothing to do with you. You're here as a customer and none of this should matter. I can tell you it's a beautiful ring that any girl would be crazy for, and I can assure you that the price is right."

Randy reached for the box and sprung the lid. I noticed he had a tan where his wristwatch usually must be.

"You're not kidding," he said very slowly. "I've never seen a ring like this. Not that I've looked at that many—but, boy, this is something."

Randy slid the ring from its slit and onto the top of his index finger, to see how it would look, as best as he could imagine it shining on Roseanne's hand, just below that dot of a beauty mark on her knuckle. Then he peered very closely into the stone. "You can see all kinds of things in here!" he gushed, grinning and looking sideways at me and then back into the stone. He was like somebody getting his first look through a telescope. There might as well have been planets in there. Spaceships orbiting. Maybe somebody waving at him from the driver's seat of one of them.

He turned to the lamp and flipped the ring this way and that in front of the shade. Then he got as much of his head under it as he could and seemed to be looking straight into the light bulb. I heard him whistle, and then he laughed.

I sat with my arms around myself. Randy was there getting a kick out of what he was seeing, and something somewhere in me knew that joy. I suddenly missed Eddie, but kicked away that big hole of a feeling as quickly as it had come to me.

"My dad has got to see this," Randy said, his back still to me, the Living section of the paper being creased under his thigh.

"You think he'd want to see it?" I jostled Randy from his inspection and he knocked his head against the shade.

"It's part of the deal," he said, and he steadied the rocking lamp. "He pays, but he gets the final say. I didn't figure it sounded so bad."

"Sounds fair to me," I said. "How many rings has he looked at with you?"

"This is the first one I've even looked at. But I've got to bring him to see it. I know he'll think it's fine—more than fine—I think he'll say OK, that he'll pay for it."

"Well, you know how to get in touch," I said. I took Randy's cap from the hat rack and handed it to him at the door.

"Look, I know it doesn't matter in the sale, but I really am sorry. About whatever happened. It's none of my business, but I just wanted to say something. You know?"

I scratched the back of my neck, for no reason that I knew of. Then I had that feeling again, stronger this time: that Randy could be the one. He could be the answer here, both for Roseanne and for the ring. "Thanks," I said to him with a smile, trying to appear warm so that he really would want to get his father over here, not just say to me that he was going to so I wouldn't feel bad. "Maybe I'll see you at the Quick Stop."

"Maybe. But I'll call. To bring my dad."

He swept back his hair and planted the cap on his head and walked backward the first few steps out the door. Then he turned and I watched as his number 11 got smaller and smaller the farther away he got.

BY 5:15 ON EASTER MORNING, THE NOON MEAL WAS NEARLY cooked and both my parents were fully dressed and polished for the day. The house smelled of simmering borscht and baking ham and Brut. On the kitchen table, set for the family breakfast that would be eaten after we returned from the 6 A.M. sunrise service, the everyday dishes were joined by my mother's black patent leather pocketbook, our three church envelopes, and a can of Progresso minestrone soup for the poor people's food basket. Though church is only a mile away, we would be leaving soon.

When I attend mass with my parents—they prefer the 8 A.M. Polish one in which even the sermon and the announcements are in the language that the relatives who took them in advised they try to lose to better their chances of blending in with the rest of America—we almost always are the first ones there. They are afraid of not getting a seat, or, worse, of having no choice but to sit in one of the vacancies way up front, in clear view of everyone else. I remember a time during my high school years when my mother began to refuse to wait for me if I was running late in my preparations. On several occasions, I had to chase the car as it pulled away, my mother crouched over the wheel, my father sympathetically looking back at me, then quickly at the driver, and again at me, my high heels clacking and my handbag flapping. It was pretty embarrassing and pretty much unnecessary, as aside from major Holy Days of Obligation, there always are lots of empty seats throughout the church.

Even so, my parents are determined each week to get their same pew—fifth from the last row on the left. The location allows for a quick exit, and is on the side of the church on which the priest—not the extraordinary minister—distributes communion. My mother never has accepted the idea of extraordinary ministers, and long ago made it clear that while she has no problem buying a pair of sensible pumps from him, she doesn't want that shoe salesman—that divorced shoe salesman, no less—placing on her tongue the Body of Christ.

So there we sat that Easter morning, five seats from the back, with only a handful of people beating us to the place. When my mother spotted their three or four cars parked in the prime spaces edging the front walk of the church, she said to no one in particular, "I told you," and raised high her eyebrows. I felt no guilt—any tardiness that prevented us from getting there right at the point when the nuns were unlocking the doors was not my fault. Today I had been ready on time. Everybody in the world went to this mass on Easter, and I knew Eddie would be one of them.

Slowly, the rest of the pews began to fill. Old sons held the door as their much older mothers maneuvered walkers over the threshold. Young mothers in tight floral dresses herded elaborately outfitted toddlers, and elbowed them when they played too much with the elastic strings holding the straw hats on their heads. To my left, my father, in the old brown suit he must have had forever, was praying on a set of rosary beads his own father had received on the day of his First Communion. The beads were dark and oval and I always have thought they looked like the coffee beans I once saw being ground up at the A & P. A long time ago I was snooping in their room for nothing special and I found the rosary in its place in a brown leather box on my father's dresser. I sat on the bed and swung it around, then admired the beads and their smoothness. Then I bit one, just to see if they were indeed some kind of food. I left in the first Our Father bead the straight impression of an incisor in what I finally found out was wood.

Now the beads were passing through my father's fingers at the rate of a clock's big hand: if you watched, you wouldn't see them moving. But all of a sudden you would notice he had gone through an entire decade.

I wondered what it was he prayed for. Were there things he'd wanted since he was a boy that he still hoped to get? Money? Property? Renown? Somehow, I couldn't see my father hoping to be famous, to be somebody who would get bothered for his autograph while scooping a bag of tenpenny nails from a bin down at Chudy's. He always had money—not in the bank, maybe, but I know there were wads of large bills jammed into at least three Chock Full o'Nuts cans on the top shelves of his workshop. He owned his own house, with three acres for his Macs and Spencers, so it couldn't be that. He was married, so it couldn't be love he wanted. Or could it?

To my right, my mother sat with her hands in her lap. If she had her Austrian crystal rosary with her, rather than leaving it in a velvet sack in her top dresser drawer, from where, my father and I are reminded periodically, it is to be taken on the day she dies so the undertaker can lace it through her fingers for eternity, I know her prayers would have something to do with me. And, I am certain, they would not be in thanksgiving.

One of the few women in our church who continue to wear a hat to mass in our church, my mother alternately darted and glared her eyes from beneath the small round brim of orchid and white satin hung with a drape of royal blue Russian lace.

I was staring at the foam rubber that poked through the cracked vinyl on the kneeler at my feet when she jammed her elbow into my side. "Hey!" I whispered sharply, and looked at her. Her own face was set straight ahead, but her eyes were flitting in some sort of code: to the right, back to the center, and to the right again. So I looked to the right, too, and saw Eddie taking a seat across the aisle and up a few rows. I felt my heart quicken and I lowered my head.

From the corner of my eye, I saw Eddie kneel in the silence broken only once in a while by a *ssshhhh* to some child or by somebody having a coughing fit. On Easter Sunday in my church, no music plays until the priest comes out in front of the little altar that the nuns, using papier-mâché and gray paint, have transformed into the cave in which Jesus was buried—the same cave they used about four months before as the one in which he was born. The priest stands there in front of the empty hole and, in a big, long line of Polish, informs everyone that Christ has risen. Then the music swells up and the choir pipes out a harmonized Alleluia! Alleluia!

That is what it is doing right now, in a church so packed that people are standing on tiptoe outside next to the open windows to hear what is going on. The choir is blasting out Alleluia! We are responding Alleluia! Some of us, like me, who can't sing, only mouth the words. But all of us can feel the hope of a resurrection, of the fact that things can begin anew. One of us, and that is me, can feel the hope of something almost more unbelievable than God rising from the dead: the reality that Eddie Balicki has turned and that he has spotted me and that our eyes have met and that he right now is whispering Happy Easter, right to me.

Alleluia! the choir rings. Alleluia! on Easter Sunday. Christ is risen! And Eddie looked at you! Even said something!

Because I was with my parents, that one look and those two words were all I got of him that morning. There would be no staying behind for a prayer—they liked to be up and out of there and at the drugstore for the Sunday papers as soon as possible. They did oblige the priest's frequent request that everyone stay, not charge out of their pews immediately after the last amen, but that was about it. After the first chorus of *"Wesoły Nam Dziś Dzien Nastał,"* which exalts about the happy new day that is beginning, the three of us were pulled into the stream pouring out of the building, everybody smiling and greeting and looking forward to the rest of that happy new day.

I shuffled toward the door, but glanced back. Eddie had moved to the group that surrounded the empty crypt, and was standing there staring into the cave, resting his hand on the marble baptismal font next to it. I realized with a pleasing twinge that both of us, eight years apart, had been lowered into that very same marble bowl, howling because of our salted tongues, anointed foreheads, and dripping scalps, not realizing that we had just been made one of a holy nation, a people set apart.

Lottie Balicki had given birth to Eddie less than twenty minutes after her sister had rushed her to the hospital. With another sister, she had been baking a babka that day, and had just begun to brush the melted butter on top, so when it came out of the oven, the loaf would have that sheen. The pains began then. "It was something like I wouldn't wish on my worst enemy." This is what she told me when she and I had gotten to the point where people who are soon to find themselves related sit over tea and cake and come to say such things. Anyway, Lottie got that pain and her sister, Mania, got a panic attack. She backed away from Lottie with her hands up to her face, then turned quickly and dumped her entire drawer of dishcloths onto the floor and took on the job of folding them each very carefully.

"I had to scream 'Mania! Get me out of here! I am going to have the baby!' But she just bent down to the pile and began separating them, by color. She told me later it had seemed like the only thing to do, because she is not good with a crisis and she needed something that would take her mind off it."

What Lottie needed was to go to the hospital. She hefted herself off the kitchen chair and shuffled through the pile of clothes Mania had yet to fold. She grabbed the set of car keys from the nail near the back door, and, moaning many times, she remembered in great detail, waddled to the old bronze-colored Chrysler Mania's husband earned in trade for a year of woodworking in a dentist's new home in Bondsville.

"I thank God to this day that she lived on the first floor—that there were no stairs to go down," Lottie said, folding her hands as if to say her prayer of thanks. "She was useless to me. Absolutely useless."

Lottie remembered reaching into the car and pushing on the horn in long blasts. As she had hoped, her other sister, Binia, who lived on the third floor, appeared on her porch to see what all the noise was about. So did Gen Sakowski, in an apron and stirring a mixing bowl. And Joe Dunaj, who had on coveralls and was holding a paintbrush dripping white.

" 'What? What?' they yelled. By then I was on the ground." Lottie was speaking faster and faster at this point, and was looking like she was having a great time retelling everything. "I yelled for somebody to get me please to the hospital. Binia ran down from the porch and then Joe Dunaj. Gen Sakowski just kept on mixing, and she watched the whole thing, wondering, I knew, where was my husband at a time like this?"

Lottie leaned close to me at that point and confided that she had been wondering the exact same thing—why wasn't he there to help her? But there were no electronic beepers in those days, she explained, and no way to know into whose Frigidaire Mike was placing a half gallon of Hillstretch dairy products at that moment.

"No one knew where he was on his route, so they didn't bother to go looking for him," she continued matter-of-factly. "They just helped me into the backseat of Mania's car and Binia sped off to the hospital. It seemed like forever, but we got there. Such pain! I was in such pain!"

It was then that Lottie looked right at me and covered my hand, which was returning to me from selecting another Stella Doro Milano. She patted me and told me, "But you know, when they handed me my precious, precious Eddie, I just looked up to the heavens and I said this is the most wonderful day. God has given me a son—just like he had! I had to look down then, because there was this big operating room light shining in my eyes, but God knew I was talking to him. I made the sign of the cross on Eddie's forehead and told him he had come from God and he would go back to God someday. Then I raised Eddie up toward the light in a sign that he was as great as the universe—not as great as God, of course, you know—but he was a wonder to behold."

Except for the electric light and the cross on the forehead parts, I think I had seen something similar on that "Roots" miniseries. A father in Africa had done pretty much the same thing with his newborn son, hoisting him toward the full moon and proclaiming his greatness. I know Lottie watches an awful lot of television and probably had collected that little detail from there. In reality, I felt, she had been so knocked out she didn't know Eddie was a boy until she came out of it about three days later and first changed a diaper. But I just gave her half a smile, and she asked me if I wanted more tea.

According to Lottie, Eddie had been a very happy child. Just about his only problem was getting a terrible sunburn a couple times each summer, his skin being so fair. When that happened, she poured into the bathtub gallons and gallons of Hillstretch milk and made him soak in it for hours. When he was allowed to emerge, Lottie would blast him with Solarcaine from a bottle shaped like a fire extinguisher.

Eddie, she told me, had been an altar boy since first grade and volunteered to serve at every mass, including those on weekday mornings. His parents never complained about having to rise to drive him to church—as his mother pointed out, there were a lot worse places he could beg to go.

Their boy loved the quiet of the sanctuary, the way the church could roar when it was filled, the incense, the vestments, the flames put to long wicks. Throughout his childhood, on a calendar hung beneath the crucifix over his bed, he crossed off the dates to the next Holy Day. At Christmas he hinted for gifts by clipping newspaper advertisements for a local religious supply store and leaving them on the breakfast table. Chalices, or huge crosses, or monstrances studded with jewels, he thought, were perfect gifts.

In his basement, Eddie regularly cleared his mother's ironing board and brought out a plastic crucifix, a cracked dinner plate, a worn facecloth, his mother's souvenir bell from the Eastern States Exposition, and a roll of Necco wafers. Recruiting a few neighborhood girls to act as nuns, he celebrated mass next to the water heater.

When Lottie was telling me all this—actually, at the point

when I think I smirked at the thought of a little Eddie reenacting the last Supper beneath clotheslines hung with his father's boxer shorts—she pointed out with great seriousness that religion to her son never had been merely a plaything. For example, she said, when the Yankees—his favorites, making him more of a weirdo to his Red Sox-loving neighborhood—lost the 1964 World Series, he had collapsed onto the porch and cried. "Then," she said with a look of great pride, "he immediately went down to the cellar and said mass."

I also was told that though Eddie had wanted at some short intervals to become a quarterback and a sports announcer, his childhood answer to the question of what did he want to be when he grew up was "a priest, of course," and that he said so in a tone that wordlessly asked the inquirer what else was there that anyone would want to be?

I remember thinking that some of this seemed odd, but then I recalled that most kids in my class had considered the religious life for at least a moment or two. The inspiration came from a variety of worldly sources: the way the rectory cook always had a freshly baked and ornately frosted layer cake on display beneath a crystal dome on the priest's kitchen table; how the nuns could be seen each January sitting in the front row at the Ice Capades, their tickets and their popcorn and their souvenirs free, courtesy of the extra collection on the second Sunday of Advent.

For me, the lure was emotional. It was the way Sister Benicia could take out her guitar and play and sing just about anything you wanted to hear. During one recess at which about a dozen of us girls sat at her feet while she mournfully delivered all the choruses to "Five Hundred Miles" at the edge of the woods behind the school, I took in the adoring faces of my classmates, smelled the pine air breezing over us, heard Sister's lament that she had not a shirt on her back, not a penny to her name, and I knew what I wanted to do with my life. A few days later, however, Diane broke it to me that nuns had no hair under their veils—they were required to shave their heads, she whispered—and I was relieved that I hadn't rushed out and signed any papers.

For Eddie, it seemed, interest in a life dedicated to God took a while longer to cool.

He had wept on the day he was graduated from the parish grammar school, and, Lottie told me, the nuns had wailed in turn when Eddie read both the touching salutatory and the valedictory speeches (there had been no argument that both those honors should go to that stellar student). But they hadn't seen the last of him. He returned each weekend and most weekday mornings to assist at mass. The priest had to order a special set of extra-large altar boy clothes because no one that old had ever kept on with it for that long. In the public high school that everyone in town attended, Eddie studied hard and kept in with a small group of boys he'd known at the parish school. They were good kids, though many called them boring—or worse. Having worn the same outfit each day for eight years, they suddenly found themselves in a secular world with freedom of wardrobe. It took Eddie and some of his friends until their junior year to get the hang of choosing a decent outfit that did not make them look, in the words of my mother, who used the expression even though that is how she herself got here, "like they just got off the boat."

However, by that junior year, they had been written off by everyone but the friends with whom they had entered the place. Eddie once told me he felt that being an outcast had been a benefit: there were no social distractions to interrupt his studies. In what could be a testimonial for Sans-a-Belt trousers, he ended up entering the accounting program at Holy Cross on scholarships totaling far more than four years at the place actually cost.

Just about that time in Eddie's life, I was halfway

through the parish school, unaware that I was treading water in his still rippling wake. Eddie had been a star there, but I was less than remarkable, preferring to stay on the sidelines and in the back of the line—something that was easy because we were lined up by height for everything from a bathroom break to Confirmation practice. For eight long years I was paired with just-as-tall Appolonia Kowalczyk, one of the few kids I knew who was allowed to watch "Dark Shadows" on TV each day at four-thirty.

I entered high school with a small selection of anonymous polyester separates from Sears just as Eddie was exiting Holy Cross with a huge collection of honors and awards and a special citation from the priests who ran the place: never before, it said in elaborately calligraphied Latin, had they seen such a dedicated, hard-working student.

All those plaques and trophies and the contents of his dormitory room then were stored in his childhood bedroom while Eddie rode a Greyhound bus on a six-month pass that allowed him unlimited mileage, and, Eddie being Eddie, the opportunity to travel from one squalid rundown city to the next, working for a network of church groups that served the disadvantaged.

When his ticket became void, Eddie gathered his things from home and moved to Boston. He entered the working world, showing off to the adoring secretaries who asked to examine it his Holy Cross class ring, with the tiny golden cross embedded in fake amethyst. Right about that time, in our parallel universe, I was showing to a much less enthusiastic reception the *LOVE* on my finger.

The afternoon of the Easter on which Eddie looked at me, I had yet to know much of his history. As I dried the dishes, I tried making one up for him, but my story of an Eddie who had done little with his life other than go to an honest job and hope to meet a nice hometown girl kept getting interrupted by my mother's explaining to Cioci Wanda why she did not use the dishwasher I had bought her and my father for their thirtieth anniversary. I had selected at Papuga's Home Appliance Center a gleaming white model that was so powerful it could even clean pots and pans, and after eight months of paying what I could every week, it was mine—theirs—and I arranged to have it delivered and installed on a Saturday they were to be out hunting for cabbage. I even went to the florist and bought a big red bow to string across the front of it so it would look like a prize on one of my father's television game shows.

"What's that?" my mother had asked when she came in the kitchen that afternoon, two cabbage-filled grocery bags in her arms. "Where did that come from? Who put that there?" She looked at me and then back at the dishwasher, which stood in a space previously occupied by a cabinet holding neatly arranged empty plastic containers from cottage cheese and deli orders and the like, all waiting to be filled with leftovers.

"Happy anniversary!" I shouted, then went to hug her, the cabbages between us. My father, who just had staggered into the room carrying a teetering mountain of the vegetables, stopped and looked at us, then followed my mother's blank stare to the machine.

"Stanislaus—look at what the kid did. Now why did you go and spend all your money on that? We don't need that—"

I stopped her: "No arguments. It's for your thirtieth. You'll enjoy it. You'll have more time. Just fill it, and run it when it fills up."

My mother shook her head and clucked. "What a waste. More time for what? It's just the three of us. And that's what I'm here for—to take care of you two. To wash, to clean, to make it nice. I don't need a machine."

My father walked over to the dishwasher and leaned real close to examine its controls.

"Pot scrubber," he said thoughtfully, tilting his head and smiling.

"It says it scrubs pots?" my mother asked incredulously and hurried over to the thing. "How can it do that? Tell me. They lied to you."

I bit my lip. Even though I had predicted there would be some sort of scene, it still felt bad to witness.

My mother went on and on about her "place." How it was her place to run the household, to see that things were kept neat. In between her making coffee and examining each of the cabbages in the same way I know she had when buying them, she continued for the better part of an hour to underline her importance in her home. I tried to make my points about saving time and energy, but got no reply. I did finally get her to open the dishwasher, and my mother searched in vain for the arms that would scrub the pots. We'll never know if they were in there, because the machine has yet to be used.

That is what she right now is telling Rudyka, a cousin from a farm in North Adams. Actually, Rudyka is married to my father's cousin Rudy, and that happened only pretty recently. Like overnight. Rudy, a dairy farmer who hardly ever left his barn, went to the feed store for bag balm and fell for the new clerk.

Rudy is exactly the same size as his huge and long-dead brother Alex, a guy who had been so large, my father tells me when he is in the mood to tell things, that they had to bury him in a piano case. Another of my father's favorite stories is how Alex, when he wedged himself into it one New Year's Day visit, split the arms on the easy chair that preceded my father's La-Z-Boy. And now quiet, plain, old farmer Rudy is married to a talkative, cursing, cosmetic-wearing brunette with a Donna Reed flip of a hairdo and a waist the size of her husband's forearm.

There was a small wedding we didn't attend because my mother had picked up beforehand that Rudyka was a divorcée, and my mother didn't go for such things at all. I remember her trying to fit the words "out of town that day" into the little space on the reply card. We would have learned her name had we attended the wedding—it would had to have been somewhere in the vows—but we didn't. So, behind her back only, we refer to her as Rudyka. We are waiting for Rudy to call her something, but the only times we've seen them together, she is the one who does all the talking.

Rudyka is out of her mind over the fact that my mother uses the appliance as just another cabinet. That she stores all her large mixing bowls and roasting pans in the dishwasher, that she keeps her best carving knives in its utensil basket, that the top rack my mother has found convenient for arranging all those plastic storage containers the machine had displaced.

"If I had one of these, I'd be putting the laundry in it," she laughs with a cackle. "The furniture. The truck. The cows, for Christssake!"

"It's a waste of water, a waste of electricity," my mother responds as she swirls a sinkful of greasy water around and around. I catch how she bows her head quickly after Rudyka said the Christ part of her curse. Then my mother looks at me and sees me looking at her. I have no particular expression on my face. This, to me, is an old story.

"Telephone!" Cioci Julie, a hand-embroidered HAPPY EASTER apron wrapping her, is yelling from the hall. She has the receiver in her hand and is waving it like an SOS in my direction. I love Cioci Julie, and once, when my mother had asked me why I couldn't be more like Cioci Julie's sweet little Marcia, I asked my mother why she couldn't be more like sweet Cioci Julie. I got whacked aside the head by her for that one, which really was not fair, because I was more asking a genuine question that being smart.

When she hears Cioci Julie, Rudyka snickers and winks to my mother: "Probably a boy." My mother returns to her a limp smile. My mother knows better. She knows it will be Anna, who also must be trapped for a long holiday afternoon in a houseful of relatives who are working off their meals by watching sports on television or playing board games on the cleared dining room table or dozing in uncomfortable chairs. Maybe Anna wants to go to Friendly's.

I would have to agree with my mother's assumption, so I don't rush to the phone. And when I finally get to it, I don't bother to cover the receiver as Cioci Julie beams at me and drawls, "He sounds attractive." I just say, "Sure, Cioci," and I take the phone.

"Hello. This is Eddie," someone says, sounding very much like Eddie. I realize it is Eddie.

I am mortified. Cioci Julie lights on the edge of the couch, Rudy takes up the rest of it. Both of them watch me. In horror, I look back at them as I wonder if Eddie has heard the disbelief in my comment. "Eddie—I'm sorry. It's so crazy here," I say and I duck around the corner as far as the cord will allow. "With lots of crazy relatives. Joking and such, you know?"

I clench my fist to make myself slow down, to make sense.

"I know," he tells me. "We just got back from the same thing."

"Oh, are you at your parents'?"

"I'm just about to leave. I thought maybe on my way home I could stop by. But if you have a houseful, maybe I shouldn't."

Everything suddenly is going in slow motion. I see my father stick his head around the corner and pick the phone cord away from the wall, where it had caught on a loosened seam of wallpaper. He gives me a smile that seems to last a few minutes. Rudyka sidles by, and it has to take her an hour to get to the coat tree and to her pocketbook, from which she removes an envelope of photographs. I begin to wonder what in Rudyka's life has she deemed fit to document. From somewhere far away, I hear a small voice. Eddie is hanging on the line, maybe by now thinking he shouldn't stop by. Maybe he will hang up.

"Hello?"

"What?" he asks. "Is your phone having problems?"

"No, sorry, look—it's the crowd. It's not somewhere you'd want to be, believe me."

Eddie doesn't say anything and I quickly realize I sound like I am sending him away even before he has arrived. And that is not what I want. So I jump right back with, "But how about going somewhere else? Maybe get a tea or something somewhere?"

"Sounds good to me," Eddie says and I can hear him sounding happy, I am sure. "How about if I come over in about fifteen minutes?"

"Fine. I'll be waiting on the porch."

"You'll freeze—it's still very cold," Eddie tells me and I am loving how he does not want me to turn blue and die. "I'll just run up and ring the bell."

"No, we won't be able to hear you—too much noise," I quickly lie. There is no way he is coming into this place. "I'll watch for you," I say.

"See you," Eddie tells me and he hangs up. I just stand there and hold the phone, listening to the hum that buzzes with the echo of Eddie's last word—*you,* which is me.

Me.

So then I run right up the stairs. Somebody is in the bathroom so I go into my bedroom and check myself in the dresser mirror, which is very high and shows me only from the collarbones up. That part of me appears OK, but I get from the top drawer a pair of cotton briefs and wipe the shine from my face. Then I take a hand mirror and check the rest of me for any food that might be sticking to me from clearing the table, anything like that. Then I realize Eddie is probably on his way over, and I fly back down the stairs.

"I'm going out," I tell my mother as I take my coat from the kitchen closet.

"Tell that girl to bring that jar of borscht to her parents. I ladled some out for them. They have told me mine is the best." My mother says all this without bothering to turn to me from the last of the dishes, or to think anyone else would want my time.

I button my coat and pick up the jar, which once held Hellman's mayonnaise. A small sheet of aluminum foil has been screwed between the jar and lid as an extra seal, so that the soup will not escape if the container is toppled. I say I'll be back to whoever is listening, and I go out the front door and into the fresh air. On the porch, I hop up onto the flat, wide railing and lean my back against the house. I take in slow, long breaths of cold air, calming myself just with the reminder that I am out of there. I sniff my coat sleeve. It doesn't smell too much like a kitchen.

Eddie's car rolls to the curb. I feel my heart doing many pounding things. I hop off the railing and walk off the porch, trying not to make too much noise on the old boards. From the corner of my field of vision, I notice a piece of living room curtain move aside. Somebody is watching this.

Even though I am walking toward the car, Eddie gets out and starts coming toward me. I hope he doesn't want to go back in the house, but it will be hard to refuse him much of anything—he looks so good in his church coat, and I can see the knot of a maroon necktie behind part of his gray scarf. I have a guy on my front lawn who is wearing a suit and is coming to get me.

We both say hi at the same time. Then we both laugh and I look into his face and he does the same to mine. We are halfway up the walk and we are just standing there. I am not sure where we are going, but I know I don't want to stay here much longer.

"You've probably had enough dessert—how about a coffee somewhere?" I suggest. "Friendly's?"

Eddie smiles and says, "Great. Let's go. But how about tea—I don't drink coffee."

"Neither do I." That we have something in common is a kind of sign to me.

Eddie walks around to the passenger side of the car and opens the door. I get in and then he closes it.

I have seen this car many times, but this is my first ride in it. The interior is immaculate, like someone has just finished vacuuming it. The dashboard holds no maps or papers or cups. The only thing in sight that probably didn't come as part of the original equipment is a Saint Christopher key chain that holds no keys and dangles from the cigarette lighter knob. Everything else is factory condition. It is like the car is for sale, or just has been purchased. "Had this long?" I ask as Eddie, who has hopped into his side, is slowly steering into the street.

"Ten years this May," he answers.

I tell him that he sure keeps it nice.

"Well, I'm usually the only person ever in it," he says, and I like the answer.

I also like that Eddie is driving, because I can look over at him and, unless he is a careless operator, he really can't look at me. In that way this reminds me of us in church, of me studying what I can see of the left side of him. Now I am on the right. The view is very similar, and just as wondrous.

We go a little while in silence. Eddie has a tape player and he pushes in a cassette of country-western music. First there is the end of a song about runnin' from you, then begins a song about layin' with you. It is kind of embarrassing to me, considering I really don't know Eddie, to be listening with him about somebody's time in what I know must be a bed. So I start a conversation. I ask him how work is going and he says it is fine. That it is much nicer to be working around here. "The people are friendlier," he tells me. "In the city, people just seem to be lost, but don't want to ask for help."

"I can understand," I say. "Cities are big places. I got lost in Springfield once. They have a West Columbus Avenue and an East Columbus Avenue and I once got very confused looking for the Victoria Restaurant."

"Well, I meant they seem lost as people," Eddie clarifies in a kind tone. "Like they're looking for something, but they're having no luck, because they're maybe not even sure what it is they want. It's a very anonymous place. That's what I was trying to say."

"Oh, yes." I feel dumb for not knowing that in the first place.

In case I am turning red from embarrassment, I look out the window to my right. We are driving along the river, which is almost free of ice. A family in pastel Easter outfits has driven a car down next to the bridge and is posing for photographs on the bank. I know I will probably see them again soon, passing through my machine, standing there by the water, and hunting eggs in their side yard and slicing a cherry-dotted glazed ham on the kitchen counter. They also will be welcoming into their living room the boy who has come to visit the daughter. He will get warm handshakes and a seat on the couch and his own bowl of potato chips on a TV tray conveniently within reach. He will get an invitation to return. Why not tomorrow night, for leftovers? We're so glad to meet you, they will tell him, and will succeed in making him feel right at home.

Eddie tells me about his hours, which he says are long, and he speaks of his need for relaxation, which he explains was great enough to cause him to move from the city.

He asks me what I do in my spare time. I just shrug and

grin and say, "Oh, you know." It is a poor answer, and I realize that even before I say it. I am pretty sure, at this point within walking distance from my still-parted front-room curtains, that I am a flop as a date. Here I am in the big city of Eddie, and though I am lost, I do not want to ask for help.

But he is there, offering it. "Well, like what, exactly? Sports? Reading? TV?"

"I like sports," I say, and I try to put expression in my voice, to make my words perhaps more interesting to hear. "But I don't do any. I like to read, but nothing fancy. I like magazines. You can read for a few minutes and you finish something. It's not like a book, where it could take you months."

"You have a point," Eddie says and he nods.

There is hope. I keep on. "TV I like a lot. I always have. I once wanted to be on the 'Brady Bunch.' Not just on it, in the show. When you're the only kid in the family, something like that sounds pretty good—lots of people always around, you not being the only one, a pair of parents like that. But maybe that wouldn't have been so great. Who knows without trying?"

"It's something to think about," Eddie says as he flips the directional and makes a left into the parking lot. "I wanted Wally Cleaver for a big brother. I even wrote to Santa for him one year."

I laugh. That's pretty good—little Eddie, hard at work on that big blotter on that pine desk, printing on lined paper that he could do without the Louisville Slugger and the subscription to *Boys' Life*. Maybe even without the gold-plated Last Rites kit. Just send me Wally.

Eddie is at my car door, and he opens it. He extends his hand and I look into it, thinking he is holding something he wants me to see. Then I understand and I put my hand in his and he helps me from the seat. We have touched.

He holds the Friendly's door for me, and when the waitress comes to lead us to our booth, he makes a motion for me to walk first. As I unbutton my coat, he helps me remove it, and then he carefully hangs it on a peg nailed into the paneled wall across from us.

When the waitress returns to put napkins and silver on the table, he tells her we will have two teas, and then looks over and asks if that is fine with me.

I nod. He has the manners I have seen only in old men in old movies.

"Tell me about your job," Eddie asks. "It must be fascinating."

"My job? Well it's always something different."

"You must be very good at photography from being there all the time," he says. He is loosening his tie a little. It has little yellow crest things on it. I see part of a brown leather watch strap under his right cuff, from which some wrist hair is poking. I find myself wanting to stroke it.

"I don't even own a camera, to be truthful," I tell him. "I really don't know how to operate one. But Mr. Herrman—he's the owner, a very nice man—he is big on getting me to learn how. Once in a while he will say 'Let's just try this camera, for the fun of it.' He uses that expression a lot, and it usually doesn't fit. Like he says 'For the fun of it, let's clean the chemical tanks.' 'For the fun of it, let's go over the books.' I say that doesn't sound like fun, and he says 'Let's just do it, come on, for the fun of it.' "

When I do the Mr. Herrman part, I put on my German accent. I have Eddie laughing, and all this is seeming less scary as it goes on.

Eddie tells me I am pretty funny. But what I am saying is the truth. My ignorance of cameras once in a while gets to Mr. Herrman, and he places in my hand a small plastic model—instant focus, instant advance, instant on and off—the kind, he says, "a monkey could run."

"For the fun of it," he'll say, "just try to make a photograph." I know he is doing this to be nice. He does not really approve of these plastic cameras. He has owned only one camera in his entire life—a sturdy metal Leica. Small, compact, without a meter. Mr. Herrman does not need automatic anything. He knows how to read light like he knows how to breathe. He is a Leica man, but the Leica would not sell in his store. What sells are small plastic cameras in bubble gum pink or fire engine red, the kind you can throw into your beach bag, or give to a young child. The kind you just point and shoot. The kind I know he sees as a travesty. But the kind that are perfect for somebody like me.

"I think you might like to try," Eddie says. "It's so beautiful around here. Lots of scenery—you always see out-of-towners on the roadsides with their cameras. Did you see those people at the river on the way here?"

"Yes," I say, and I remember how he had seemed to have his eyes on the road all the time he had been driving. "But we were never the kind of family I see coming into the shop—those that take a picture every day of something, sometimes of nothing. They make photos of people eating cereal and doing the laundry. Pointing at road signs. We never really did anything and we never really went anywhere. To me, I don't know, there isn't a whole lot of sense to it. I guess if I thought something noteworthy was happening, I'd want to record it. Otherwise, I don't get it at all."

I was trying to say to Eddie that it always has gone along pretty much the same in my life. That my every days are not as wide-eyed and howling and vibrant as some of the ones I see on film. These people are doing things. They are going somewhere. They are making faces at parties and they are on vacation and are being pushed into joyous group shots. They line up their dogs and collect their awards and beam over the food and the garages and the babies they made all by themselves.

They all seem to be taking in a whole different kind of

air than am I, and they don't have to be running into a surf or standing with a congressman to give me this impression. It is even, to me, found in someone standing at the shady edge of a weedy lawn. This is my rhododendron right here, they are saying, and they are doing this so loudly that you can hear it coming off the paper. I planted it! I watered it! Look at it explode into magenta! All because of what I did.

I would like to take Eddie in there and show him these people, show him that they would make him feel the same way. But then maybe they wouldn't. Here he is in an ice cream shop in his hometown, and he has a look on his face like he is in Madrid. I have seen this same expression on people who actually were there, smiling even though they were at the very tail end of a long line for some important show at the Prado. They were somewhere, and it was where they wanted to be.

Our tea arrives and we fill our cups from little aluminum pitchers. We both use the same amount of sugar—just less than a pack—and we both push aside the little plastic barrels of cream. I notice there is only a rose decorating the tea bag tag, not a fortune. I am not going to get any help with this, I guess.

I ask Eddie if he takes pictures. "I get a discount, and I could get you a break on developing. Or on film, or anything else. We have frames, albums, tripods, lens cleaner. Some things are very good quality."

"Once in a while," Eddie answers. "I have an old camera that my mother no longer uses. It takes one twenty film."

"That is old," I say, because I know. That type of film, too large for our machines so it must be sent to a commercial processor in Providence, fits the kind of camera that you hold against yourself and look down into the glass to see what you are shooting. Whatever you are viewing is upside-down.

"I learned to use it on family vacations," Eddie says, and

one of his feet hits one of mine under the table. Both jump away from each other. "My parents are nuts about the Cape. We'd go there for two weeks every summer. Hyannis, which has to be the most crowded place there. But my mother liked it because she could attend the same church as Rose Kennedy."

"She was there?" I am amazed. I would think someone as big a big shot as she is could get a priest to come right to her house.

"Once in a while," Eddie says. "One time we saw Bobby—a long, long time ago, of course. And Ethel, too. My mother was awestruck the day that we saw the three of them. She got Ethel to autograph a church paper and spent the rest of the day on the pay phone at the hotel calling up every relative and going over the story again and again."

I tell Eddie of my interest in Caroline Kennedy, how I often take note of what was happening to her. Despite the fact that she was a famous rich person, I say, she has always seemed like a normal person. My mother, though, doesn't like the way she keeps her hair. Then I stop my talking, mainly because that is the end of that story, and partly because Eddie is looking at me with this pleasant, and I guess you could call it entranced, expression. I have never taken him for a person who could get a look like that on his face while looking at me. But there he is, doing so. So I ask "What?" And he just says, "Nothing at all," in a kind of whisper as he keeps on looking.

Eddie pays the check at the cash register, then comes back to leave two dollars for the waitress, for whom, he says, he feels sorry because she is working on a holiday. Then he helps me on with my coat and has me walk before him over to the door. At the car, he unlocks my door and makes sure that all my limbs are inside before he gently closes me in.

We drive back to my house as the sun is just about to set. Eddie plays the country tape again, this time just a twangy, slow instrumental that makes me move my feet a little. The trees look ready to explode in buds. A robin settles on a branch overhead. Bright green bunches of skunk cabbage already have blasted up through the dark, wet floor of the woods along the river. I look quickly to my left and see Eddie look quickly to his right, at me. We are driving through promise so thick we almost need the windshield wipers.

"I'd ask you in, but I'm sure you had a long day," I say quickly once we are in view of my house, and of the relatives' cars. Lights are on in the living room and I can see the television screen blinking colors.

"You know, I should get going," Eddie agrees in a voice that makes it sound like I have had a really great idea. I am relieved.

"I've been up since five," he says. "You know that—you have, too, I bet."

"I guess I'm beat as well," I say. "Thanks. I had a nice time. It was fun."

"Let's do this again," suggests Eddie as we reach the curb. He shuts off the motor and starts to unclick his seat belt.

"Don't get out," I say, maybe a little too fast. "Why don't you get going? I can get to the door. Thanks."

Eddie looks a little confused. He says "Sure? OK, well, I'll be seeing you."

I open my door and take my handbag from the floor. The jar of borscht had been behind it. I just pick it up, like it is something I take everywhere with me, and get out of the car. Then I poke my head back in and look at Eddie. "A nice time. Really," I say. Then neither of us says anything. So I nod and smile and shut the door.

Eddie can't stop himself from being polite. He waits in the car until I open the front door, just in case, I am guessing, somebody jumps out from behind the arborvitae and makes off with me. I turn and give him a wave once just before I make it safely inside.

My father is asleep on the La-Z-Boy. Rudy is staring into the TV set. I hear voices from the kitchen, where, I know, the rest of them are battling in a game of Scrabble. "Just take your two letters," I hear Cioci Wanda snarl. "We don't want to be here all night." I hear somebody else pick up the game box lid and swish the tiles it contains. I smell coffee brewing. Without bothering to remove my coat, I start up the stairs, wondering what I am going to do with the sloshing jar I am carrying. A hand comes through the railing and catches my ankle. It is the hand of Cioci Julie.

"How's Anna?" she asks, using an exaggerated tone like you would if you were on stage, in a play. Then she winks.

"Fine. Just fine," I say, seriously.

Then—and this is fun—I wink back.

TWO ROUND, FLOWERED HATS YOU COULD STORE LAYER CAKES IN. Two prim, tailored dark blue winter coats with Virgin Mary Sodality pins decorating the lapels. Two sets of silver-rimmed glasses hanging by two lengths of etched silver beads circling two deeply creased necks.

Two of everything.

I had only expected one, but Cecelia Osiewicki had brought along her old-maid sister, Bronia, and the two of them were standing on my doorstep in their Sunday best one chilling Saturday afternoon in November. They were numbers forty-three and forty-four, respectively, in a long line of prospective customers for an engagement ring that was entering its thirteenth month of semi-public display and had been pushed across the coffee table to the fingers of eager strangers so many times that it was amazing to me that a groove hadn't been worn into the wood.

I would have had trouble recalling each of the forty-two visits if I hadn't begun a little notebook listing the appointments—and if I didn't have my mother and her memory and her opinions. She needed no tally card to know that I was no closer to getting rid of the ring than I was the day Dick Wilkins rolled his wallpaper van up to my door. Last month—the one-year anniversary of my effort—had been particularly difficult for my mother. "How long?" she moaned when I asked her to move a pot so I could boil some water for the short and soft-spoken middle-aged electrical engineer who had been hoping to make mine the second and final engagement ring he would present in his life. The man—Rollie somebody—had been recounting in gruesome detail how the first person he'd given one to had died after stepping on something called a stonefish the first and last time they'd visited the Indo-Pacific. They had been wading near a reef. The thing looked like a stone—how was she supposed to know it wasn't? I said I didn't know how, and that I didn't blame her for thinking it was just a rock.

"Needles of pain shot into her foot," he recalled dramatically, running his thumb back and forth on the sharp edge of the coffee table. "I don't know this for sure—exactly how it felt—but I imagine that to be true. She couldn't walk over to me. She simply fell into the water. It was instantaneous. Do you have some tea? Decaffeinated?"

I was more than happy to perform a chore at that point, and I left him in the parlor with his thoughts and all.

"How much longer?" my mother had asked me when I entered the kitchen. She comes to listen at the door to the various stories customers have to tell, so I thought she was referring to Rollie and his loss.

"I don't know," I said as I rummaged through the cabinet. "It must have been awful to see that happen. They say you can't rush getting over grief like that, you know."

"I don't mean him—I mean you. A year you've been doing this and where has it gotten you? Just keep giving out more free food and wasting your time."

"It's one tea bag. Maybe a spoon of sugar. Now do we have decaffeinated tea or not?"

"I never heard of such a thing," my mother said. I took that to mean about decaffeinated tea.

I have made mention of Dick Wilkins because he passed me just today. Not in the Nu Design van, but on a roll of film, where he and a tiny doll-like woman he no doubt takes great pride in seriously calling "the little woman" were waving as they entered a shining black limousine. The plan to slim down obviously had failed: except for a rented tuxedo and some dry hair, Dick looked just about how he had when he sat on my couch that night so long ago. He looked the same in the photo of him and his bride standing with a beefy set of parents that had to be Dick's, and he looked the same in the one of him and his bride standing with a blank-faced tiny older man who tightly clutched the little woman's arm like there was no way you were going to pry him loose.

The roll ended and I looked up and into the plastic panel that covers the developing controls. In it I could see myself, and I, too, looked much the same as I had on the night Dick had visited. Maybe my hair was a little longer, maybe a little flatter on this particular day. But here was Dick Wilkins, having gone in some oblique full circle, and here was I, with no bend in sight that I might turn.

That was no concern of Mrs. Osiewicki, who refused to step into my house before I would say it was fine that she had brought her sister along without first calling to tell me. "It isn't a problem, is it? The two of us?"

I told her not to worry about it, and to please come in. I really didn't know much about Bronia, except that she lived in Southbridge. I knew Mrs. Osiewicki from church, and from going to school with her son, John Paul.

John Paul.

That said it right there. Somebody who was twenty-eight and who still went by two names. You can imagine the fuss

Mrs. Osiewicki made when the newly elected pope chose as his name the same one she had selected for her son way back when. She went absolutely hysterical for a while, seeing the selection as a message from God that her own John Paul was destined for greatness. The Sunday after we got a Pope John Paul, the priest read from the pulpit that an anonymous donation of forty-five dollars had been made to the church "from a grateful mother, for a true sign from Our Heavenly Father." Mrs. Osiewicki even had hung a white wreath on the front door of her home, and some said she was having delusions that the John Paul in the Vatican was the one she'd given birth to—even though he was about her same age.

I ended up going to confession over it, but because of Mrs. Osiewicki, Anna and I had the biggest laugh when Pope John Paul I up and died before he really even got to unpack at the Vatican. Mrs. Osiewicki, however, didn't find it funny. She appeared publicly only in church after that—nowhere else—looking very sad. I think the first time I saw a prayer directly answered was when the next pope ended up choosing the same name as his predecessor.

Other than being noteworthy for the pope business, Mrs. Osiewicki was known for her bus trips to shrines—both the famous ones, like those in Quebec, and others that no one had ever heard of before she publicized them in the fliers she stacks next to the lost and found box in the back of the church. The mystery destinations, unfortunately for those who don't know better, make up most of her itinerary. Yet she regularly manages to pack a chartered coach full of people who pay twenty-five dollars each to leave the church parking lot by 6 A.M. and ride a bus for two or three hours, with only a dry Danish and a single cup of coffee as sustenance, to usually someplace no more elaborate than a backyard in Connecticut that contains a concrete statue at which some small miracle like the curing of a toothache or the return to church of a confused eldest child supposedly once took place. En route, Mrs. Osiewicki crochets and sells flimsy string rosaries and collects donations. She always says that a portion of her proceeds benefit the church, but it is not known just what percentage that is. Most people suspect it is a low figure, as Mrs. Osiewicki always is able to take John Paul to Atlantic City for a couple weeks each June.

John Paul is the produce manager at Fruit Fair, which, despite its name, actually carries everything a grocery store does. Randy, who sells John Paul regular unleaded for the panel truck with which the store delivers its trademark fruit baskets, has pointed out to me that a simple change of that name could increase the store's profits measurably—OK so you're driving down the road and you all of a sudden get the idea to make a rib roast, he said, setting the scene. You're not going to slam on your brakes for that fruit store up ahead. For a Food Fair, maybe. Even a Fruit and Food Fair. But then, I point out, fruit and food are the same two things. These are the kinds of conversations we have about every other week, when he calls to check if the ring is still available but ends up talking about anything. Like how Fruit Fair, not really a competitor, but another store nonetheless, has a stupid name. When my mother asks what does Randy want in these telephone calls, I don't know what to say.

Promotional manners do not concern John Paul, who has all he can handle trying to remember each day to bring to work the red polyester blazer with both his names embroidered on the right front, just above a plastic pocket protector always jammed with felt markers and the case for his out-of-style aviator glasses with photo-sensitive lenses. The bulbs in the store are of the intensity that gets his glasses just dark enough so you can't see his eyes. My mother says that's why John Paul is especially lousy at sorting tangerines.

He is pleasant, an all right person, I guess, but to hear

Mrs. Osiewicki speak of him, you'd think John Paul was the catch of the century. Apparently that is what Dorota, the only girl he ever has gone out with, and the one who one day will be Mrs. John Paul Osiewicki, also thinks.

John Paul's mother says that even though they had only recently decided to wed, the two have most of the details settled—even down to the banner that will hang above the punch bowl. "To a Fruitful Life," it is to read. "The store is going to donate an entire table of exotic fruit, as its gift," his mother informs me. "So that will be very fitting, that being his job and all."

I smile at her, as does Bronia.

Mrs. Osiewicki straightens in her seat, and pushes her shoulder blades back and together. "I won't lie to you, dear," she says to me. "Though we have money for a nice wedding, we are not a wealthy family. When my John Paul asked me if he could marry the girl, I told him that while I had no objections, he should realize we couldn't afford too grand an affair. His father—God rest his soul—left me a sum, but over the years it's depleted. As we—as John Paul and she—marry, we have to watch our pennies."

As I wonder why we—they—have to, she answers my question.

"Dorota's father, you know, does not work, due to his, um"—she stops and looks over at Bronia, who offers only a confused expression—"they call it a substance abuse problem."

I know she would like to have called him a drunk, but that she wanted to appear more sensitive than that.

"I have offered to pay for the wedding, but, like I said, I am not wealthy," Mrs. Osiewicki reiterates. "That's why we answered your ad. It is important to be frugal, to look for a bargain, at all times in life. I know you know what I mean, with your situation. I don't really know it, but I've heard. What I mean to say is you know how it is to plan a wedding."

Not long ago, such a comment would have had me turning my head to see what program was on the television, so the visitor couldn't see my brimming eyes. But Mrs. Osiewicki, and anything she could think of saying, had become part of a process that had become part of my life. There was no selling this thing without being on display somehow, and I had come to take people like her, and whatever she and they had to say, rather in stride.

"I sure do," I say cheerily. "Now, here's the ring." I take the little box from atop the fan of magazines and flip it open. Bronia adjusts her bifocals and leans toward it. Mrs. Osiewicki snatches the ring from her view and rotates the box in front of her own face.

Neither of them says one word.

Then Mrs. Osiewicki makes a *tsk tsk tsk* sound and looks up at me. "You poor dear," she says. "So close you came."

"You're right," I agree, again without being snide. Well, she was correct. There was no arguing it. Just about now, I know, Eddie and I would have been a year and a half into our marriage. There would have been a little tarnish on the candle extinguisher, maybe some crusty burnt-on stuff at the edges of the Corning Ware. The porcelain soap dishes would have a coating of film, and we long ago would have abandoned wearing the matching pajama set for wearing nothing at all. But instead, all those things and more either were still on the store shelf—repackaged to make them look brand-new—or now lived in the home of someone who actually had made it to her wedding day, and beyond. For me, the only concrete evidence that Eddie Balicki had ever wanted a life with me is being mashed onto the right finger of somebody whose only connection to him is a few letters of her last name.

Mrs. Osiewicki puts on the glasses that have been resting against her chest. She also has taken from another chain around her neck a small decorative magnifying glass. As she lifts it, the chain catches on a golden cross also dangling there, and Bronia reaches over to help her untangle.

To her obvious dismay, the ring will not move past the first bend in Mrs. Osiewicki's finger. She hands it to Bronia, whose fingers are large but less flabby, and devoid of any adornment. Bronia pushes it onto her ring finger and it actually looks quite elegant there. For a second I wonder what Bronia's story is, but know better than to ask, as I might get the entire story, blow by blow, of what a sorry life she had without ever once knowing a man's love.

"Hmmm," goes Mrs. Osiewicki, reaching over for her sister's hand. She holds it out and positions the magnifying glass so closely as to examine the stone. From where I am sitting, I have a new, greatly enlarged view of the fleshy mole that has grown just below the right-hand corner of Mrs. Osiewicki's mouth. With the help of the magnifier, the three hairs thrusting from it appear as sparse trees struggling for survival on a tiny island. The island quakes: "Hmmm," Mrs. Osiewicki hums again, and I think I hear her say something like, "So this was his . . ."

Just then, a slice of midafternoon sun settles through the window, hits the stone, and zaps back, greatly intensified by the magnifying aids, into Mrs. Osiewicki's eyes. She grimaces and recoils as if somebody has hit her. *"Oooooww-wooooh!"* she howls. Bronia's hand is sent flying. The ring falls to the floor, and lands without a sound.

Mrs. Osiewicki fumbles in her bag for a hanky and holds it over her right eye. She makes a little sniffing sound. Bronia rubs her ring finger.

"Forgive me," Mrs. Osiewicki whines in a higher pitch than she normally uses. Then she clears her throat.

"That's OK, it's right here somewhere," I tell her, and bend to find the ring.

"No, I mean I'm sorry, we're not interested. Bronia, let's go."

I am down on the floor right then, and I spot the ring

wedged between the leg of the coffee table and the toe of Mrs. Osiewicki's sandal. I reach for it and her foot comes down on my finger.

"Hey!" I shout, because she is crushing me.

Mrs. Osiewicki quickly answers, "Sorry again. We have to leave. Thank you for your time." I still am under the table, and am level with ten then another ten nyloned toes that rock past me.

I get up off the floor and see that Mrs. Osiewicki and Bronia already are at the coat tree, fixing their hats onto their heads. I brush off my knees and walk over there.

"So you're not interested?"

"I think not. I really don't know what I was thinking. I really don't at all. John Paul should just go to a store." I see Mrs. Osiewicki is shaking as she says this, and Bronia at one point puts a hand onto her sister's shoulder.

I suddenly get a feeling that I merely have been something to do for the afternoon, the way you might ride by the place where a car had been wrecked the night before and stare at the empty space in the road where it came to rest.

I also get the feeling that they would have stayed here and stared a little longer, had it not been for that piece of light hitting her so timely, so sharply and directly. We all just say good-bye stiffly and I close the door. I realized I still have the ring in my hand, which I open and take a look into. I see that Mrs. Osiewicki could have something here, that this very well could be seen as one of the pieces of glass scattered at the curb, sparkling at the end of the short but pronounced skid mark.

The ring looked fake to Estelle Konopka, so I was able to get to work early.

She and her fiancé, some nervous guy she introduced only as "my fiancé," had arrived on time, just after supper, at 6 P.M., and it wasn't 6:05 when she opened the box and protested in a huff, "Oh no, no, this is not for me—I want real diamond," and the two of them got up off the couch and let themselves out. It wasn't worth getting upset over. These meetings are chances I take, and they're usually entertaining to some degree. At least I'd only wasted five minutes on the sourpuss, and now I had an entire batch of still-warm chocolate chip cookies, which I'd made for the appointment, to take to work.

Mr. Herrman was training a new high school kid to work at the counter, when he needed the help. Meghan Ziskowicz, a diligent worker except for her frequent trips to hairspray her hairdo in the rest room, left us two weeks ago, when her brother opened his frozen yogurt stand near the reservoir entrance. Mr. Herrman had been hoping Kara Ogrodnik would be as good an employee as her guidance counselor had predicted, and there were signs of that on her first night, when she suggested placing some of the overprints in the frames for sale, and hanging up a sign offering a discount on the frames to those persons who found themselves on display.

Having acquired a great interest in such marketing ploys over the years since he'd abandoned his art, Mr. Herrman immediately was impressed.

"I'm going to like her," he whispered to me when he came by to get his coat.

I agreed, only for the fact that he liked her enough to have hired her and therefore to have rescued me from working the cash register, as I many times had been forced to since the departure of Meghan and her assorted styling products. I was back at my machine.

"Are my pictures ready yet?"

I must hear this fifty times a day, but as long as I'm at the machine I don't have to get up and find the answer. So I didn't turn around when somebody said this.

"Go ahead, ignore me—I'll take my business elsewhere," said the customer, who I realized was Anna, and who, I also realized, would never go anywhere else because she gets free developing from Mr. Herrman. In contrast if we're talking about family, twenty-five years into my friendship with Anna, my mother usually refers to her only as "that girl."

Right then, that girl was leaning over the counter, sticking her head through the doorway of the glass booth in which I work. "You can let her back," I told Kara, who was protecting her new turf by placing her hands firmly on the half-door that keeps the public where they belong. "It's my sister."

"Oh," Kara said apologetically and hurried to unlatch the gate. "I didn't know. I'm so sorry. Go right in. Please."

Anna hung up her jacket and put on one of the white lab coats that Mr. Herrman wants worn in the developing area, both to keep street dust out and to make us look like a professional operation, like your photographs are of utmost importance to us.

"Where's my pictures?" Anna wanted to know again.

"OK, OK. I just got here. I'll do them now."

"Right—how'd it go with that woman? Did she like it?"

I remembered Estelle, and her disappointment. "I guess she's used to something better," I said.

"She's gotta be crazy," Anna said.

I inserted her roll into the end of the printer and took my seat. Head-and-shoulders portraits of Anna began advancing past. Then came a series of a rather elegant young woman. I exposed about six frames before realizing the next person looked familiar. "Who is this, some relative?"

Anna laughed. "It's me—can you believe it?"

I moved for a closer look, and even from only the negative image, I realized she wasn't kidding. It was Anna—hair swept back, eyes made up, lips darkened, pearl earrings dangling. In one shot she even placed her hand to the side of her face, and her nails were colored.

"Val got to me—the night you were supposed to come over but the pig man wanted to see the ring."

So while I had a truck full of swill outside my house, and Gary Popko on my porch, downwind, trying to get me to lower the price so he could really wow his intended, who one day will inherit her father's rendering company near Turners Falls, Anna was being moisturized and plucked and decorated and photographed. It had been my lucky night, and I didn't even know it.

She ran over to me with her prints, which had just fallen into the bin at the end of the machine. "Look! Before and after," Anna said excitedly, holding pale, flat-haired, turtle-necked Anna in one hand, and glamorous, blow-dried, almost unrecognizable Anna, shoulders peeking from a wrap of satin fabric, in the other. "I don't know—you know I hate posing, and I wasn't too excited about this when she first wanted to do it—but it's kind of fun to look at now."

"You look nice. I have work." I was annoyed. Out of thin air had come the thought that maybe Anna and I would have gotten made up together for my wedding. Something to look a little special, something other than the regular Chapstick. I wondered if I would have been as transformed as Anna, if I would have been able to take Eddie's breath away. When was I going to drop all this?

"I'll just get an envelope," Anna said, figuring that something was wrong. "Are you all right?"

I didn't say anything, then I figured, why lie? "Sometimes I think about Eddie." Anna, who now officially hated Eddie, but who always loved me, said kindly and only, "Of course you do."

Anna left after she gathered her things together, and I charged through a couple dozen rolls, one after the other after the next. I saw a 4-H group on a tour of the Statehouse, many shots of locomotives taken from an overpass, an anniversary party, and a lady posing at Rockefeller Center with an irritated-looking Tom Brokaw. Somebody had caught a pickerel and had it swimming in their bathtub. On one roll there was only eleven close-up shots of a scaling skin condition on somebody's forearm.

By the time I finished all the films, Kara was long gone, picked up at nine by a father who purchased a pocket photo album just so he could watch her operate the cash register. "I am so proud of you, honey," was what he told her just before the door closed behind them.

I cut and matched the negatives with the envelopes, then with the sets of prints. I bundled the tour group and the fish and the arm and then I spotted Randy. Being handed an infant, who was screaming and fighting. Randy was trying to smile for the camera, but was way too concerned about the baby really to look as good as I knew he was able. In the next shot—I had to look, of course—the baby was a little more at ease with this stranger, but Randy still looked worried that he was holding it incorrectly, or that he might drop it and kill it. In the next shot, the baby was nowhere to be seen. Instead, Randy was holding in his lap a fully grown woman, made up as much as the "after" Anna, wearing a low-cut shiny black dress, cuddling up so close to Randy that half her pile of blond curls hid half his face. The part that was visible looked as anxious as it had with the baby.

I checked the envelope: "Malachowski, Roseanne," was written boldly, marking the owner of the photographs taken at what, after noting that they all looked like pushy blonds, I guessed to be an anniversary party for some of her relatives.

I found the right negative strip and placed it in the machine. In minutes I had a five-by-seven of Roseanne and my friend Randy—well, mostly of Roseanne—to insert into a paper frame that went into an envelope I marked with a sticker reading WITH OUR COMPLIMENTS.

SO THERE I WAS, ON A BLANKET, AT THE EDGE OF A LAKE, FLAT on the ground, leaning my head against the bare and bony and hairy and naked and wonderful knee of a man. A man who had invited me to come here with him. A man who had called me and asked "Why don't you take the Feast of the Assumption off and we can do something?"

It was August, our fifth month of keeping steady company.

Ever since Easter, we had been doing things together—dates, you could say. First it was a weekend night, to the movies or to walk, in public, down the street. And, of course, we would run into each other at church and talk for a while until our two cars were almost the only ones in the parking lot—staying so long we nearly outlasted the Chapels. Then we began making Sunday afternoon plans. We met and took car rides, or walked at the reservoir, or just sat somewhere, on a bench at the Common or in his car, and learned about each other. Like how, in an effort to make some reparation, Eddie sends a fifty-dollar donation to the National Wildlife Foundation each time he, accidentally, of course, runs over a squirrel or some other animal he couldn't have avoided on the road. How I, for a joke he didn't get, once bought my father a can of hairspray to replace his daily Vitalis when all those "wethead is dead" commercials were playing on TV. How Eddie has a list of the hundred things he wants to do before he dies, and how each time he crosses one off—after visiting some historical landmark or reading a specific book or taking up a new sport or learning how to count a hundred in another language—he adds another to replace it. How the one time I made graham cracker crumbs for a cheesecake I did so in the blender, but with the top accidentally left off and the pieces dusting the whole kitchen. How he'll use the second side of an envelope or a piece of correspondence for scrap paper, which is cut and stapled and kept in a pile next to his phone. How, in fifth grade on a dare after school with no nuns or boys around, I ran into the boy's lavatory to flush a urinal and it wouldn't stop running. How familiar to me is the menu in his home. How strange to him it is that such a wonderful girl is not taken. How similar is the sequence of prayers we both say in Polish, on our knees, at the edge of our beds, every morning and every night.

In late July, my mother began asking me what it was that Eddie Balicki wanted. She was unable to ask him personally because he had yet to come into the house. As I would tell Eddie at the end of each night, crossing hidden fingers, the floor had just been waxed. Or somebody was sick with something contagious. Or the house needed cleaning. I wasn't ready to put him and them in the same room. Not yet. So it was to me, rather than Eddie, that my mother would pose the question: "What does he want?" And I would say I didn't know. Because that was true—I was having a little trouble believing that what someone as charged and as alive as Eddie Balicki wanted was somebody as, well, me as me.

But he must have. Because there we were, selecting the same pew, genuflecting at the same time, and shuffling sideways to our places. It was the 7:30 A.M. mass, and it had a fair turnout for an easily forgotten Holy Day stuck on a Thursday in the middle of a long and sweaty month that finds most people asleep on a beach somewhere. I had often thought this was poor treatment for celebration of the day on which the world's only Virgin Mary had been lifted all the way up to heaven, without even really having to die.

As we took our seats, we got a sideways glance from old Mrs. Lega, the butcher's wife (GET YOUR LEGS AT LEGA'S reads the backs of the jerseys worn by the store's softball team). But other than she, nobody turned. It was like none of them noticed that one of my greatest dreams finally had come true—that I was seated right next to Eddie in that holy and exalted pew I had stared at for so long.

The organist plugged in her instrument. Its motor whirred like a blender, then quieted to almost an inaudible little hum. Eddie and I still were saying our prayers, though, actually, I was just kneeling and taking this all in. When she began to hit the keys, I looked up at the altar and I thanked God for this present, to be the one bumping my elbow into Eddie's, before him and all these people.

Because there were all those people, I knew I would be hearing from my mother what my mother soon would be hearing from someone else: "Edna, I saw your girl in church with Lottie's boy. What were they doing there?" There would be dumb questions like that, but people think they have to ask these things, feeling it is their business.

Eddie crossed himself at the end of his prayer and slid back onto the seat. I did the same. He took a missalette from the seat and handed it to me, then reached for a copy of his own. "Someone's crying, Lord, kumbayaaa," sang the organist. I knew to expect something like this from her. She was not our regular one. She was Peggy Turner, who practiced at home on one of those electronic keyboards that has the build-in drum sounds (I have seen it in her Christmas pictures, Peggy dressed as an elf, playing to adoring nieces and nephews), and who fills in when Basia Sekula cannot make it to mass. Basia knows what music to play in this church and would be loved for no reason other than that she never sang kumbaya. And if she did, she'd do it in Polish and bring tears to everyone's eyes. Basia came to this country as a child and began playing the organ at church when she was a teenager. She never sings in English, except on Sundays that coincide with national holidays, when she does "God Bless America"—or, as she puts it, "Got Bless America"—and has everybody joining in. Then, just when you think the mass is over and you can leave, she launches into *"Boże Coś Polskę"*—"God Save Poland"—figuring it's a national holiday, so why not?

Basia is a coloratura soprano, self-taught. But that month, at age forty-one and, as she put it to my mother, "through Got's grace," she was a mother for the first time. So she'd been out for a couple of weeks, and, in the interim, we were forced to sing the English standards from the back of the missalettes like a bunch of Protestants.

"Someone's laughing, Lord, kumbayaaa," Peggy wailed, dragging out the last syllable like her tail was caught in something.

"Someone's laughing, Lord," Eddie sang softly on the second line, then he turned into that someone. It began with little movements at the corners of his mouth, then at the corners of his eyes, and then his head began to shake a little. He coughed, but really he was laughing and trying to disguise it. I turned to my left and looked over at my regular pew, which was occupied by Anna's cousin, Val, a former Grange Queen whose IMVAL license plate I had noticed in the parking lot adorning the new mauve convertible she had earned from her record Mary Kay sales. She was looking at the altar from beneath lowered lids perfectly blended in subtle shades probably named something like Fawn and Desert, but, I wondered, if she turned our way, would she see the view I see every time I'm here: Eddie looking devout enough to be on the cover of the Bible. Or would she see somebody who was ready to crack up laughing. That's what I was seeing—Eddie all set to laugh his head off. In church of all places.

I whispered, "Knock it off," feeling I was ready to join him. Eddie smirked, then put both hands over his mouth, as if to sneeze into them. But he just laughed some more.

I was hearing it over his noise: "Edna, I saw your girl in church with Lottie's boy. They were laughing!"

"You're bad," I told Eddie, feigning disgust as we left the building. Eddie's fit had lasted through the first reading, then had subsided. It almost was kicked off again when Peggy cackled three alleluias just prior to the Gospel reading. But Eddie had managed to control himself through the end of the recessional.

"I'm really sorry," Eddie replied, very seriously. "I've never done anything like that before. Not even when I was a kid. I can't believe it. I just can't. I don't know what came over me."

"Maybe Peggy Turner?"

Then we both cracked up, and I told him my image of her tail, and Eddie swore he would never be able again to listen to her without thinking of that. We laughed again.

We had Eddie's car, and, as he always did, he let me in my side and closed the door for me. He had the trunk filled with picnic items, but we needed some more ice, so we headed for town. The day was bright and there was an excitement about being free to just up and go, with most people around you up and going to somewhere they probably didn't want to be. It was still early enough that some could be seen leaving their homes for work and we made some jokes about feeling sorry for them.

At the Quick Stop, Eddie parked the car in a space in front of the door and went inside to get some change for the ice machine. I stayed in the car and watched him walk to the door and hold it open for an old man who was hobbling out with a loaf of bread. The man slowly tipped his hat to Eddie, and Eddie told him to have a pleasant day.

Eddie then got in line behind a young woman who had an armful of magazines and a Frostee. I could see it was strawberry or cherry because she had greatly overfilled the container and there was a huge peak of pink ice, speared by a white plastic spoon. Her breakfast, I figured. The man behind the counter, a tall, lanky guy with little tails of blond hair falling over the back of his white shirt collar, rummaged under the cash register and came out with a larger dish into which he placed the Frostee so, I figured, it would not damage the woman's upholstery if it tipped over while she was making the sharp turn from the parking lot. I saw her try to hand him a coin to pay for the dish, but he put his hand out flat toward her, as if he was trying to stop something from hitting him, and he smiled and shook his head no, for "no charge."

Then it was Eddie's turn. He handed the guy some paper money and the clerk handed him a fistful of change. Eddie nodded thanks and headed toward the door. Then the clerk waved and shouted something, and Eddie turned and came over to the other side of the register. He handed Eddie a stack of dollar bills and Eddie just stared at them there in his hand, like they were foreign currency he was trying to calculate. Then he extended his hand and the two men shook. Eddie, looking very serious, was saying something to him slowly and deliberately. He waved good-bye at him before going out the door.

"What was going on in there?" I of course wanted to know when Eddie returned to the car.

"You wouldn't believe it," he said, lifting himself off the seat so he could get his wallet from his back pocket. "I thought I gave the guy a dollar bill. But I don't know—I must have been tired or something—I gave him a fifty—then almost walked away with only four quarters. He could have kept forty-nine dollars for himself. How would I have known were it went?"

We both looked into the store window, where the clerk was fishing a hot dog from a steaming metal cooker. He fit it into a bun and wrapped it for a man wearing a tan hat pinned with a fishing license.

"That in there is a fine person," Eddie said of the clerk. "An honest person. I'll tell you, I almost lost a lot of money, but having this experience was worth some risk, to see that this kind of person still exists."

We both sat in the front seat of the car that hadn't been started, just sat there and looked into the store. We saw the clerk select a pickle from a small green plastic barrel next to the display of chewing tobacco, and he put it in a piece of waxed paper and handed it to the fisherman. We knew he wasn't going to charge him for it.

"He looks like a nice guy," I agreed.

"Well I for one know I'd put my trust in him," Eddie said. Then he stopped. "All this and here I am, forgetting the ice."

Eddie left the car and walked to the machine labeled ICE in big blue letters that had icicles hanging from the top of the *I* and the *C* and the *E*. I watched Eddie and his handsomeness as he reached into the machine, and enjoyed the fact that he would be coming back to the car, not to any of the other ones parked here. I looked straight ahead and saw the clerk looking out the window right at me. Then Eddie opened the car door and I turned away.

We headed for Pittsfield, taking the turnpike, playing his music. Eddie let me choose the tapes, and there were about a dozen of them arranged in alphabetical order inside a small brown vinyl case he kept on the floor behind the passenger's seat. I'd yet to see his car a mess. Usually there were just a few newspapers in the backseat, piled neatly. Today there were a couple back there, and on top of them was some kind of pamphlet printed with a full-color painting of Jesus tending a flock. There was a small black retractable umbrella, and there was an old green vinyl gym bag that held the clothes into which Eddie would change once we got to the lake.

He had thrown my bag in the trunk when he picked me up at the house. I had seen the upstairs curtain jerk a little when I got to the curb and I knew my mother was up there shaking her head and repeating what she had asked me as I was leaving the house: "Going out so early, and with a bag of clothing—what will people say?"

I told her that I didn't know what they would say, so she filled me in: "That you're sneaking off somewhere, somewhere you don't want anybody to know about. That's what."

"We're going to church."

"That's to make it look good."

This is why I tell Eddie the house is a mess, that my parents are tired, that we're painting the walls.

Anna says her father believes that anybody who wants to take you out should be man enough to come to the door. My own father seems to have no problem with my waiting on the porch for my date to arrive, but once in a while he will say, "Ask the boy in"—which I've yet to do. Usually, though, my father only wishes me good night or that he hopes I have fun. That's about it.

I have been to Eddie's parents' house, but only to cook or do some other church business. I have not been there with him, nor do I yet want to be. It is one thing to be someone who in theory might be wonderful for your son, but it is another thing actually to turn out to be that person.

It's a whole new light, and one that I don't yet want Lottie Balicki shining on me.

I have not been inside Eddie's apartment, though on occasion I drive by, and one time shortly after all this began, on the way home from working late, I even dared to park my car across the street and tried to see what I could of what was going on inside, where a golden glow illuminated the two front windows. It wasn't too long before I saw movement, and there was Eddie, bisected by the blinds, picking up the telephone and nodding his head. He stood there listening for a few moments, then said something into the receiver and hung up. He turned toward the front of the house, and my heart jumped as I wondered if he'd spotted my car. He moved closer to the wall, but his head was turned toward the space between the two windows, and he stared at that place, arms folded across his front, head cocked and face—what I could see of it—in placid concentration for what the digital clock on my dashboard told me was a whole seven minutes before I put the car in neutral and, lights off, rolled down the incline and out of sight.

So the few thank-you notes for some particularly nice times we have had are all of me that has entered 12 Eden Street, apartment 1. But that seems to be OK with Eddie. He continues to be the person who allows me to walk first into Friendly's, and who holds my coat and selects my restaurant meals and makes sure I am buckled in.

And as he has done ever since that first lovely kiss he set slowly and wonderfully on my lips, on top of Mount Sugarloaf, on the fifth Sunday after Easter, the day the Gospel told us to ask and we shall receive and our joy will be full, he never attempts a second without first asking, "Do you mind?" And I never say anything. I just let him. And let him. And let him, he who will be the one I will let do anything. But while I will say Eddie and I have been close, the only thing he has taken off me so far has been a shoe during one walk where I slipped and hit my ankle on a rock. When he asks me into his apartment and I say I don't have the time—when I actually don't yet have the nerve to face the unleashed passion my mother, reciting parables about the sad fates of girls whose lives were ruined when they forgot their good upbringings, has warned me I would be up against in a private setting—he just smooths my hand and pulls me close and says somewhere into my neck that he hopes someday I will find the time. You could not make up somebody so good.

I think exactly that at the lake, on the blanket, on his knee, as I stare out at the mountains and feel the sun. Once in a while, Eddie touches my shoulder or puts a little piece of grass on the tip of my nose. We are a greeting card waiting to be written on.

A set of parents and five grade-schoolers clop down the path in rubber flip-flops, dragging their folding chairs and coolers and baskets of water toys toward us. "Here! Over here!" yells one of the little kids, throwing a towel and a black inner tube onto the grass under the tree that's shading us. "I'm going in the water!"

"No, no—let's go nearer to the rest rooms," his father shouts as he eyes us and grabs the boy by the arm so he doesn't get too close to our blanket. It amazes and thrills me that I am part of something that can send an entire family running. With Eddie, it seems, anything is possible.

"They're gone," says Eddie, and he sounds genuinely relieved.

I turn and admire that kneecap. There is a little freckle there and I envy it, thinking how it would be to be that small mark stuck to him for life, to be able to be with Eddie at all times, every minute of the day, something he could never get rid of.

I could see myself as something like that, not so much as a mole but as a person, a long-time girlfriend, a fiancée, even—if dare I think it—a wife, Mrs. Eddie Balicki, who gets to cook his meals and make his bed and balance his checkbook and mow his lawn and do all those other daily things that for anyone else would be mundane, but done for him would be sacred acts. To bear all the many Eddies and Edwinas we would send into the world to spread the great and unconditional love they would inherit from their father. To be the one who gets to say to everyone—though it was not really the case but is an excuse that sounds plausible—you were wondering why I waited so long to be with somebody? This life is why. I knew he would come to me sooner or later.

"I'm glad," Eddie says as he watches the family march away. "There's something I wanted to do, and I didn't want anybody around."

His comment gives me a little stirring and I don't know what to do. He sits up and I do the same, though I am wondering if I should stay there on the ground. "Edna, I saw your girl at the lake with Lottie's boy. They were rolling around on the ground." I can hear it now, but I can't worry about it right now.

Eddie stands and takes my hand. I will follow him anywhere, but he only goes over to the big tree. I realize that I have no idea what he is doing, and that neither does the old black couple on the matching flowered chaise lounges, who have been watching us when not reading from their *USA Today* and sipping from their cans of something tucked into foam rubber insulators that say they've had A HALIBUT TIME AT MISQUAMICUT.

The two of them stare as Eddie has me sit down in front of the tree and then goes back to his bag and searches for something. His hand comes out holding The Future—a slim black and silver plastic rectangle with a corny name, a camera that I recognize as Mr. Herrman's top-of-the-line point-and-shoot.

"Eddie—what are you doing with that?" I stand up and ask this, and he walks over and shows it to me proudly.

"I went in and introduced myself, and Mr. Herrman was more than happy to tell me which one would be best—'Anythink for you,' he told me. He gave me a lesson and everything—it's really quite easy. I had to be sure to get to the shop when you weren't there. It was tricky, but I did it."

Eddie looks very pleased, like he for the first time has pulled off something illegal, and that it feels good.

"And what are you going to do with it?" I ask.

"I'm going to take your picture," he tells me. "Stand still. Smile!"

I walk over to him. I don't want this. We do a little tussling thing as I try to get the camera from him. "Come on," I plead. "I hate this. Let me get a photo of you. Go over and stand by the water. I'll get the mountains in the back. I'll make the sky real blue."

"No," Eddie says to me like he means it. "Go over by the tree. All my hard work, learning which button to push, and you don't want to cooperate."

I feel foolish. The two old people have put down their paper and are taking this all in. I look over at them, but they don't look embarrassed, as I would be if I were them.

Eddie stands there with his hands on the camera, ready to shoot. "You're ruining this for me, you know."

"Sorry," I say. "He shouldn't have made you buy the expensive one. I know how much that one is. You can get one for ten dollars and ninety-nine cents—he should have told you that."

"I didn't care," Eddie says. "I wanted the best one he had. This is an important shot—something's happening here."

I look behind me and see that could be true—I am about a foot away from the tree and the tree is a couple feet away from the drop off into the water, where one of the kids we would have corrupted is snorkeling very close to a woman floating in an inner tube. I can see some roots waving from the eroded embankment, and rocks jutting out, ready to crash onto the beach. Something definitely could happen here. But Eddie is staring at me like he means something other than falling in.

"Here," he announces rather loudly, "I am going to record that this is when we said that we love each other. We do—don't we?"

I take a step back. Then another. The tree stops me from going farther, from going off the cliff, off the edge of the earth.

I nod my head yes. Eddie smiles, more what you'd call a loving smile than a regular happy one, and says, "Perfect." Then he brings the camera to his eye. I look into the lens only because I know he is on the other side. I'm not sure exactly what you would call it, but I have an expression on my face that says this is who I am, in the out-of-doors, with the mountains and the water, and with the tree to hold me up. I can stand here on this day and say that somebody loves me.

I hear the click.

I hear the angels.

I am going up to heaven and I haven't even died.

BOLAC KOZIOL TALKS LIKE THERE IS AN EXTRA SPACE BETWEEN each of the words he says. This habit, it is widely known by everybody around here, was one result of his studies with an elocution expert hired by Bolac's parents right around the time the boy was learning to speak English. He was the first member of his family to be born in America, and his parents wanted him to live his life as an American, speaking as Americans do, however that might be. There would be no thick Eastern European accent for this child, so extra money from the cobbler shop went for private lessons with the high school's English teacher, and that's why, more than sixty-five years later, Bolac Koziol is sitting on my couch making his long-dead parents proud by responding yes, he'd like the cherry, rather than the cheddy, soda.

"Coming right up," I say and I leave the room. I don't know why I have offered him anything—I just want him to leave, and felt that way even before he arrived. In my eyes, Bolac Koziol is not an altogether pleasant person.

Take how he treats the customers who browse the selection of candy and magazines he keeps in a corner of the cobbler shop. They have to hear the man who stocked them ask, with slow and perfect enunciation, how can they read such trash, or do they know how those things will ruin their teeth?

And they and all other customers have not to mind being sucked into a conversation during which, no matter how hard they resist, Bolac Koziol will work a little piece of their lives to the surface, where he will net it and add it to his great collection of knowledge that really is nobody else's business.

And so, the next person who comes in to collect their resoled dress bucks gets not only their pair, but that little something you left behind. In with the next customer's change, he might slip in that you needed your galoshes reglued as soon as possible because the hospital in Worcester where you take your husband for treatments has an expensive parking garage, so you drop him off there and walk from a cheaper lot four and a half blocks away. Or that you ruined these suede loafers when you had to fly down to North Carolina in a rainstorm because your brother landed in jail there and you had to see him. Or that you hoped the shoes for your neighbor's wedding hadn't been dyed yet, because the whole thing has been called off: Eddie Balicki just dumped her—didn't you just know it wouldn't last? The first two examples I know for a fact actually happened. The third I can only speculate on. But I know that somehow, Bolac Koziol was well aware what had happened to me. He had a look that said so.

"Did he say why he wants it?" My mother is attacking the freezer floor with a spatula, smashing the built-up ice and sending pieces flying as she works to free a pound of hamburger that has been claimed by thick layers of frost. When the dishwasher gift had flopped, I had offered to exchange it for a frost-free refrigerator. "And just what is wrong with this one? And the freezer in the cellar—what about that? Just let it sit there?" My mother had challenged me with these questions, her eyes popping. So I gave up. From watching my father's daily rolling over and playing dead, I had figured out long ago that it was always easier to just let my mother win—even when she didn't, she felt she had anyhow, so it wasn't worth getting exasperated over. That's what I would tell myself, but I often forgot my own advice.

I go around the other side of her and open the bottom of the appliance to find the bottle of cherry soda. "He wants some," I tell her, and she keeps chipping away. "I'll make it a small glass."

"Don't say I'm in here," she whispers.

My mother is not wild about Bolac Koziol. However, like the rest of the people in town, she has pretty much no choice but to have to bring her shoes to him. "Being the only cobbler around makes him act like he owns the world," she has said many times, including this one. "You'd think that guy owns the world," she says right then and there, in between a couple of choppings.

"I'm sure he can hear the noise you're making," I point out.

"Just say I'm a workman."

I go back to find Bolac in the same exact position in which I'd left him, hands primly folded in the lap of his gray pin-striped suit, knees and feet straight together, eyes focused directly across the room, into the small bookshelf next to my father's La-Z-Boy, staring right into the center of the ruby-red spine of the *Better Homes and Gardens Handyman's Encyclopedia*.

He turns and accepts the soda with gratitude: "Ah—thank you very much, young lady. I sometimes greatly crave a cherry soda."

As he lifts it to his mouth, I am reminded how his head

very much resembles a potato, with its dusty brown-gray skin pierced by little pointy white eyes.

"Have you a coaster?" Bolac inquires, and I jump to get one, nervous that he can tell exactly which vegetable image is running through my head.

I give him a circle from a set of crocheted coasters my father long ago brought home from a Christmas bazaar at work. They are of thick woolen rug yarn and each of them is decorated with a symbol of a season of the year: a flower, a sailboat, a pumpkin, and a snowflake. For Bolac, and I don't know why, I choose the flower. Before he sets down his glass, he picks up the coaster and examines both sides. "Quite beautiful handwork," he decides and then puts his nearly empty glass on top of it.

"Here's the ring," I say. I push the box over to his side of the coffee table and invite him to take a look.

Bolac tilts his head, then he reaches for it in a slow movement and turns the box around and around in his hands, like that was what he has come to see.

"Lovely container," he says in the painfully slow meter Randy imitates so well that when I told him Bolac was coming over, he called me later in the day to ask, in a Bolac voice and timing, "if I would not first consider exchanging work on my entire family's footwear as a fair exchange for the piece of jewelry."

Bolac works just about as slowly as he speaks. I remember my mother once talked about how long it took him to pound a single nail into the sole of a demi-boot she had brought to him. She actually was funny that time, saying it was spring by the time he finished the one nail, and she didn't need the boot any longer.

As if on cue, I hear a series of loud smashes from behind the kitchen door. After a few, Bolac lifts his head from the study of the ring box and looks at me quizzically. "A workman," I say, and his mouth goes, "Oh."

"You may open it," I tell him, hoping to move the process

along. I have no idea why he is interested in the ring. The short but drawn-out conversation we'd had on the phone told me only that he'd like to come by and see it, "except, of course, if that would pose a problem."

I said it wouldn't, but now I am not so sure, I have to get him out of the house by the time my father comes back from the lumber yard. Bolac's father long ago denied mine a job sweeping and otherwise tidying the cobbler shop, hiring instead a young man who had been born in this country. Decades later, that remains unforgotten in my home.

"Please, open it," I tell him. "You'll love it." Bolac looks up at me as if he needs one more word of permission, then lifts the lid. He remains there with the same serious look on his face.

The only noises going on are the clock ticking and fewer and fewer sounds from the kitchen. After a couple of minutes of looking into the box, Bolac looks up at me. Then he returns his focus to the ring and reaches a finger in to loosen it from its slot. He is checking, I assume, for the numbers inside the band that will tell him this is genuine gold. The real thing. He must be satisfied, because he slides the ring back down into place, clicks the lid closed, and sets the box back on the coffee table.

"I am going to tell you, my life has not been an easy one," Bolac says to me.

I don't know what to answer, so I don't say anything. I mean, what do you say?

"You're young. You'll see how difficult it gets . . . your health, world morality, the cost of living—everything changes."

"So do you like the ring?" It is sounding like he is going to lecture me, and I don't want that.

"Just a moment," he says and he holds up a finger to silence me. "I'm trying to explain myself. What I am getting at is life is not easy. Who would have thought forty-two years ago, when my Lydia met me at the altar on that glorious spring day, that we would have such a life ahead of us. Three children. A successful business enterprise. A respected place in the community."

Here I turn my head away and take a deep breath. It is the point at which I know I am going to have a great tale to tell when he leaves and my mother asks, in case she missed anything, "What did he say?"

"But it has not been easy," Bolac continues. "It has taken a great deal of hard work to achieve what the Koziols have, wouldn't you imagine?"

I really am not sure. From what I know, the kids—Bolac Jr., Kenny, and Karen—are three young potato heads years older than I am but yet to do a day's work. There had been some talk of lumpy little Kenny going into the television business, but all he really does is intern during the summer at the public television station in Springfield. He doesn't get paid a cent, but he does appear on the television screen, in the background, his little gray hands clutching the ends of giant cardboard gift certificates during the station's annual fund-raising auction. Dour Karen, who wears oversized glasses she believes make her pointy eyes appear less so, is her mother's chauffeur. When Bolac and Lydia married, he was opposed to his wife being at the wheel. So she gave up driving. Since age sixteen, Karen has motored Mrs. Koziol around all week, doing errands at a leisurely pace. Though when Bolac Jr. first was graduated from high school his father said he was headed for a pre-law program somewhere, that son has yet to leave town. Once in a while you'll see him in the shop, his huge loafers up on the blotter of his grandfather's oak business desk while he minds the register and watches the soap operas playing on a miniature television that fits into one of the drawers.

Even so, to answer his question, I have to agree that Bolac Koziol has three kids and a wife who have stayed with him all these years, that he has a steady business, and a pristine vinyl-sided ranch—one he accents with pointily trimmed shrubs and a carpetlike lawn he routinely cuts and vacuums. I have to agree, even though all of it, to my mind—even his rigorous work on the lawn, out in nature—is without evident joy or great purpose, lacking heart. Just something obtained or done so people might look and envy.

So I say "Yes, an achievement." I know my mother, if she is listening on the other side of the kitchen door, probably is gagging right now.

"Well I am now in need of a special sign of appreciation," Bolac tells me.

"This would be a fine present," I say. "Forty-two years is a long time. It's a nice thing you would be doing."

Bolac nods yes and leans to open the box again. He leaves it on the table and looks at it from where he is sitting. I know the light from the stone is such that it can be seen from afar. It is shining back into Bolac's face, and even makes one of his potato eyes glisten as if a tear is ready to fall. Bolac shifts in his seat and I see that really is the case.

"It's a fine ring, but it's far from enough," he says, jerking back a nostril and inserting an extra beat of space between each word he says. He just keeps his eyes on the box. Who but he knows what is going on in his head?

"Why don't you think about it? Take your time and let me know. You know the number."

Bolac takes the suggestion and reaches for his hat. He stands up and bows a little toward me. I smile, and do the same, then just nod my head. I don't know what I am doing and I feel strange, bowing to the guy who has installed arch supports in every pair of shoes I have ever worn.

"Thanks for coming by," I say. Bolac answers yes and turns. His not being himself makes me uneasy. He walks toward the door, then stops. And there is a glimmer of the

Bolac we all know and avoid as much as possible when he points at the little wooden school desk my mother uses as a plant stand for her African violets.

"Interesting," he notes. "That looks almost like the desks that used to be in the old first grade. An inkwell . . . I often wondered where these went when the church bought the new plastic desks for the school."

"My father helped Father move them out to the auctioneer's truck, and so he was told to take one home, as thanks. I used to play school with it," I say. Then I remember that when the desk had been brought home so many years ago, I had been warned not to tell a soul where it had come from. I now realize that even in his altered state, Bolac Koziol has gotten something out of me. I almost would laugh, but I realize that the next time my mother brings a loosened tongue into Koziol the Cobbler, she will be told what a fine old desk she has her plants on, and wasn't it nice of Father to single her family out to present one to, free of charge?

WE WERE PASSING THIS GIGANTIC MAPLE TREE WHEN HE SAID it, and I remember I all of a sudden wished that I were that tree, which by then was about a half mile back, where it would be staying for the rest of its life, a span of seven or eight decades that never would include having to introduce its mother to its boyfriend.

Maybe during that time a few cars would slam into its trunk. Or somebody would take a chain saw to one of its limbs. Or some disgusting strain of beetles would bore through its bark and implant there an infestation of worms that would slowly eat into the wood and little by little, in a grossly disfiguring manner, kill it. Any of that I would have preferred to the prospect of subjecting perfect Eddie to the disapproving eyes through which my mother views everything but her own reflection.

So when Eddie said, "I think it's about time I met your parents," I turned and stared jealously at the maple, then said, "Nah, why don't we wait a while?"

Eddie said he didn't think that was a good idea. "It's been eight months—and we're in love," he said. "Don't you think it's important that I get to know them, and they me?"

Eddie often said things like "and they me?" where I might say "and them get to know me." The thing is, I never felt inferior because I realized my incorrect grammar through just listening to him—not his correcting me. As I thought of this, and of the fact that he unabashedly said things like "we're in love," I had another pang of affection for him, and thought OK, whatever he wants he can have.

When I backed down and told Eddie that we'd have to set something up someday, he asked how about Thanksgiving, since that was practically right around the corner? "In the same day," he pointed out, "we could visit with both my family and yours." This was said with great expression, like it was some kind of a good idea.

So that's why I was up at 5 A.M., as I had been on Easter. Only this time I was watching my mother, who had just pushed the back of a safety pin into its catch and gently patted the engagement ring she had safely secured to the front of her apron, lean forward, and plunge her left hand far into a gaping cavity that not twenty-four hours ago held the functioning, pulsating vital organs of the bird that was to be our Thanksgiving turkey. Her eyes were fixed on the pantry door as she felt around inside the body for anything that might be out of place. "You never know," she told me, "they could leave anything in here." I didn't want to know exactly what that might be. I had my own guts to think about, and right then they felt just like the turkey's, pulled from their attachments and all gushed together in a little waxed paper bag before being shoved back into the space from which they had been removed: Eddie was formally coming to Thanksgiving dinner to meet my family for the first time.

My mother was in an all right mood for at least one reason I could think of. Thirty-six Thanksgivings ago, she and my father had been married. This was one of the Thanksgivings that fell on the exact date, and it was another chance for her to talk about herself, about her life, how hard it has been, and, of course, how easy is mine.

Every once in a while she'd look up at the clock and would say something about what she had been up to thirty-six years ago that day. Like at 5 A.M., she thought, she probably had been braiding her hair. "I could make beautiful braids on my own head—I had to," she said, telling me something that long ago had been ingrained on my brain: "I had no mother to do it for me."

When my mother was seventeen, her mother sent her to America. "There is nothing but potatoes here. You will have no life," my mother remembers her mother telling her out of the blue one day. "Go and forget about me." So my mother and her sack of things were put onto a cart with a few of her cousins headed to live over here with a couple other cousins. That cart took them to a train. The train took them to a boat. The boat took them to Philadelphia. From there, it had to be a train or a bus—she never says which—to Massachusetts. "I never looked back," is how my mother always finishes that story. It just sort of ends right there.

My father's is similar, except that he was the one who made the decision. Looking into his hand one payday at the nine cents he was pulling in every week for pick-axing blocks of salt, he said who needs this, and he boarded a similar cart, train and boat, and found his way to North Adams, where he ended up fighting Alex and Rudy for desserts.

My parents chose Thanksgiving as their wedding day because a big meal would be planned by somebody, and people would have the day off anyway. It would be a small ceremony, with just a handful of people to celebrate after the Mass, and with music on the radio for any dancing. Afterward, Stanislaus would move into Edna's rented room, and the next day they both would be up at five again, this time so the groom could walk to his job at the lumberyard and the bride could get to the carding room on time.

"I really had no mother," mine reminded me. "You're lucky." Then, having found no stray entrails or pieces of hardware that might have been left behind by the turkey farmer, she slid her hand out of the bird and went to the sink to wash the slime from her hands.

Except for carrying the plate of Brussels sprouts and a package of stuffing mix into the church this morning so they could be blessed during the mass—and thus bless our entire Thanksgiving meal and everyone who would partake of it—my father kept out of the preparations. But at 11 A.M. he had his first real job of the day: keeping Rudy and Rudyka, the first to arrive when there's a feast in the works, company in the living room. The three of them had the TV tuned to the Macy's Thanksgiving Day Parade and were watching Willard Scott doing a last-minute weather report from a tall building overlooking some street in New York City. He had ropes pinned to his suitcoat and a ring of little kids dressed as elves surrounded him and held the cords to make it look like he was a balloon they would be walking with in the parade. Willard made a couple of jokes about being fat, then pointed to a map of the country. The sun was shining everywhere but over us. Then he wished a happy 102nd birthday to Ramona Zimmerman of Hopewell, New Jersey. "It says here she was left at the altar, but she says that it was the best thing that ever happened to her," Willard told us. "Now there's a new key to longevity!"

*"Paciara,"* my father said, calling Willard one of his favorite derogatory names—the one that means leftovers, something pushed to the side of the plate and then thrown to the pigs. I many times have been called a *paciara* by my mother, but I remind myself that it's only food.

She actually called me that just a couple of minutes ago, when I was putting on my coat so I could go and wait on the porch for Eddie. *"Paciara,"* she jeered. "Sitting out front and waiting for a boy, where everybody can see you . . ."

That's exactly what I'm doing right now—being a *paciara*, out on the porch, sitting on the wide railing, hoping both that he gets here soon and that he never shows up. But here comes the green Datsun, and I can see him smiling from half a block away. It looks like he has shined his car, and something about that makes me feel lucky to have a guy like this, the kind of person who might straighten his sock drawer before company comes, even though he knows nobody is going to be looking in there.

Eddie rolls his car to a halt in the space behind Rudy's truck. I am sure right now he is looking at the IF GUNS ARE OUTLAWED ONLY OUTLAWS WILL HAVE GUNS bumper sticker Rudy proudly has adhered to his rusting tailgate. He is taking a few seconds to unlatch his seat belt and turn off his radio and remove his keys from the ignition. It is too long a time for me, so I slide from the railing and walk quickly off the porch and down the walk and over to the curb. Small pieces of snow are falling, and some hit my face as I near the car from which Eddie is finally stepping.

"Hi!" he calls, and waves with one hand, which is inside a black leather glove. The other hand, and glove, holds a flat, gift-wrapped package, gold and white striped with a gold bow, all matching perfectly. He slams the car door and comes over to me.

As Eddie usually does, he looks perfect. He has on the gray woolen tailored overcoat, with a little gray-and-white checked scarf at the neck. His hair is neatly trimmed. From the trousers I see, I can tell he has on the same suit he wore when we went to Friendly's at Easter. It must be a multiseason fabric. I am thinking about this when he walks up in front of me. I am hoping he does not want to kiss me hello, here, in daylight, on the lawn in front of my house, where I know somebody must be looking out the window at us. So I don't get too close.

"You look great," Eddie grins. "Are you ready for this?" I shrug and murmur, "Too late now, right?" He laughs, but I did not mean that as a joke. I want him to say "No, I can just go to my parents' and pick you up later, and maybe we'll never come back." But he just takes the crook of my elbow and says, "Let's go in. It'll be fine."

This is one of the things that makes Eddie Eddie. He is anticipating a pleasant and insightful experience, a chance to get to know my family and learn more about me on my own turf. I, however, can see only the guillotine erected behind the front door, and my mother standing to the side, holding a bucket with Eddie's name on it.

"Well?" he asks, and I realize I haven't moved toward the house. I look at him, and his unflawed neck, and realize there's no turning back. We head to the porch. Though I fear it might start me hyperventilating, I dare one last big lungful of the cold air and push the front door open.

The TV is very loud so that whoever goes into the kitchen can hear the commentators describe the Macy's parade. Right now, you don't need an announcer to know that the Rockettes are doing a dance in front of the store itself. They are wearing red leotards with white fur trim, and Santa caps bounce on their heads. Their feet are tied into clunky high heels, and they are kicking those shoes and their legs way up in the air. Then, all of a sudden, each one grabs a huge ornament and runs toward and almost into the television camera, making a sharp left or right at the last moment before they have no choice but to leap through the screen and into the living room. Just before they disappear to either side, they flash big smiles into the camera.

Rudy, who appears transfixed by the performance, comments to nobody in particular how "they can dance, but close up, they're nothing special." Nobody answers him because he is the only one there. Eddie and I start to take our coats off and we distract him. He looks over at us and says, "Parade's on," motioning toward the set with his head.

"Rudy, this is Eddie. Eddie Balicki," I say, thinking what does Rudy care? Eddie drapes his coat over his arm and strides toward the couch. He extends his hand and Rudy makes one of those leaning-forward efforts, like he is going to try to get up off the couch but it is going to take a minute. "Don't get up," Eddie says, and they shake.

"Nice to meet ya," says Rudy. "Ya like Snoopy?"

Eddie is looking at Rudy like he doesn't know what he is talking about, because he probably doesn't. So, to explain, Rudy lifts his chin at the TV, in an over-there gesture. Eddie turns and sees Snoopy floating among the skyscrapers. Macy's employees hold on to him with long ropes, and I don't know if it's their skill or just the wind, but Snoopy's head seems to be very, very slowly moving from side to side, as if he's looking down and seeing the world for the first time. They show a shot of the crowd, and people are cheering as the dog floats overhead, like it is the great accomplishment that it is, and that he can hear what they're saying: Wonderful job! Safe trip! Come back again! Some of the spectators just wear blank expressions and stare straight ahead into the street, as if the people with the ropes are what they're supposed to be watching.

"I had a dog named Snoopy," Eddie says, telling Rudy something he never told me. Rudy doesn't answer, so I say, "Really?"

"Eddie—I'm Joyce," says Rudyka, who has just swooped into the room and is telling Eddie something she never has told any of us—maybe, for all we know, not even Rudy. "Nice to finally meet you. There's something different about my cousin since she met you—all good, you understand."

Eddie smiles widely at me. I begin to return the same

kind, but it falls into a grimace when I hear my mother in the kitchen, telling Cioci Wanda that "he better get here on time. I hate to keep food warming. It just loses its taste, forget about how mushy it gets just sitting there." She has said this at a volume high enough for all of us, and the Rockettes, to hear. Rudyka-Joyce goes to turn the Motorola down.

"Hey!" my mother yells from the other room. "What happened? The parade!"

"We have a guest," Rudyka calls back. I finally go over to the coat tree and hang our things. In the mirror there, I notice a bright blotch of red overtaking my neck.

I see also that my mother has come into the living room, and that she stops just at the doorway. She puts on one-half of a pleasant face and makes small nods toward Eddie when Rudyka pats him on the shoulder and says, "Edna, Eddie." Eddie nods, too, and walks over to give her the package, which he had been holding. "A little something," he says. "I appreciate the invitation today."

My mother is holding the box and is staring down at it. She gives it a little shake. "Chocolate-covered cherries," Eddie says. "My mom said you like them at the Ladies Guild parties."

That gets her to give somewhat of a real smile, but she has a monotone when she responds, "How thoughtful. Thank you." Then she turns into the kitchen and calls for my father. "Stashu!"

He appears in the doorway with two small glasses of what looks to be whiskey. "Hi," he says to Eddie as he goes over and gives one to Rudy, then the other to Rudyka. Then my father walks over to Eddie and shakes his hand in a real, genuine way, like all of this is OK with him. My mother is still standing there with the box of cherries, taking in the scene.

"Your neck . . . ," Rudyka whispers to me. My mother, who can read lips moving a mile away, announces from across the room, "She gets that when she's nervous. I always thought she'd outgrow it."

I want to know if Eddie has heard this, but I am too embarrassed to look and see if I can tell. Just as Rudyka quickly jumps in and asks Eddie what he'd like to drink, the doorbell rings and in comes Cioci Julie and Uncle Louie. "Hey, hey, kid," Uncle Louie says, half-laughing. "How are ya?" I go over and he smashes his cold face into mine. "Got that guy here today? Is that him?"

Uncle Louie already has his coat off and is steaming over to Eddie like a train on a rail. "Hello, young man, I'm Lou." My uncle shakes Eddie's hand so vigorously that half of all of Eddie shakes at the same time. They are both laughing at each other like this is some kind of long-awaited reunion. Cioci Julie wraps me in a big hug, and, with the tail of her vermeil peacock lapel pin jabbing into my cheek, holds me a long time and whispers to me how special I am and how she has looked forward to seeing me—that with both her Marcia and Agnes living so far away, I am the daughter she has left.

I pull away only because I can't stand it—the tail—anymore, and put my hand to my pierced cheek in what I hope Cioci Julie will interpret as a gesture that I am deeply touched by what she has said. Over the little bit of pain, I wonder about my age-old theory that maybe Cioci Julie, out of the goodness of her heart and because maybe at one point long ago she and Louie had been too poor to feed another mouth, had presented my parents with me when I was too small to remember such a thing, and that this was the kind of open and unashamed love and emotion that was supposed to have been mine to soak in every single day of my life.

I tell Cioci Julie to wait right there, then I go and get Eddie away from Uncle Louie, who is trying to get him to agree to help him hang draperies on the weekends. "It's good money for a young guy like you," Louie is telling him, and then he starts winking and adds, "plus, if you get there early enough, lots of gals who didn't expect you so soon are running around in their houses au naturel, if you know what I mean . . ."

I glare at Uncle Louie and pull on Eddie's arm. "Meet my Cioci Julie," I say, and the next second she has him in a handshake that gets her many gold bracelets jangling with every syllable as she tells him what a good girl I have always been and what a fine young woman I am now.

She gets cut off when the front door flies open and Uncle Mitzi stamps onto the roll of green plastic runner that extends several feet onto the blue shag. "It's awful out there," he says through chattering dentures. "Wanda! *Prędko! Prędko!* The heat is on in here!"

"I'm hurrying—do you want me to fall and kill myself?" We hear this, and the tap tap of little heels, as Cioci Wanda comes in off the porch. She enters with her hand holding a scarf over her mouth to warm the air that is entering her lungs. She keeps the wrap there, and nods hello to everyone as Uncle Mitzi slams the door behind her and begins to dust snowflakes from her shoulders.

"Stash, Edna—glad you have the room because we might be stuck here," Mitzi announces, grinning from the side of his mouth like he does. Normally, this would be good news to me. Their all having to stay because of the weather actually happened once in a while, and I just loved how our house for that night and the next morning had each of its rooms used by different people all at the same time. There was someone to bump into in the hall, or to have to get off the telephone for, people rummaging around in the kitchen at night. One big meal blended into the next and the next until, when everything was put away for the night, somebody got hungry again and it started all over. And in the middle there I would be, wishing it would snow the next day, too.

But today I don't want to be stuck here any longer that

is absolutely necessary. We will sit, we will eat, we will sit some more, then we will leave, to do the same at the Balickis'. Then, formally, Eddie will have met my parents and I will have met his, and that all will be over with. Eddie and I can go back to just driving around and going to movies, and walking in the dark, as we are doing nearly every single night now.

"It's supposed to clear," I say, though I haven't heard a weather forecast. I often predict the weather to other people along the lines of what I would like to see, in case my wishes have anything to do with what actually is going to happen.

"No, no," says Mitzi, shaking his head grimly. "Big storm. Big. You can smell it."

"He's right—you can," says Cioci Wanda, who bends one eyebrow and adds in Eddie's direction, "who's that?" She finally has taken the scarf from her face and I see that some of the royal blue fluff that makes up her angora muffler has stuck to the crevices in her pink lips. As she purses her mouth and waits for an answer, the breath from her nose causes the strands to wave wildly.

"This is my friend. Eddie," I answer. I have made it sound like I met him this afternoon during recess.

Eddie shakes hands with Mitzi, then with Wanda, who both look over at me and make big eyes, like they can't believe I have a friend who is a man. A handsome man. One who looks like a fine and decent person.

My father is distributing more shots of whiskey. He gives one to all the men, including Eddie, then hands one to Rudyka, the only woman ever to drink such a thing in this house. My mother has glasses of brandy arranged on a little wooden tray, and she gives one each to Wanda and Julie, then takes one for herself.

"*Nazdrowie!* Happy Thanksgiving!" my father wishes, then swings his glass forward and brings it back to his mouth. Everybody else does the same. Because I am not offered alcoholic beverages in my home, I stand and watch. Mostly I watch Eddie, who gulps the shot without a wince.

*"Sto lat!"* Louie shouts, wishing everyone another hundred years of times such as this.

"Another one!" Rudyka commands, and Wanda and my mother connect eyes for a second.

"Be right back," chirps my father, and he heads for the kitchen. Holidays put him in a spirited mood. It's like he saves up his life to live during four or five days each year. On these occasions, he speaks quite often, with animation, and to many people. He tells stories. He laughs loudly. He pats people on the back and rushes around them, making sure they have whatever it is they need to make the event a perfect one. Holidays are the only times he ever swears, and he makes them pretty good ones. Everything is the goddamn politicians or the goddamn Red Sox, and that sends my mother out of the room with her hands over her ears when she is not blessing herself. When she comes back, he even will try to plant a kiss onto her cheek, and she'll shoot her shoulder up into his jaw and snap that he should behave himself. And he will come over to me, usually at the end of the day, and will put his hand on my shoulder and say to whoever else is there, "Here's the best gal in town." It all makes me happy, but it can make me sad if I think of maybe this is how he was every single day of his life before my mother began stomping him down. Before he decided to just let her.

"OK, OK," she says loudly over the talking and laughing that is filling the room. "Get your drinks, but it's almost time to come to the table. Very soon, now, so don't get too comfortable."

"Santa!" Rudy yells, and he looks quickly around at each of us to make sure we have heard him. On the TV, an elaborate sleigh is gliding into Herald Square. Seated between a huge swan's wings is a magnificent Santa Claus.

"I love Santa!" shouts Rudyka, who seats herself on the

floor smack in front of the television to get the best view. "Look at him—he looks how he should look."

"Yeah, I'd say that's his real beard," Rudy notes.

"I don't mean that," she says, in the first time I ever have heard them converse with one another other than his "time to hit the road" and her "okeydoke."

"I mean look at how he is radiating to the crowd. It's like he's sending out his love to the world—to those people on the sidewalk, to us here in the living room."

Santa waves his gloved hand at the camera, and Rudyka fans hers back enthusiastically. I know this is the right time to look at my mother. She is rolling her eyes at nobody in particular. Unless they are of a religious nature, she does not like belief in the things that cannot be seen.

"Come and eat," she blurts and starts motioning her hand toward the table just about at the same speed Rudyka had been flagging at Santa.

We file through the doorway, and I feel Eddie touch me on the small of my back. I turn. From the pleasant look on his face, he does not seem to be finding this so bad. Maybe it won't be.

"You, there. You, there. You, there," my mother instructs, pointing alternately at each of us, then to a chair. "You, there," she says to Eddie, setting him to the left of Rudyka.

"You," she orders me, pointing to a seat across the table from my date, "there. You're not a guest, you know. I still need help in the kitchen."

I reluctantly pull back the chair and sit down. My mother circles the table, filling champagne glasses. Across from me, Rudyka is whispering something funny to Eddie, and both manage to laugh without making a sound.

"Excuse me," my mother orders in their direction. "It is time for grace."

She sits down and we all join hands in a circle. We used to simply fold our hands in a silent prayer prior to a special meal. But a couple of years ago Cioci Julie offered to say grace, and asked us to all join hands. That custom stuck, and that's why, right now, my father is clamped onto both Mitzi, whose face is skewing and turning redder by the minute, and Rudy, who is waving the hand that is holding on to that of another man, and he is telling us that hey, he's just realized this feels kinda good.

Rudyka, who gets to hold on to Eddie, snickers. I insert my hand limply into my mother's cold right hand and slide my own right into Cioci Julie's warm, soft left.

"Let us pray," she begins, and bows her head. I do the same, as I am pretty sure everyone else is. "Let us pray that we may be truly thankful for all our riches here in this great country, to which we came like the Pilgrims of old, seeking better lives . . ."

In the circle of china that is my dinner plate, one of a set of Thanksgiving-themed dishes my mother earned by having a card punched at the Fruit Fair each time she bought an order of ten dollars or more, there is the *Mayflower*. And there I am, on the bow of that ship, dressed in a Pilgrim's drab gown, holding on for dear life as the craft pitches and yaws in angry waters made even more dangerous by the presence of the mother shark below. Through torrential rain, I see the land of Eddie straight ahead. There, the sun is shining, and somebody is signaling a welcome to me from his place atop a rock.

"Please, God in Heaven," I intone, "let me get there alive . . ."

"Amen," I hear my mother snort, and she tosses my hand back into my lap like it is a damp dishrag she is pitching into her sink. I wonder for a second if I had been pleading to God aloud, here in front of my whole family and Eddie. But then I hear Eddie say, "That was beautiful," and I hear my Cioci Julie, who has worked herself into a state, sniffle shakily, "Thank you, Eddie. I just have so much to be thankful for."

She gives my hand a squeeze and I realize it is still connected to hers. I leave it there for a few extra seconds, just because it feels so nice, then draw it away. As I head for the kitchen, I hear Eddie tell her, "So do I—I know what you mean."

"Such a show," my mother huffs as the kitchen door closes behind her. She takes her place at the stove, where a cloud of cabbage soup steam envelopes her head as she leans over the pot for one final tasting. Without turning, she tells me not to just stand there—get the rolls on the table before they harden to rocks.

I undo the twist tie on the plastic bag and remove a dozen of Pytka Bakery's best, the black poppy seeds raining from them. When I bring the basket into the dining room, Rudyka claps once and grins. These are her favorite, something she can't get back home. She asks everybody to remember to remind her to get a couple dozen next time she's here—she could freeze them, you know. Eddie, who had been listening to Uncle Louie try to connect the Balicki heritage with our own—something that, because I knew it could probably prove we were related, I hoped he stopped before too long—raised his head for a look into what I'd set onto the table.

"They're only rolls," I said with a little smile.

"Oh, but in your hands, gold to those who love you," Cioci Julie said, glowing at me. I patted her shoulder, and, reddening, turned for the kitchen, and walked right into the door, which my mother was shoving open with her foot.

I jumped back as the door jerked. "Do you want to give me third-degree burns?" my mother gasped in anger. I love her always using questions like this—like there is a yes or no answer to something like that. There is only an apology, but she won't hear it. "This is my tureen, you know," she blasted protectively, stringing out the word like it had a few extra *e*'s in it.

I knew well what it was, mostly because it is a rare

thing—it is real and it is connected to something I have a hard time thinking ever was true: that my parents ever were crazy about each other. So crazy that after they met and they danced that one dance Stanislaus stayed up all of two more nights in a row and carved Edna the graceful and generous cherry ladle she is now taking into her grasp, so crazy that he walked to her house the hour the oil had dried—though that was just before dawn—and would set it onto the porch rail for her to find, tagged with a piece of paper onto which he had written her name, underlined twice. So crazy that when she asked him why he had made it and he said it was because she had given him a dance, she wrote, "If you give me a ladle for one waltz, if we had a date I could expect to see a tureen to use it in" and so crazy that she had paid Mitzi three homemade apple-cranberry pies to sneak into the mill at night and leave the note in the pocket of Stanislaus's leather apron. So crazy that leaving for seven-thirty mass the morning after the first night of dancing each and every number with Stanislaus and no one else, Edna found just to the side of the front door this same good-size heavy-handled cream-colored tureen, a hydrangea branch with a pink bow around it stuck in the opening where the ladle was to fit.

"It's a nice tureen," Eddie says because, I know, he feels sorry for me and must have some inkling that we are all better off when my mother is happy.

"Thank you, yes," she says soberly, setting it onto a hot plate between the candles. I know better than to expect her to offer more to him about it—the story never even was told to me. It's just something I heard joked about a long time ago, my mother recalling to somebody "such silliness, people risking trespassing, risking cutting a finger off in all that hurry—but you know, he said at that time that he wouldn't have cared if he had to bleed for me."

I saw my father run his thumb slowly into the thumb groove he had cut so long ago into the handle of the ladle, then he scooped a helping of soup into his bowl. I wondered what he was thinking of and, without being asked, he told us all as he set it back into the tureen: "Got this cabbage at four cents a pound."

Cioci Wanda's mouth fell open. "I have never heard of such a price—it had to be half-bad."

My mother, who had been watching everyone draw their portions, glared in Wanda's direction: "I'm going to be serving you, and our guest"—she lifted her chin in Eddie's direction—"something rotten?"

"I didn't mean that—but there had to be a part you had to cut out, something wormy," Wanda said, still in disbelief. "Four cents! Why didn't you call us?"

"He didn't have that many," my father told her. "He just wanted to get rid of them. He was having a bad year and just wanted to get it over with."

"Al Szyszko?" Rudy asked, his mouth full. "I heard nothing grew for him this year."

"No," my father said. "Lenny Duda. On River Road."

"Never heard of the guy," Rudy said as he mushed the end of a roll into his soup.

I had. I remember being a little kid going to the Duda farm—they had a daughter, Heddy, a sweating and freckled girl who would let me pet her Shetland pony while our parents argued over price per head, deals that increased per dozen purchased. Except for her problem of extreme perspiration, which caused her hair to stick to her head almost year-round, and which, one day we were there, led a string of boys to ride their bicycles past the farmstand while loudly singing, "Who's the ugliest girl in town? Duda! Duda!", Heddy was living my fantasy life. That basically consisted of having a horse to ride whenever I wanted. Obviously, her mother never had snorted over and over "she'll never take care of it" when her father, spotting a tiny well-mannered pinto with an oaktag FOR SALE sign hung around its neck at the Grange tag sale, said pleadingly, "Can't we get this for her, Edna?"

No. Heddy's mother hadn't protested when her husband got the idea and Heddy's father just up and bought Star, a sleepy buckskin who never ventured beyond a fast trot. Lenny Duda was not one of those men who need permission.

"Remember Heddy?" I asked, then tried to make eye contact with everybody else—Eddie first. "His daughter."

"That girl—she's the reason for the terrible year," my mother piped up. "Her parents want to give her the farm—Lenny's discs are in such bad shape they cut him open every so often just to shock the medical students at Baystate—but she doesn't want to run the place. She's got some career—if you can call it that—handing out free meals to all the bums in Springfield. She thinks catering to the free-loading Puerto Ricans is more important than getting a husband and having him run the family business."

I cringed down at the tablecloth, not able to look over at my mother, who had no problem spouting off like this even though hunger was what had driven her here from another place. She wastes no time picking on other nationalities, but no matter where she is, she actually will spit on the ground—or the sidewalk or somebody's wall-to-wall rug—if she hears a Polish joke being told.

And I couldn't look up at Eddie, who had chosen to spend this day with me, rather than how he usually spends a good portion of his holidays: delivering foil-wrapped meals to people who he told me live in certain spaces under Route 91.

"Edna—that's not the whole story," my father said, daring as he would only on such a day to challenge her. "He said Heddy had offered to write on some kind of grant that would let the place she works buy the farm, so they can grow their food there for feeding the people. She would make it so nobody could ever build there—that they would only use it to be a farm. It would be nice, I think, but Lenny will not be happy with that. He wants her to have it as a money-making business."

"It's making him sick," my mother pleaded to my father, as if he had some influence over a girl he didn't even know. "Why can't she do what he wants?"

"She has her own life, Edna."

My mother just shook her head and blessed herself rapidly. Then she rose to clear the bowls, which everyone had emptied silently, and she quoted as she backed into the kitchen door, arms full, "Honor thy father and mother."

"So, Eddie," Cioci Julie said quickly, "I understand you enjoy charitable work."

"When I have the time," he said, and I dared a look at him. He appeared fine, unbothered. "I think it's important for each of us to do—"

My mother's electric carving knife roars to life in the other room, loudly enough to obliterate whatever answer Eddie is giving.

"What?" Uncle Mitzi asks, cocking his head. Eddie gives up and shrugs and we all laugh, though you can't hear that either.

I know I should help, so I get up and go into the kitchen, straight to the empty serving bowls ready to receive the side dishes. I ignore my mother, who is still noisily sectioning the bird while chewing on a fold of greasy turkey skin. I empty the warming pots of mushroom stuffing, mashed potatoes with bacon pieces, whole cranberry sauce, broiled butternut squash, buttered baby peas, sautéed Brussels sprouts. I place the bowls on a tray, as many as I can fit, and stick a serving spoon into each. I carry them past my mother, who, despite being aided by electricity, is using the moving knife to saw back and fork a drumstick that will not part from its hip.

When I enter the dining room, I can't hear it, but I see

that I get an Ooooh from everybody. They all can see the steam and the colors, and the garnishes of parsley I had almost forgotten to slip into the edge of each offering, and they are impressed. They are a table edged with the anticipation and excitement I usually print again and again the entire first week of December. Photographs of people wide-eyed like they never before have seen a roasted turkey. People smacking their lips as the block of butter disappear into the baby carrots. People, forks still in their mouths, rolling their eyes in disbelief over how wonderful the taste is. People who are so incredulous simply to be eating a meal that I might as well be Heddy coming toward them with representatives of all the four food groups ice cream-scooped onto a partitioned Styrofoam plate.

There is something I like about this attention, and I pretend this is my family. That they are here to see me. That I have made this for them. That they will go away saying all the way home nobody can cook like I can. Nobody.

The Oooooh comes again. This time I can hear it, because it is directed at my knifeless mother and her platter of light and dark meat, all of which are right on my heels. "Move."

"That is beautiful," Rudy says in awe to my mother, who smiles and tells everyone the hour at which she rose to make it so.

"I'm sure you couldn't have done all this without your beautiful daughter," Cioci Julie says, tapping a Himalaya of potatoes onto her plate.

I don't hear an answer. Then I hear my father say an enthusiastic, "That's for sure."

Then he goes on: "Did you know she developed some vacation film for a selectman? A celebrity! He runs the town and he allows my daughter to develop his pictures."

"Who?" asks Rudyka, even though she doesn't really live around here and wouldn't know the person.

"His name is Vic Baldyga," I say.

Rudyka again: "Where'd he go?"

I push a forkful of stuffing across the port side of the *Mayflower* and set it to rest in the stern, where I could imagine there might be a place to keep some food with which to sustain yourself while you were at the wheel, aiming for your destiny. I shouldn't answer: There is a company policy—Mr. Herrman's policy, actually—that says I am not supposed to talk about what people bring in to be processed. "You will be in a position of trust," he told me as he reviewed my application way back when, his bifocals slipping down his nose. "People don't want it blabbed all over town where they went or with whom they went." I really even shouldn't have acknowledged to Rudyka that Vic Baldyga had come into the shop, but I already have said that once: He will be running for office in March, and as he filled out his film envelope he asked if my family would consider displaying one of his signs in our front yard, once it thawed out. So I had to tell my parents what he wanted, where I'd seen him. And when he returned to pick up his forty-eight disappointing glossy double prints, each showing the back of someone's yellow helmet, a white spray of water, a section of black rubber raft, and, way to the right of the frame, a tiny dark blue slice of what he told me was the Allagash, I had to say to Vic Baldyga that, sorry, our lawn is to be reseeded in the spring—not that his request got any farther than my mother's waving hand and the word *crook*.

"She can't tell you," my father is informing Rudyka. "It's like working for the government—there are some things she is not supposed to tell. It's an important job, you know."

Rudyka looked at me like to ask if he was joking and I said, "Boss' rule. We never see anything too exciting, but he likes to keep confidentiality." I am telling her the truth. I have seen shots of a few rear ends of college kids mooning at parties, I think though that no totally naked people have come through the machine yet because wouldn't they send something like that out of state?

Rudyka, who reached for the salt and shot it over a pool of gravy, didn't seem too broken up about being denied some details about the only things I did see that came close to being odd: just about every other person laid out at Wazocha's, documented in their makeup, best clothes and best rosary, final portraits for the old folks back in the old country, proof that their reason for not writing any more was not because they had become successful Americans too haughty to remember where they'd come from.

"I've said I think the job must be so interesting," Eddie said. "Just to see the places and the people."

"All God's creation," Cioci Julie pointed out cheerfully, but needlessly, Eddie knowing all that, practically being God's best friend.

"What I want to know about the picture place," Uncle Mitzi said to me just as the bowl of peas passed in front of his face and for a second I couldn't see that he had one, "is when you're gonna settle down and get married?"

From my left came a snort. From my right came a "Mitzi!" From the head of the table came "When she's good and ready. Nobody is to be pushed." It was my father saying that. Then, I sense, rushing to fill the space my mother was ready to claim, he asks, "Drinks, anybody?"

The uncles and Rudy want something. I can't yet look at Eddie, but I hear him say he'd appreciate a soft drink. Rudyka thinks some wine would go nicely with all this. My mother shrieks.

"The wine! The beet salad!" She shoves her chair back, asks me gruffly why didn't I remind her of the things that have been bought and prepared just for this occasion, but that have been pushed so far back into the refrigerator they would have sat undiscovered for at least another day.

"She always does this," Cioci Wanda whispers toward

Eddie. "It's like a tradition. But I have to say usually it takes a little longer for something to be thought of."

"Good thing I said something," Rudyka pointed out, and everybody agreed.

My mother takes her plate from the table, saying that she can eat anytime, and sets the jellied salad onto her place. It was made in the round mold with the interchangeable seasonal designs—today a haystack-shaped depression my mother has filled with cream cheese and dotted with a walnut half.

I help her distribute the wineglasses, and she has Uncle Louie, who likes to show his strength, uncork the Ernest and Julio Gallo. We pour for those who are not having something else.

As the last is being filled, I tap my knife on my plate. "I want to toast—a happy anniversary to my parents," I say, lifting toward them my glass of plain water, lukewarm by now, ice long gone, like nothing when it goes down.

"Here's to the best gal in town," my father responds. I look to my mother, to see how she will handle this compliment given her here in front of all these people. But she is looking at me. Because, his arm straight out, glass pointed straight at me, that's what my father is doing, looking at the one he thinks is best.

I AM FREEZING. EDDIE'S CAR HEATER IS BROKEN AND IN THIS BLINDing snow Uncle Mitzi had been correct in predicting as being really big, there will be no getting to the Balickis' in record time. Beneath the blanket Eddie has draped over our laps so we don't get too cold on the way over, I crawl my left hand toward his leg, wanting to touch and make sure he is real, this person who has told me the minute we left the house what a nice family I have, this person who thinks Rudyka is a "hot ticket," this person who never before had such a slice of turkey, this person who responded to my apologies for my mother by saying everybody has a character or two among their relatives—you should get an earful of his Uncle Johnny. I might never: suddenly the car pitches sharply and "Look ouuuuut!" screams Eddie, who flings his right arm across the front of me as we fishtail. I clap my hand to my mouth because I am going to scream, too, and I don't want him to hear that coming from me, even if I am about to die. The headlights, which barely cut a hole into the storm, illuminate a flash of a buff-colored deer shape flying inches from the front bumper. I see a huge tree trunk in our path, then we veer. We start to spin wildly and I recite an abbreviated Act of Contrition, firmly resolving to sin no more and to avoid the near occasions of sin—even though I really don't think I am going to have any more chances. My conscience clear and my soul ready, I throw myself into Eddie's side, my hands covering my eyes.

I hear and feel myself in a long, silent, uninterrupted slide. There is a bump here and there, and a few little scratching noises. I take it all in, including the sense that there are arms around me as I fly through the darkness. Then the moving feeling and the little noises stop. The arms remain and I feel safe and protected, actually kind of excited, the same feeling I once heard described on a talk show about near-death experiences.

So this is it.

"You're OK—don't worry," I hear a voice say soothingly, and I notice the voice sounds like Eddie's. So we are both dead, both headed to God and heaven and eternity, together. Just like that. Dead with Eddie. How could I get so lucky?

"Everything's fine," the voice says. "We've stopped."

I try to make some sense of this halt before we get to the gates.

"Then is this purgatory?" I ask slowly, trying out my dead voice for the first time.

"No. I think it's Soja's field."

Wherever I am, I open an eye. And I focus on the face of God himself.

He is a lot smaller than I had expected. He is holding a sheep. Neither is moving. I squint and study him: the eyes that have seen things that haven't even happened yet; the knotty staff he grips in his scarred hand; the dark blue cape covering the rose-colored gown; the bare, strong feet, sandal-less on the dirt road. And the words. There are words. I can pick them out: "Christ the Shepherd Seminary."

None of this makes any sense to me. "God?" There is no reply. Just a stare. Then he is gone, as if whisked away. I next see the face of Eddie, staring into mine.

"I have seen God," I tell him solemnly. "We can't be too far from heaven."

"No, no," Eddie is saying as he runs his hands lightly across my forehead. "We just went off the road. We really slid. Are you OK?"

"We're not dead?" I ask, and I feel a strange and creeping disappointment.

Eddie laughs a little and puts his face next to mine and we are still for a moment, together. "Not that I know of. Isn't that great?"

I nod like I think it is, and I guess it really is. But I can't help thinking I have seen a vision. Of what, exactly, I am not sure. But it leaves me a little cold.

I tell Eddie how I am cold, and he says "We have to get out of here." I move my feet and crunch the cover of one of Eddie's cassettes. I reach for it and see that it is Johnny Cash's collection of spirituals. I say I'm sorry. "Everything got thrown around—don't worry about it," he says, gathering some papers into a pile and tossing them into the backseat. "Let's just go and we'll straighten it out tomorrow."

I find my bag and unbuckle my seat belt and open my door. There is snow past the floorboard, and I step into the storm. When I stand, I find I need to lean against the wet car for support. My knees are shaking from more than the cold: I look up the hill, and as far as I can see, which isn't that far with the snow and all, is the wild curve of tire tracks that have exposed brown grass and leaves beneath the snow. I see that had we—had Eddie—not made a sharp left once we were onto the field, we would have gone straight into the river that is so close I can it hear it now roaring right over there.

We walk and slip to the top of that hill, keeping to our tire tracks and staying out of the drifts that are starting. We have our good shoes on and one of us almost falls every so often. Not much is said. I have wrapped my scarf around my head and, like Cioci Wanda, have the ends across my nose and mouth. Eddie is bareheaded and he has his coat collar up as high as it can go. His hair is turning white.

"If somebody comes by, we'll flag them down for a ride," Eddie shouts to me once we get up to the road. "But we have to keep moving. Let's walk this way—my place isn't that far." He says all this with a jaw that is shaking. He heads to the right and leads me by the hand.

I let myself get led. This is not how I had dreamed going to Eddie's apartment would be, but right now I do not care. I am wearing nylons and a pair of patent leather flats and I have been trudging through what seems to be a good half a foot of snow. My feet feel curiously like they belong to someone else. All I want to do is go somewhere warm and dry. I feel so sorry for myself that I start to whimper a little, the scarf and the wind keeping any of that from Eddie. I don't know what he is doing because I am a little in back of him, my right hand in his left. He is leading us down the road, into any traffic that might come, placing himself nearer to any cars so he, rather than I, will get struck if we are not seen.

I have my head down into the falling snow, and some of the time my eyes are shut so that his hand is my only link with where we were going. Once in a while, Eddie squeezes my hand. At the first house we come to, we almost run to the front door and knock to ask if we can use the phone. But no lights are on and nobody answers, except for some small dog whose bark is softened by the covers of the bed he must be hiding under. Eddie says something about how he thinks his house is about a half a mile farther, and asks me if I can make it. I don't remember telling him yes, but I do recall seeing, when I peeked, a streetlight, a house, another house, then another, more lights, then several more houses, closer and closer together, and then, right now, we are shuffling up the front walk on Eden Street and Eddie is swinging open the front door and we are collapsing on the stairway.

Eddie works at the buttons of his overcoat, which is stiff with frozen snow. He manages to bring out his keys, and his hand shakes as he tries to fit the correct one into the doorknob. The lock clicks open and he gestures to allow me in first.

I take a step, toward him, then another, into the apartment. "Sink?" I ask politely. This, I realize quickly somewhere in my mind, is not the first word I thought I might be saying in Eddie's home. I thought it might be something like *this is lovely* or *where'd you get that chair?* Not *sink*. But that's what I say, and Eddie is hooking a finger into my coat cuff and leading me through one dark room and into another, where he pulls a cord to illuminate a small and tidy kitchen, very white and outdated, like his mother's, but with accents of pale green.

Eddie grabs a pair of dish towels that had been hanging on the oven door and he throws them to me. Then he reaches into a drawer and pulls out a pile of them, all folded, all in the same rose color. I peel off my scarf and throw it into the sink, where it keeps its frozen shape. I kick off my shoes and throw them in there, too, along with my gloves. I see a small kitchen set and I pull out a chair and try to rub some life into my feet. Eddie stands at the sink and picks the ice from his hair, then leans on his elbows and rubs his head with a towel.

Neither of us says anything. I stare straight ahead as I work on my feet, and I catch sight of the clock built into the stove. "It's, it's eight P.M.—Eddie—it's eight," I say and I can't believe it. We were supposed to have been at Eddie's parents' two hours ago.

Eddie stops and lifts his head so the rose towel frames his face, as in my vision of God. Then he looks at the clock and then at me. "My mother must have the cops out for us," he says.

At the sound of the word, I recall my own mother—a person I have not thought of since before I died. Since before the split-second image of the variations of amber in the deer's pointed hoof. Since just after the dessert and tea and three games of Scrabble and one half of a televised football game, when we got our coats and said our good-byes and I heard from behind me, rather than a farewell, only a "Wear your boots—you'll be wishing you did."

"Soja's field. We barely missed the riverbank," Eddie is telling his mother on the telephone in the other room, which, now that he has lit it with a terra-cotta table lamp on a small shelf next to the door, I can see is his living room. "But the main thing is we're fine. I just don't think you'll be seeing us tonight. We're not going anywhere."

His last words, for me, hang there in the air, and I realized that my first visit to Eddie's is going to last a lot longer than I had thought it would be in the many times I had thought about it.

Eddie comes back into the kitchen and pulls back the other chair. The pants of his suit are damp to the knees and he peels off sopping gray socks decorated with little red triangles. His feet look very white and very pink, both at the same time. "You know, I have no way to get you home," he says, looking at me and at the socks, alternately. "And even if you had a way to get home, it would be too dangerous and I wouldn't allow it."

"OK," I say, not knowing what else to give as an answer. Most of me wants to get up and do some kind of wild dance, I am so thrilled. But I don't want to look too excited so I just sit there. "OK. Fine."

"Do you want to use the shower first—to warm up?"

"You go," I tell him. "I have to call home, too."

"The phone's in here," Eddie tells me, and gets up and takes my hand. Suddenly he has me in a big hug that jars the pieces of snow stuck to my coat and knocks them to the floor. "What would I have done if something had happened to you out there?" He wants to know this, and it is what I honestly would describe as a desperation in his voice that convinces me he isn't kidding. He has just stuck a flag into a whole other piece of my heart, which already should be named for him if they ever make a map of me.

I follow him into the living room, where he shows me a white princess phone, the style Anna and I had always dreamed of having installed in our bedrooms. Eddie goes through another door and down a hall. I stand and stare at the receiver, steeling myself for the conversation.

"Happy Thanksgiving!" Rudyka cheerfully answers.

"Same to you. Is my mother there?"

"Oh—hi! How's your supper going? I'll tell you—he was a big hit here. What a hunk—those eyes! I see now why you kept him a secret."

"Can I speak to my mother—or my father?"

"Sure. We'll see you later, OK?"

I tell Rudyka that will be OK, and wait to see who picks up the phone.

"Yes, yes, what is it?"

"We're fine," I begin to tell my mother, "but—"

"You've been in an accident—I knew it—you should stay in your own home with your own family on a holiday, but no—"

"We're fine," I was able to stick in there somehow, cutting into her speech. "Eddie's car went off the road and we had to walk to his house and there isn't a way to get to his parents' or any way I can get home probably until this clears so I will be staying at Eddie's tonight."

There are no sounds coming from the person on the

other end of the line, but I know we haven't been disconnected because I hear Uncle Mitzi ask who wants another beer, and I hear Cioci Wanda tell somebody that a zander is a fish, not a word she was making up to get rid of a *z*. I hear her say they can look it up. Then I hear my mother clear her throat.

But there is nothing else from her, so I say, "I just wanted to let you know."

"Do what you want. You're an adult," she tells me in a falsely diplomatic tone. "Make your own choices."

"I could walk back home, but I have to wait for the feeling to return to my feet," I snap, and quickly realize that I have touched upon the wrong subject.

"I told you to wear boots, didn't I? But what does an old lady know? You want to look fashionable. A blizzard out and you're interested in how you look. That's where it gets you. Pneumonia. Just let me know what kind of flowers you want for your funeral."

"I could have just left a message with Rudyka, you know. I thought you might want to hear from me that I was all right."

"I'm tired," she sighs. "I've had a long day—up at four-thirty and now it looks like I'm going to have a full house for the night. I have to get back to the kitchen—there are so many dishes yet to wash."

"Fine. Good night."

She says nothing, then speaks: "If the weather changes, I expect you to come home. But if you stay there, remember who you are."

Then she hangs up.

Had she remained on the line, I would have assured her that there is no chance I will be forgetting who I am. This is the sort of thing that happens to other people, people who co-star with Cary Grant in stories where their cars break down in rainstorms and they have no choice but to disrobe and sit around in his pajamas. This is the sort of thing that never happens to any real people I can think of, to anybody I know. Stranded. At the house of a man. A man I love. A man who says he loves me. I am thirty-two and this is the biggest thrill of my life. I think for a second how that realization is pretty sad. "If you'd like to make a call, please hang up and dial again," a mechanical voice is saying. "If you need help, dial your operator." I replace the receiver, having made my call, and not feeling in need of any assistance, right just yet.

I stand in Eddie's living room, next to a rust-colored tweed couch, listening to water running and sloshing somewhere down the hallway. The room is cozy, with a worn orangey Persian rug taking up most of the floor, and two fat armchairs holding extra pillows. The walls are covered by a very old and white flocked wallpaper that I can't help but pet. Over that, Eddie has hung a few simply framed woodcuts of the faces of people who look famous but to me are unfamiliar.

Heat has begun to blast from a big metal grate in the baseboard, and I go and stand in front of it. I see that both of the end tables flanking the couch are piled with books that don't fit on the ceiling-high set of shelves, the sides of which have been covered by the fuzzy wallpaper. Eddie seems to favor biographies and self-help books and titles on social change. It is a serious-looking room fit for a serious person. The only thing that looks out of place is the small stack of *People* magazines under the telephone.

I hear the water stop and that sends me into the kitchen, where I sit and massage my feet as needles begin to wave through them. The room is beginning to get so warm that my face pulses as it defrosts.

"Your turn," Eddie says to me. He is in the doorway and, from what I can see by just turning sideways from examining my feet, he is wearing at least a pair of beat-up jeans. "Did you call home?"

I tell him I have, and I raise my eyes to see he also has

on some kind of baggy sports jersey with the number 11 stitched to it in blue and yellow. There are a couple of holes in the fabric, and some corners of the number have begun to tear away. Eddie notices me looking at it and pulls the shirt away from his front. "I don't know who eleven is—some roommate somewhere left it behind. Want to use the shower? I'll try to find something to eat."

"Where is it?" I ask, though I am still stuck in some sort of amazement and maybe an envy that in the time Eddie has spent living away from home he has done so with so many people that he can't even recall all of them. Then I am hit with something else: "You don't happen to have a dryer or something—I could just dry out these clothes and put them back on."

"I wish, but no," Eddie says. "I do my laundry at my parents' house." I see him climb the snowbank with a basket of what I know to be underwear. And into my head rolls my mother, gunning the engine and tsk-tsking about his manhood. I should have known that she of all people would have no trouble making it here through the storm.

Eddie assures me that he has lots of sweatshirts and things, and that something here ought to fit me. "If not," he adds, "there's always the Crevier sisters upstairs. We could both get something to match." I smirk through my shivering. The Creviers are twins who have to be about eighty and who still wear identical dresses, shoes, handbags, hats, and the like. In good weather, they walk side by side each morning to the 7 A.M. mass at Saint Yvonne's, and do the same on the way back. Unless you are one of them, there is no way to tell if the same sister who was walking on the right before mass is on the same side on the way back.

Eddie's bathroom, the first door off the little hall off the living room, is compact. There is a shiny aqua vanity to the right, a toilet of the same color and in the same state of cleanliness next to that, and a white claw-foot tub straight ahead. There is a window over the tub, and someone—his mother, I bet—has sewn Eddie a plastic curtain to go over it. The window curtain—aqua—matches the shower curtain that hangs from a circular pipe clamped to the showerhead. The walls and floor are white tile, and are immaculate.

The mirror is steamed from the water Eddie has drawn for me, and heat is pumping from a register under the sink. I stand in the middle of all this and I start to take my clothes off. Slowly. I peel them from me like I am some kind of rare and expensive fruit.

In Eddie's mirror, which just is a little lower than the one in my bedroom, I see what Eddie would see of me if I were naked on a TV show. He would see my pink face and my straggly head of hair, and my white neck and shoulders, Cioci Julie's pearl the only decoration. The rest of me is censored from the viewing public, but I can look down and see what else there is, and it suddenly and impulsively comes to me that maybe in this God-given circumstance, Eddie could, also.

It takes me about a half a second to do this thing that I can't believe I am doing, and now I actually really do crack the bathroom door enough to look into the hall, enough to see if he is out there for some reason, like maybe waiting for me to open the door and give myself to him, finely and amazingly, I hope. But I see nothing except a bicycle and a cardboard box, not the man who could have made some kind of history here, with me, with no one else around. There is no one walking the track behind the high school or driving up next to us at the game preserve or choosing the second-to-the-last row at the theater, no one at all anywhere near to mar, as they regularly have so many times in these past eight months, the perfect moments in which I have far more than half considered giving myself to Eddie.

But no Eddie in the hall, I shut the door quickly, shaking for various reasons, one of them relief.

* * *

Eddie is staring at me. "You . . . you are incredible," he manages to get out, and I say it this way because it looks like it takes him some effort. His expression is so serious I believe him.

"It must be the outfit," I shrug, and I adjust the cuffs I have rolled on the red chamois shirt he has left me. Eddie also has found for me a pair of gray running pants that he says never were the right size for his waist. He has given me a white T-shirt with a volleyball stenciled onto the breast pocket, and he has brought out a pair of red woolen socks like you would wear to hike. There was no proper underwear to lend.

"I mean it—incredible. There's something about you, in those clothes. I don't know," Eddie says and he goes to kiss me for one long time. We both smell like the same soap, and we slowly comb our hands through each other's wet hair and find that we both taste like the same biodynamic apricot lip balm I'd found on the toilet tank. I also notice that Eddie in general smells like he does at the beginning of a date, and I take that in slowly and with great disbelief that all of this is happening to me.

"Do you want," he breathes warmly into my ear, then stops. "Do you . . . want vermicelli?"

While I was in the bath, sitting with utter amazement in the same spot that I knew for sure he had been naked only moments before, Eddie boiled some pasta. Now he empties the pot of it onto two plates. He has set the little table and, in the middle of it, has lit what is left of a green candle in a tall glass jar. It looks very familiar.

"My mother has one of these." I point to the glass, which is decorated with an image of Saint Jude and a prayer to him. You are supposed to light the candle and pray your hopes and dreams to this patron saint of hopeless cases. Thanks to me, my mother says, her candle is no more than a stub. I am surprised to see that Eddie's is almost as short.

"Have you had this a long time—the candle?" I ask

Eddie, who is reaching for something way back in a cabinet. The jersey lifts with his arm and I see for a moment a part of the skin on his back, something I have not seen since the summer.

"I've had it long enough, as you can see," Eddie replies, with a little laugh. He brings to the table two wineglasses and a bottle that he must take a dishcloth to and dust. "Would you like something to drink?"

"Sure. Anything is fine."

This is the scene: Eddie uncorking whatever that is and sitting down and pouring it into my glass, then into his, then reaching over to pull the string that shuts off the round and buzzing fluorescent light in the ceiling above the kitchen table. The candle flame bounces in a draft, and our shadows shift on the wall.

"I like this a lot," I tell Eddie. He slides his chair over and bumps it into mine. We lean into each other and watch the light, which is whitest behind one part of the prayer: "Come to my aid in my great need so I may receive the heavenly consolation and help in all my needs, especially . . ." Then there is a space in which to insert what the candle calls your petition—your request or concern.

I want desperately to know when exactly all hope was gone for Eddie, and what great needs did he have that required heavenly consolation and help. What requests did he insert into those parentheses so many times? But I can't ask him that. I do, however, ask him if the candle works for him.

Eddie nods slowly. He doesn't say anything. Then he opens his mouth like he is going to tell me, but he seems to change his mind. So I start in about how my mother prayed with her own candle for me to pass algebra, and it worked. I passed. I didn't get great marks, but I passed. That's what she'd asked for.

"You know," Eddie says, looking more at the light than at anything else, "that shows you why you have to be careful what you pray for. If she wanted you to get good grades, that should have been her prayer. You get exactly what you ask for—when it's in the plan that you should get it."

"I know," I tell him as I look at him, who is still looking at the flame. I have heard that said before.

The meal is good, once we get to it. The pasta had cooled while we had been staring at St. Jude, so Eddie dumped it back into the pot and swirled it around over the burner, adding some more sauce and getting the whole thing bubbling again. We eat it all, and quickly, like there never had been all those platters and bowls and baskets paraded from the kitchen, plus the helpings of homemade pecan pie and raspberry jelly roll, and a politely opened box of cherry cordials.

In the living room, Eddie removes a few stacks of books from the coffee table and invites me onto the couch to put my feet up. From where we sit, there is a view of thick snow flying around under the streetlight.

"Do you know these people?" I ask, pointing at the portraits.

"I wish I had known them, but no," Eddie says. "I once had a roommate who was artistic, and he did them up for me. They're just people I admire for one thing or another."

He stands up and goes over to the portrait between his two front windows. He looks at it closely, like you might into a mirror, then points to the face: "This is Saint Paul. He was given a preview of heaven and came back to tell people that they have never seen or heard or even could imagine how great it is there. Like you don't even have it in your mind to comprehend, in this life, how terrific it'll be there. Isn't that something to think of? I always liked that."

I nod my head yes. It is something to think of. I am Saint Paul here in Eddie's home, and when I leave I will tell Anna you would not believe it—you could never, ever imagine it.

Then Eddie goes over behind a Christmas cactus and tells me that the one hanging there is of Henry David Thoreau, who wrote a lot of great things, in isolation. The thing he wrote that Eddie likes the best is something about "the mass of men lead lives of quiet desperation." He quotes that to me, then looks back at the face for a moment or two, like he might be waiting for it to say something else right there.

Eddie points to the pictures of the man over his stereo and says he is Roger Maris, a ball player who hit a home run the first time he batted in a World Series.

"You believe that?"

"It's in all the record books—want to see?" Eddie starts for the bookcase, and the cactus wobbles on its stand.

"No," I say. "I mean about the mass of men. You think everybody's miserable?"

"To an extent, I believe most people are," Eddie says with some certainty.

"Are you?"

"I have been." He turns to the window and looks out at the snow. "That's why I came back here. I was so happy living in this town as a kid. But then, you know, you leave and things happen so quickly. I've enjoyed my jobs and my traveling and being able to say I've done this or I've been here or I have that. But when it got to where I would hear myself telling people about all that, I would say to myself, so what—what's the big deal about that? Are you the places you've been, are you the things you've done?"

He looks at me as if he wants an answer. I have never thought about such a thing, so I make a guess. "No?"

"Right," says Eddie. "You know that, but I needed to find that out. I needed some time and some direction, because I didn't think that was true. So I came back here. Some people told me I should go to Alaska or somewhere remote, go live in a cabin, like Thoreau. But this town was it for me. I think it's working."

"Is that why the candle is so low?" Then figure I might as well add "You have had lots of petitions?"

Eddie smiles his smile. "Lots of them. You know—what should I really be doing? That's the big one. I think I kept the pace I did so I wouldn't have time for that question. But it's really been hanging over my head for as long as I can remember—even when I was pretty convinced I knew the answer, that I should become an accountant and go make some money. Even when I was a kid here, I think it burned in me more than it does in most people. And I'm not saying that to be dramatic. It's not what *should* I be doing with my life that I'm asking, I want to know what I *really* should be doing with my life. There's a difference."

I look down at his red socks on my feet and think how this never has been an issue with me, how I have never wondered what I should be doing. It's like I was born, I went to school, I graduated, I got a job, I make some money and I do all right. Of course, realizing this makes me feel greatly inferior to Eddie, who I hope will not turn the conversation my way.

But he does. "Does that whole thing bother you? I bet it doesn't. I envy you, how—and I'm not being condescending—how you live your life and that's it. You seem not to need much. That's where I want to get to. I've prayed about it. Is that what you did?"

I think about that. What did I do to get to where I was? I find the answer: "All I did was end up with the mother that I did. She didn't give me any goals other than being good."

Eddie is studying my hands, and keeps to himself any comments about their size. "Well that's one fine goal," he says. "I admire her for wanting that for you. I think it must be so difficult to be a parent. Who knows what made her put so much importance on it? You probably can't even imagine what the situation is like until you yourself get to that point."

That's Eddie, always right there with a large supply of the benefit of the doubt. He will say that the man who is driving hazardously might be having chest pains, that the kid who bagged the soup cans on top of the potato chips seemed to be new to the job. I sometimes think he had looked at me and said to himself, Well, it probably takes somebody like this about a year to get really interesting.

Whatever it is that Eddie thinks of me, it has him here right now, right next to me, with no signs of going away. I have to admit I have pinched myself a couple times since I got to this apartment, and more than just to check if the feeling had returned to my feet. But I did not wake up from all this to wonder who was bothering me and to see those same feet poking up under my yellow and orange floral twin bedspread, my white spindled footboard beyond that, and then my molded orange plastic chair set in front of my small white wooden desk standing against the sill of my window through which I can see my backyard and the farthest row of Macs.

Instead, I am totally conscious, here at Eddie's, and he wants to know if I would like some tea, would I want to watch the news, how about some music, should he turn up the thermostat, is there anything I need? When Eddie has the opportunity to have me, a more than grown woman, alone in his home, in what my mother calls this day and age, he is not ripping my clothes off and forcing me into a corner and doing God knows what. As far as I know, I am the only one here who has entertained thoughts even remotely like that.

No, we are only standing at the stove, where water has been put to boil in a copper kettle Eddie tells me he has owned since he first used it on a hot plate in college. It is the kind of scene I have seen photographed many times, usually at the end of rolls, when people are at the point where they just want to bring the film in, but there are a few frames yet to spend and they do not want to be wasteful. So they snap people brushing their teeth or drying their hair, sleepily filling the coffee maker. A baby splashes in its kitchen sink bathtub. A couple hugs for the camera while waiting for the kettle to boil.

Eddie asks me to select a type of tea, and he opens a cabinet. I take in not only the chamomile and the English breakfast and the ginseng, but the long boxes of lasagna noodles, the cellophane bags of spaghetti, the huge carton of oatmeal, the sack of brown rice. These are the things Eddie is made of—all wholesome and good, nothing fake or preserved, all chemical free and pure. I am not surprised.

I shuffle a few boxes but can't find the one with the friendly old man lifting his teacup. "What would you suggest?" I ask, having no idea what any other type tastes like.

Eddie walks over and hugs me from behind. He rests his chin on top of my head. That's how tall he is. I lean back into him. He is strong and as solid as a wall.

"I like this one," he says. He reaches for a dusky blue box decorated with a drawing of a napping bear and says, like he is in a commercial, "It's perfect this time of night."

I look closely at the artwork. The bear, suddenly a tall and handsome one, rests on his rust-colored tweed couch, his corduroy slippers set on the worn Persian rug. On the arm of the couch, a young woman bear has seated herself. She wears an oversize red chamois shirt and a pair of gray running pants and she looks incredibly beautiful. She holds a cup of tea in her left paw, and, with her right, she strokes the delicate and soft ear of the tall bear, who makes small and contented bear sounds.

"Want to sit on the couch with this?" asks Eddie, taking the box and the scene from me.

In the living room, he presses the button on an old television set on a straight-backed chair across from the couch. Because it has a tall stack of books on top of it, I haven't noticed it before. Now that I have, I see that on top of that pile Eddie is displaying the Thanksgiving card I had sent him. Because it is the first somewhat suggestive greeting card I have sent to him, I am at the same time horrified and elated to see he has put it out there for whoever it is that comes here to see.

"It's Thanksgiving—let's head into the woods and look for turkeys" reads the front, which has a cartoon of a shapely little Pilgrim woman holding a musket. Inside are the words "Well, it's a good excuse!" and a cartoon of the Pilgrim and her Pilgrim man racing happily into a dark forest.

The television picture starts with a small white dot, then blasts to fill the screen with the heads of the two people the announcer tells us is "the award-winning Channel Twenty-one news team of Kiki Cunningham and Spence Turbly."

Kiki, a giggly bleached blond in her mid-twenties and usually in some shade of pink, and Spence, a deep-voiced veteran of local radio who needed only a blond hairpiece to make the leap into television, are frowning into the camera. The word *BLIZZARD!* is printed on a sign hanging on the wall behind them.

"Bbbbrrrr!" shivers Kiki, shaking exaggeratedly and hugging herself so tightly that the carnations in the holiday corsage pinned beneath the "21" pin on her lapel lose a few leaves. "And a Happy Thanksgiving to you out there—and to you, Spence."

"It's happy only for a few, I'm afraid," Spence sighs, squinting at the TelePrompTer. "An unexpected blizzard already has dumped a record two or more feet of snow on western Massachusetts, turning a joyous holiday into a nightmare for many travelers."

Spence turns to Kiki, who grimaces and tells the camera, "We have reports that power and phones are out in many parts of the area. We don't know how many parts, because the phones are out, so people can't get through to tell us. This is really a nightmare. For all of us."

Kiki swings back toward Spence, and Spence says, "That it is. News Team Twenty-one's award-winning meteorologist, Buzz Muraska, is tracking the storm. We urge all of you to stay where you are. Do not use the roads unless you have an extreme emergency."

I silently thank Buzz. His plea will come in handy as ammunition if I ever again see my mother. I know she has heard him, because she never misses News Team 21. "Buzz said rain, you know," she will remind me. Or "Spence promised the prices will be going down." Kiki, she is in love with, and had a friend who owns a videocassette recorder tape the segment of the news that showed Kiki getting married last summer. "She was a vision—a mother could be proud of a girl like that," I was told when my mother returned from viewing the tape over and over for an entire afternoon.

It is funny to think that here I am, snuggled up to Eddie, his clothes right next to my skin, wearing no underwear and drinking an exotic tea while looking at the very same television picture my mother is staring at. Right now. I get a little closer to Eddie and put my head on his shoulder. He whispers his love for me. I am across town, but I am so far away from home I might as well be speaking another language.

Buzz is standing in front of a map of the area, and you can hardly see it because it is covered by drawings of clouds. His artificial tan is all the more striking against the billows of white.

"Do not, I repeat, do not, leave your homes," he sternly orders us. Then he adds one of his trademark humorous comments that my mother just loves: "It'll be just you and the leftovers—and, hey, hope those in-laws got out of there before this hit!"

Buzz sweeps his hand from here to Albany. He is big on

dramatic gestures at the map. "It's especially bad all through this section. When will it let up? We'll take a look at that following this important message."

He and his tan and his map instantly are sucked into a snowy static. "The cable's out," Eddie determines, after hopping up to flip the dial and find nothing but more snow. He shuts off the set and returns to me. "Well, at least we know we shouldn't go anywhere."

"I figured that."

From behind a pillow, Eddie takes a crocheted afghan of white acrylic yarn, something he tells me his Cioci Lorraine down in Phoenix sent him last Christmas, and he covers us. We look out the window, and there is only a small space clear now to see the snow, which still is falling like somebody is up on the roof dumping it out from buckets. I don't know how long we sit there, but it is long enough to get so comfortable that I know I couldn't move if I had to. Then, somewhere in this, I feel Eddie's head on my shoulder and hear only his steady breathing.

In my dream, we are flying together. I am just above the surface of the ocean, Eddie is just below. To anybody seeing this, we are headed in the same direction, and are very close. But to be one of us is to feel there is something in the middle that can be seen through, but that still separates us. It is the kind of dream that makes absolutely no sense to me, and I awake confused about it—but not about where I am. I do not ask what am I doing here. I do not wonder how this has happened. To be lying on Eddie's couch under his aunt's afghan feels about as good as dying did. I turn myself toward the windows, which are white with ice and lit from the sun that has come out this morning. On a table next to the armchair I spot something in a small frame—a photograph of a woman standing in front of a tree, with the blue water and the blue sky and the blue mountains behind her. The look on her face—unbelieving and grateful—I have never seen on my own.

In the armchair next to the television, I then see Eddie, wrapped in a blue blanket, looking at me. In the small voice you have when you first wake, he tells me that I am the very most wonderful thing. That he couldn't even leave the room knowing I was here.

I wonder first how I must look right now. Then I don't care. On this day of this day and age, I, a more than grown woman, pull the afghan and slide against the back of the couch. Eddie stands up, walks over to me, takes up that empty space, and for the first time we know what it is like to lie next to each other. There are things I know we could do, there are things I know we probably even want to do. But I let him decide, and lie there is all we do. And it is good and it is right.

Across the room, the Pilgrims are miles ahead of us. Saint Paul just watches. He promises me that what waits ahead is at this point indescribable to me—things I haven't ever seen and things I haven't ever heard and things that haven't even entered my mind.

THAT. IN THERE. THAT IS NO WOMAN."

My mother was whispering this loudly. I just had swung the kitchen door smack into something solid on the other side of it. I heard a quick shuffling of bedroom slippers and realized what the obstacle had been. And it repeated that the woman on the couch, the woman here to see the ring, was not a woman.

"Ma. Please. I'm in no mood," I told her, shooing her from her post.

But my mother, a crazed look on her face, continued in a louder tone: "That is no woman. Get it out of here. To think—in my house, such a thing."

By that time I was already on my way out of the kitchen, carrying the napkins I had forgotten to set out when preparing for prospective customer fifty-six, Jane Lowney. "Please keep your voice down," I asked her in a whisper. My mother glared at me, her arms anchored across her chest.

When I reentered the living room, Jane was busily

searching for something in her purse, a rectangle of dark brown embossed leather that I only now noticed had a small stuffed alligatorlike animal stitched to the top of it. Its tail dipped down and made up part of the catch. I thought of Randy's last visit—when he popped in just to say his father was trying to rearrange his schedule to get out here finally—and his hopes for a Florida honeymoon. Jane noticed me taking in her accessory and she held it out to me. "Vintage shops. I love them! You never know what you'll find! Ever go?"

"I've never been to one," I said, and wanted to say that this type of merchandise was exactly why. But I didn't. As usual, I gave the compliment I knew the other person would like to hear.

"What a find!"

"I think so," Jane said, glowing with confidence, putting great emphasis on the *I*. "I used to shop at Sears. For everything. One day I said I'm going to try something new. I went about as far away from Sears as I could get. In fact, nearly this entire outfit is from those types of shops—antique places, the Goodwill, Salvation Army . . ."

She then stood up and turned in a circle, so I could take in the black wool smoking jacket with sleeves rolled up a ways to expose its subtly printed burgundy and navy satin lining. The classic high-necked white linen blouse. The yards of dark gray tweed that made up the long and many-gored riding skirt. The brown boots indented with the same pattern found on her handbag, and on the animal.

I noticed that each item of clothing was of a larger size than you'd usually see a woman wearing. But then, Jane Lowney was a larger-size woman than you'd usually see.

"Not one piece was over twenty-five dollars," she confided in her raspy voice, and added a pajama party-style giggle. "Not only is it cheap, but they're of wonderful quality, and I know I'm not going to see someone looking the same way I do!"

From the kitchen came the noise of something dropping to the floor, and clanging when it landed.

"I have the same hope for this ring," Jane continued, not seeming the least bit distracted. "I search for the unusual. No more white bread for me, no ma'am. When I saw your advertisement, I felt this was something worth taking a look at. The stone. The combinations of gold. The size alone—there aren't many rings that could come ready-to-wear for me."

I looked over at Jane's hands, and it was like looking at my own, only these had been dusted with a bit of makeup powder, the same shade as the one applied a little heavier to her neck and face, where, right then, two elaborately shadowed eyes were blinking with expectation.

"May I see it?"

I not only had forgotten to put out napkins, I had left the ring up in my room. "Just a second," I told her, then climbed the stairs. The box was on the desk, and when I went to grab it, I saw that my mother was out in the backyard, trying to pull my father by his coat sleeve away from the garage, where he was repairing a downspout so water would not collect in the gutter and maybe rot holes in the roof, and our cars, should we ever park them in there, would get as wet as if we had left them outside. My mother was pointing excitedly toward the house, and I could see her trying to get my father interested enough to come in and take a look at who—or what—I had in there.

I didn't wait to see if she was successful. I took the box downstairs, where Jane was standing at the bookcase. She had pulled out the *Better Homes and Gardens Handyman's Encyclopedia,* and was scanning its index with her formidable index finger.

"Hope you don't mind," she said. "I used to love this book."

"You're handy. That's good," I said, making little nods with my head, not sure what other comment to add. "Here's the ring."

Jane rushed over, bringing the book, and flew to her spot on the couch. Her skirt made a grand swirl as she turned and took a seat.

"Will you look at this," she said slowly and seriously, and removed the ring from the box. "May I?" She turned to the light next to her, and soon was holding the ring all sorts of ways, examining it from many angles, both in and out of the path of the lamplight.

Almost every time Jane changed her view of it, she let out a breathless sound of amazement. Her intensity really allowed me the opportunity to take in her physical appearance. I admired her mass of carefully tended black curls. I noted the clunky gold chain that encircled one big-boned wrist. I observed the space she used on the couch cushion. I had no conclusion to reach, other than there sat a confident, friendly, larger woman.

"May I use your telephone?" Jane asked, startling me a little when she looked up and I was still looking her over.

"In the hall—right there," I said, pointing. Jane placed the ring in the box and then removed a small leather-covered address book from below the legs of the alligator.

She went over to the telephone and I watched her wait for her connection. It came and she turned away.

"Psssttt!"

The sound came from a crack in the kitchen door, where my mother was signaling me furiously. "Psssttt!" she hissed again.

To quiet her, I got up, took the ring, and rushed over. "Give me a few minutes, OK? She'll be gone soon. She's using the phone."

My mother reached through the opening in the door and grabbed my arm, pulling me with surprising force into the kitchen, where my father was standing with his hands in his pockets.

She pointed to him. "He's sure that's a guy that used to work at the lumberyard—Jay somebody," my mother giddily told me, in a hushed volume and with much delight. The disgust over the possibility of having this unusual person in her home apparently had turned into glee over a story that could win her great attention when she related it at the next Ladies Guild meeting.

I looked at my father, who tilted his head and lifted his shoulders once.

"Ask him—her—him," my mother urged. She still was gripping my arm and she shook it strongly as she spoke. "Ask this person where he used to work."

"She seems nice. You're going to embarrass me," I told her sternly, pulling away. "Please!"

"Oh, excuse me," my mother said with false horror, and she put her hand to the side of her face. "I forgot—you love everybody."

Though that was not entirely true, I just said a defeated "yeah" and left the room.

Jane remained on the line in some conversation, so I reached for a magazine. RELIGION IS MORE THAN AN ACT, boldfaced the headline of an article that accompanied a huge close-up photograph of Martin Sheen receiving communion. The story told how so many stars are returning to their spiritual roots, or how they never really left them, even though they became big shots. There was a photo of an extremely good-looking young man flashing a confident smile from his place behind a news desk. "A New Life," began the paragraph below his portrait. "Philadelphia's favorite news anchor-hunk, Patrick Josephs of WPHI-TV, last month stunned his many thousands of fans by turning down a prime network job offer in order to enter a seminary in eastern Massachusetts specially designed for those with delayed vocations. 'I prayed for my true goal in life,' the future Father Pat told us. 'I encourage everyone to do the same.' "

I slapped the magazine shut and shot it onto the pile just as Jane came back to the couch.

"I didn't mean to be on there for so long, but there's a friend I'd like to have take a look at the ring. He's very smart about jewelry. He tried to work it out, but he can't come over right now. Do you think we could come back?"

"Whenever. You have the number," I said from Philadelphia.

"You've been very nice," Jane told me.

"No problem."

"Well I've never done anything like this before," she said, "just to go into somebody's house and shop. It's different. But, you know, lately I'm doing a lot of things I never did before. It feels wonderful."

I didn't ask Jane what those things were, but I wanted to—only so I could get from her maybe a hint of how to go about being somebody else. Even if she never had been a man, now, obviously, she was someone other than who she had once been. That held an appeal for me. Who—or what—brings you to that, I was dying to know, as I sometimes had a strong feeling this was what I needed. A kick of some kind, or a push from somebody. I wanted to ask her what hers was, who did that for her. Or could it be possible she had done it herself—had swung around and booted herself right into her dream.

But I couldn't find the words, not while I had an audience. "Good," was all I could say to her. And I meant it. "Good for you."

I let her out the front door. She shook my hand in an admirable grip and turned away. I felt a little lonely and envious as I parted the curtain to watch her walk her no-nonsense stride over to the small white sedan she'd parked out front. She shifted into gear and waved to me as she rolled the first few feet. Her head was still turned to the side as she passed my driveway and got in sight of the garage. Something she saw there made her put her foot on the gas.

THE CHRISTMAS TREE WAS RIGHT OVER THERE, AT THE FRONT window, like it had been the night Andy Ligawiec visited so long ago. Awaiting Jesus, the manger was set up on top of the television, in the same way. The plastic candles were glowing again and I was nervous one more time. I had been here before. Andy had been right there, on the couch, smiling at me, with those teeth, saying, "Take it, take it, open it."

Only this time, it was Eddie who was there. And he did nothing but smile.

When he did say something, it was "Come here."

I was about as close to him as I was going to get, but I edged right into the side of him. We locked into a kiss like you would see on the front of a romance novel, losing our lips and our faces and our heads and the rest of us in the same kind of psychedelic whirlpool you can see on "Twilight Zone" reruns. Then we separated slowly and the both of us sat there, staring at each other. I knew what was happening right there at that moment in my life, but I figured that at any minute I was going to hear my bedroom window shades shoot up violently and my mother, who would be standing next to the swinging crocheted tabs with which she had yanked them up, would be yelling didn't I know what time it is? Church is in ten minutes.

But my mother didn't say any of that, because I was awake, and this was as real as I had ever known reality. Eddie was there, and he was holding a little white cardboard box. For me.

He cleared his throat, just like you would expect somebody would need to at a time like that. It sounded almost like how you would spell it if you had to: "Ahem."

He did it again. "Ahem."

"Yes? Eddie, what? Say it—whatever you want to say." I couldn't stand this for much longer. Then I had a thought. Here I was, thinking I knew what was in the box, but also knowing truly that something this fantastic could never happen to me. Just like what my mother had said about how she had dated my father for a year and was hoping to get from him for Christmas exactly what she had been praying for. "But instead of a small little box with maybe a ring in it, what did he come in here with?" she would still fume as she recounted this to me for the millionth time, like Stanislaus never had shown up finally with a ring and they never had been married, like all she ever had to remember him by was the silver-plated brush and comb set he had delivered that holiday, the one that was suitable enough, he proudly pointed out once she had unwrapped it, to display on one's dresser.

"A hairbrush! One year dating me and he brings a hairbrush."

I pulled myself out of Eddie's eyes and looked down at the box. It was too small to contain even a folding brush you might take in your pocket on a trip. But it could hold a key ring, maybe with a Saint Christopher on it. It could be a pair of dice. It could be one of his little trinkets. It could be many other things than a ring. But I really thought I was sure about what was in there. I just couldn't let myself believe it. And it was just as unbelievable to me how twice in the space of a few seconds my mother, snoring deeply behind a closed door behind another wall, had managed to sneak into this most holy of moments.

"What can I say to you except that I love you, and I want to do that forever."

Eddie said this to me.

To me.

I watched him take the lid off the little white box and remove from it a velvety maroon case. I saw him pull at the lid and I saw it work open. I saw a yellow-white light glowing on a golden band. I saw him take it from its place and hold it out to me.

"I am going to give you a new life," he said slowly, right at me.

And he slid the ring onto my finger.

When I really want to hurt myself, this is what I think of: How I couldn't stop staring at what he had just given me. How I just said "yes" and nothing more, how we hugged so hard we went right through each other. How over his shoulder as he held me, when I finally opened my eyes, the stone nearly glowed in the dark and gave me the feeling that whatever new life he was planning for me, I right then all of a sudden already had.

In the morning, I woke before my mother only because I never really slept. It was about five and I couldn't stand it anymore. I had to share this, and, having heard my father leave to shovel the driveway, she was the only person around to do any sharing with.

I went into their room. The Madonna and child over the bed were the only ones with their eyes open. My mother was on her back, clutching the blanket up to her neck, her short and gripping fingers visible and looking like the serious paws of something that had settled in for hibernation. There was a strip of a white cotton rag wound around her head, the hair on which had been twirled into curls secured by black bobby pins.

I went over to her side of the bed and sat on the floor. When I was little, I used to go in there and wait for her to wake up. If she didn't by the time I wanted her to, I would pull her eyelids up. She hated that, but it worked. She would come to thrashing like a drowning person. "What? What?" she would want to know, a puzzled look on her face, her arms flailing and her feet fighting off the covers. "Who's? What's wrong?" Then she would spot me, sitting there. "Don't you ever do that again," she would growl.

"Get up," I would command. If I had had a sister, I always had thought, she wouldn't have had to go through such a thing.

That morning I wanted to rouse her in a better mood. She hadn't been her same old self to me since my night at Eddie's, from which I returned, she enjoyed noting many times, "looking entirely too happy for somebody who slept all night on a couch." So I didn't need to get her more irritated. I shook her arm. My finger sunk deep into the flabby upper part. I shook her pillow, and realized it had the same consistency as my mother.

"Ma. Ma. Get up. Come on."

The gasps continued. A hand reached over and brushed the ridge of her nose.

"Ma—I want to show you something." I shook the pillow again. She rolled onto her side, the one facing me. I got real close to her.

"Ma!"

Her eyes shot open, and she looked at me like she had never seen me before. In fact, she stared at me for a long time, until I got a little worried. "Ma. It's me. Get up."

She blinked and pulled her head back. "It's you? That's

you? I was trying to figure out who it is. You don't look like you. It's dark. What time is it? What do you want?"

"It's me. It's five."

"Five what?" She was angry. "What are you doing? What's wrong with you?"

"Nothing at all. I just wanted to show you something."

She looked at me suspiciously, like maybe I was going to make her sign something while she was in this state.

"This," I said, and put my hand up where she could see it. She caught it before it came too close, and moved it into her field of focus.

"You know I can't see close up. What's that? A ring?"

Her guess dropped to the floor with a thud. "Whose is it? What are you doing with it?"

"It's Eddie's . . . it's mine. Ma, he wants to get married."

My mother just lay there and held my wrist and looked at my hand like it was something she was trying to find a name for. Could it be this? Could it be that? Could it be the hand of my daughter—who someone wants to marry?

She shook her head. "Married." She pronounced the word like she might pronounce a vegetable she had memories of throwing up from.

This was not what I had thought it would be like. OK—I knew much better, but I had hoped for more. On TV, where I really should have lived, my mother would have awoken in a glamorous cloud and would have invited me to hop onto the bed and tell her all my problems, even if it was not yet light out. Then I would have told her I had no problems, I was only there to tell her somebody had asked me to marry him and that I was going to do just that.

We would have hugged. We probably would have cried, then looked at each other and broken into laughter. She would have retrieved from her bedside drawer a silk hanky and would have dabbed each of my laughing tears individually. Then she would have taken the ringed hand in hers and would have proclaimed some kind of blessing and I would have felt so wonderful I would have given that ring right back if, in exchange, I could only be just like my mother.

But, instead, here in my own life, I was getting her bedcovers thrown half over me as my real mother hefted her feet onto the floor and gave a few loud hacks as she cleared her lungs for the day's use. I swatted the quilt from my shoulder. "What do you think?" I asked, scrambling for some semblance of approval, beating the deadest horse that every lay rotting on the ground.

My mother struggled into her robe. "Well, at least he's Catholic," she said, grinding her nose into a wadded Kleenex. "Mrs. Fijol's daughter married a Lutheran and in the ceremony they wouldn't let them go closer to the altar than the communion rail." Then she stopped, and peered at me from the doorway. "You don't have to do this, do you?"

"What?"

"You know what I mean—like Teresa Muniec?" She was waiting for an answer—was Eddie to me what Smiling Jasiu, Chicago's newest polka sensation, had been to Teresa Muniec? Had my one night at Eddie's apartment put me in the same dilemma Teresa had found herself in long after Jasiu's bus rolled out of town at the end of its one-night gig at the PACC?

"Come on, Ma," I begged. "We're getting married because we want to. Can't you at least say you're happy? You were the one who was so big on Eddie when he first got here. Now I'm with him and you're mad. You don't make sense."

She looked at me for a few seconds, then came over and gave me a quick and stingy hug. "Do you love him?"

I cocked my head. "No. I just figured, hey, who else will marry me. Of course I do! What did you think?"

She gave a look like she really didn't know what she thought. "It's early. You woke me up. What did you expect? I suppose he's a good boy. It'll be all right."

"I know that. It's going to be great. Can't you act happy?"

"I'm happy, I'm happy, OK?" she waved me away. "Now go. I have to dress up."

She left the room and I heard the bathroom door close. I sat down on the bed, which was warm from my mother like it had an electric heater in the mattress. In the dimness, the stone on my left hand sparked and I felt a little better.

With a marriage in my future, I had my first thought about what kind of mother I would be. I wasn't sure about everything, but I knew for certain I would not want to be like my own.

I JUST WANTED TO SEE HOW IT WAS GOING—I'M ON A BREAK. JUST thinking about you—you and the ring—how is the ring—has it sold? Hey! Hey you! Not on top of the donuts—next to the donuts . . ."

It was another call from Randy, who was not only the only prospective customer ever to call back, but the only one to continue to do so, almost weekly for the seven months since he first looked at the ring.

"That's OK—no, it's not been sold, not yet," I say, telling him what I always tell him. "I've got Elizabeth Taylor coming here this morning."

"Let me know if she's serious, will you? I'm still trying to get my father over there. He wants to see it, but he's always got something going on. I've been telling him it's going to go fast, that this is the one I'd like, but nothing makes any difference to him. Sometimes I wonder if he just doesn't like Roseanne. Maybe he's trying to stall me."

"Maybe," I said, sliding a handful of store-bought pecan

sandies onto a plate, for some reason kind of annoyed that he didn't get my joke. "But you've been wondering this since I've known you, and I always say why don't you just ask him. So, have you asked him?"

"No, but maybe that's because it doesn't matter to me. I mean I want to marry her, not him. Right?"

"I guess," I said. I folded three paper napkins into little pennant shapes. I didn't know if Maria Dusza would be coming here alone, and I wanted to be prepared in case she showed up with a guest.

"You sound distracted—you OK?"

I exhaled. "I'm all right. I don't know. It's just one of those in-between days."

I knew exactly what it was. Lydia Koziol had died. Last night's obituary page gave the news, next to a photograph of her that had to have been taken in 1943. She was wearing a snood, and her skin was tighter than I'd ever seen it, but it was Mrs. Koziol all right, head dramatically turned sideways and upwards, a pose that defined a sturdy collarbone and positioned her upturned eyes so they were examining with a hint of pride the adjacent headline that read:

LYDIA KOZIOL, 72

PLAYED ORGAN, DANCED

I knew none of those things about her. I only knew her to be older than most of the parents of people my age, but I did not know her to be anywhere around that number. The obituary, which read that she had left "three grieving children: Bolac Jr., a partner in the family business; Kenneth, a self-employed television program consultant; and Karen. All at home," also told me that Lydia Koziol had enjoyed playing the organ at family gatherings. My mother told me that morning that the dancing part, described in the paper as "a stint in the world of professional dance instruction," had been a part-time job as a spare practice partner who sat on a folding chair at the Arthur Murray studio in Springfield the summer before she married. All I really knew was that her "distraught and loving husband of 42 years, Bolac, proprietor of Koziol the Cobbler," in a somewhat better time not too long before Lydia, as Anna's mother later that day would put it, "went into the bathroom and never came out," had come here looking for a special sign of appreciation.

And now, according to the paper, in lieu of floral arrangements, he could only show his gratitude by making a donation to his local public television station or the hospice.

"Somebody died," I said to Randy. "It's just unsettling. Her husband looked at the ring for her. Something was going on with him and her then—I don't know what. But I guess she had been sick, and he wanted to give her something nice."

"Wow," said Randy, and I heard him take a gulp of maybe a coffee. "That's really sad. I'm sorry."

"No need," I said. "I really didn't even know her. And what I knew of her, I always laughed about a little. She was somebody's wife. Somebody's mother. Now she's dead."

I could hear Randy's store radio. It was playing some song about layin' next to you.

"I have to go, to get ready," I said. "Thanks for calling."

"I'll give a call again. As soon as I can get my dad going. I'll call back soon, I promise."

I knew he would. He always did. So I said "I know. Bye."

In the living room, I set the cookies and the napkins on the coffee table. The ring already was there, where I had left it last night, after Thaddeus and Albert Czarniecki politely had requested a moment of privacy, then had asked me back from the kitchen to say they had decided it was much too large for what they called their mother's "delicate hands."

"She's got hands the size of a gorilla's," my mother snorted after they had left and she could come out from the other side of the door. "They're just too cheap. They knew the price—why did they come here in the first place?"

I said I didn't know. My mother said she would tell me.

"To see you, of course. They're both eligible. They know you're eligible. Put two and two together, will you?"

The Czarnieckis were eligible, but they had been so for each and every one of their fifty-two and fifty-four years. I wasn't in the mood to hear my mother's reaction to the truth that it definitely had been the ring in which they were interested—not I, nor any other woman for that matter.

What I knew about Maria Dusza was much less intimate. It was limited to that she sounded old on the phone and that her last name translated to the word *soul*.

For a while after she had arrived, on time, wearing a black pantsuit and holding a typewritten sheet containing the directions I had given her during our telephone conversation, I had the feeling that those two bits were all I was ever going to know.

I welcomed her, and she said nothing, just put a kind smile on her thin, glossed lips. I offered her a seat, and she took it, smoothing her blond pageboy once settled. I told her the conditions (cash, all at once), she just made an "OK" sign with a manicured hand. I offered her something to drink, and she finally spoke: "Later, thanks."

So I just slid the box over to her, off the *People* that was featuring three or four barely recognizable television personalities, all beaming from photographs tucked in and around the cover story headline that boasted VIRGIN STARS—THEY'RE CELIBATE CELEBRITIES! My mother had been shocked to see this week's lead feature. The only thing that hit me about it was a wave of envy that I had no celebrity, which appeared to make remaining untouched a whole lot more joyous that I was finding it.

I saw Maria Dusza glance quickly at the magazine cover, then flip the ring box open. She took that first sharp breath that most—actually, I'd say all—people who look at the ring take at first, then she took it out and slid it onto the ring finger of her left hand. It fit her like it had been made for her. "Nice," she praised, dragging out the syllable and looking down at her hand. "A nice light. The ad was correct."

It had been so long that I had to think about what had been written. Then it came to me in a single, unsettling wave. "Truth in advertising," I said and I smiled at her. She smiled back.

Then she reached for the pot of tea, and poured two cups. She pushed mine toward me, and I accepted it, taking the sugar and fixing it the way I like. She did the same with hers, then sampled it and placed the cup on its saucer. Sitting on the edge of the couch cushion, Maria Dusza folded her hands onto her knees and said, just like this: "So. What happened?"

"Excuse me?"

"What happened? How did this happen?"

I had known that sooner or later I would get a kook, one who might make off with the ring and I would never see it again. Maria Dusza still had it on her hand, the fingers of which were laced into those of her other one. She moved a little and the thing glowed, even though her back was to the window.

"You're not interested? Why not put it back in the box, then," I suggested, using a friendly voice so as not to rile her and cause her to want to use any weapon she might be concealing.

"I'm very interested," she said kindly. "I want to know what happened."

"You know," I said, and I was getting aggravated, "what happened with me has nothing to do with anything. Either you want it or you don't. I really don't see that it's your business."

"Fine," Maria Dusza said, settling back onto the couch

and folding her arms across her front. "Then I'll tell you what happened to me."

"OK, but could I have the ring back first? I mean, I wouldn't want you to be hurting your finger if it doesn't fit."

"You know it fits me," Maria Dusza said, "as well as it fits you."

Her tone was not threatening. It was matter-of-fact and honest. And correct. I looked over at the grandfather clock, which told me no parents would be coming home until, probably, I was slumped here on the floor, the front door wide open, the ring box empty, my mother saying she had known this was going to happen. "My baby," I was sure she would wail over my cold body. "Why did I not love her like she wanted?"

"Pay attention, please," Maria Dusza requested, as if this was my first time at some kind of lesson. "When I was your age—maybe a little younger—I fell in love."

She spoke the last four words with great care. "He was wonderful—so polite, great at pinochle, a lover of marching band music. He could tell a good joke, could cook even. His favorite color was the same as mine, and, without consulting one another, we always chose the same numbers when we played the wheel at the park on Sundays. Nobody is perfect, but I think he was very close. A real gentleman. A good wage earner. Just my height."

Maria Dusza looked at me. "Do you see?" she asked, and I nodded that I did, though I didn't see anything except a prim, direct woman who had once been in love and who now looked a little like Carol Channing. I thought a little about that, wondering if one had anything to do with the other.

"You don't see," she said right at me, knowing that, sounding as exasperated as she all of a sudden looked. "What happened was that I thought here I am, set for my whole life. It is what I have been waiting for—the one, the right one. Didn't he sound it?"

She looked like she wanted an answer, so I said that it sounded it to me.

"You would think so, wouldn't you?" she asked me.

"I would," I answered.

"That's what I meant: you. You would think so, because you think like I used to think—he's here, my life is solved. Isn't that what you thought?"

She stared at me, waiting.

I started to say something like it was time for me to get to work, which it was. But something stopped me. And I just sat there for a minute. Then I agreed with her out loud, staring at her black leather clutch so I wouldn't have to say this to her face: "That's exactly what I thought."

I saw Maria Dusza unlace her fingers, extend her right thumb and forefinger and slowly remove the ring. She set it into its slit, snapped closed the cover of the box, and placed it onto the face of one of the untouched stars. Then she looked up at me. "You are the person who solves your life. Nobody else. This is what I want you to realize and think about now."

That said, she stood up and went over to the door. I followed her. "I really like the ring. I'll be back when you're ready," she told me. Then she opened the door, stepped outside, and closed it between us.

# 18

◆◆◆

THE DAY AFTER I GOT THE RING FROM EDDIE, I BOUGHT MYSELF a new bible, *Today's Bride,* which promised not the keys to heaven but something pretty close: all you needed to know to throw a memorable and romantic wedding—"the one day that lasts a lifetime," as the magazine put it.

"You know we can not afford much," my mother had said right to Eddie the night we sat down with my parents to begin discussing plans. She had her hands balled up on the table in front of her, and in that pose reminded me of the old Egyptian statues I'd seen in rolls of travel photos and that Mr. Herrman had explained to me are very symbolic. A clenched fist, for example—the kind my mother was displaying—was meant to show that the pharaoh the statue depicts held great power.

"Thank you, but that's not necessary," Eddie had told her kindly. His hand was flat on the table. I had never heard if that was supposed to mean anything. "I'm perfectly willing to pay for the entire day. I've been working for many years, you know. I can afford it."

My mother at that moment shoved her chair back and stood up slowly. "We are the parents of the bride," she said, reminding him angrily, shaking her finger. "It is our duty to pay for the wedding." I looked at my father, who nodded his head at me and smiled like don't worry—it'll be taken care of.

So it would be a no-frills event, which was fine with me. I did not care for the spotlight, and the less fuss the better, as far as I was concerned.

According to the *Today's Bride* wedding checklist, "preferred resources and services often are booked-up years in advance. Many couples don't hesitate to plan two years in advance." According to my mother, she needed at least one year to make all the preparations.

Eddie and I chose to have only five months. We selected May—the month of Mary and of his birthday and of fine weather that would be neither too cool nor too hot and a month that was not so far off that we might go crazy waiting. Plus, something in me told me to hook up with Eddie as soon as I could—before he, or I, woke up.

The rush meant jamming into one both the checklist's 10 TO 24 MONTHS AHEAD and 4 TO 6 MONTHS AHEAD columns. Evenings and weekends we worked at my dining room table to determine the type of wedding (informal), select the site of the ceremony (our church, of course, 2:30 P.M.), plan our reception (4 P.M. at Saint Władysław Lyceum), choose our attendants (only two—Anna, and Eddie's old grade school friend Teofil Romboletti, whose parents' Krakow- and Palermo-based union back in 1949 still was referred to as a mixed marriage) and draw up the invitation list.

One hundred and thirty-two people would be our witnesses, my mother informed us when she added her list to that sent over by eager and thrilled Mrs. Balicki—sixty-six from each side.

"You can afford this?" I asked, hoping she would realize the expense and condense the pack somewhat.

"You go to somebody's wedding, you have to invite them to yours," she explained to me. "We've been to many. Now we must pay back."

I saw my day turning into a bar of guest soap or a canned ham that could be quickly gift wrapped and presented.

"You don't even like some of these people," I pointed out, examining her list. "The Trzpits—you said last week that all they ever do is talk about how they go to Rome every year and get a private audience with the pope and how he sends them a Christmas card. You said you can't stand to be in the same room with them."

"Yes," she said. "But we went to their Stasia's wedding."

"How about Mrs. Giza—doesn't she make cracks at the card parties about how you never pay full price for anything?"

"Yes, well she'll come to this and she'll see money being spent," promised my mother, folding her arms beneath her bosom on the word *this,* which was my wedding day.

"Am I supposed to throw a party or something?" Anna, sitting on my bedroom floor, nose in *Today's Bride,* asked this with not much enthusiasm. "I guess I could . . . it's just that I'll need help. Maybe you could help me. Could you?"

Yeah, I was going to help her throw a party for me. That would look about as pathetic as it sounded. Lucky for her, my mother was miles ahead of her and already had contacted Saint Casimir's Hall about a ladies' shower. "If you're going to do this, I have to do this," she lamented when I went to thank her for planning an event I knew would have Eddie and me set for life, as far as housewares went. "She's not the only one who can spend money . . ."

The *she* was Mrs. Balicki, who, unlike my mother, did not leave the room when Eddie and I announced our engagement, but instead wrapped me and Eddie in her arms and looked at her Mike and sobbed as she told him that now, her prayers finally were answered: God had given her a daughter. The other day she called my mother to say she would be hosting a tea for me in her home. A chance to chat and relax before things got too crazy, was how she described it, nothing fancy, just some little cakes and things for me and my mother and a couple of Eddie's aunts and female cousins.

A chance to show off, was how my mother described it.

I needed a dress to wear down the aisle in front of the Trzpits and Mrs. Giza and everybody else who would be there for reasons other than to celebrate the fact that Eddie and I would be joined in Holy Matrimony, so I made that my next job. *Today's Bride* was chock full of all kinds of gowns, and I soon had bent the page corners of the styles I liked, or favored some parts of.

Some held no features that interested me: the Royal Wedding line, grandly poufy and satiny and each with a great long train that would mean hiring the local Girl Scout troop to help you drag it down the aisle, was shown on brides who stood awaiting their princes on palace balconies and private oceanliners; the Eleganza Chic woman, wrapped in many, many layers and layers of suffocating tulle, posed on a bridge next to Baby Eleganza Chic, a toddler who wore a tiny but no less nightmarish copy; the Ultimate Look bride, in an ornately beaded sheath with what I counted to be more than fifteen strings of pearls cascading from its neckline, was sprawled across a parquet marble floor, looking like she had been tripped, but that it had been fun.

I decide I like Lace Memories, a line described as "informality personified." The dresses were antiquey-looking and high-collared, which would cover any blotches should I get nervous. And they were shown on models who were sitting on chairs or standing with their fathers—something

I could see myself doing. The directory below the photo told me that Cupid's Bridal Nook in Ware carried the line, and I made a note of that next to the checklist line reminding me to "Select your dress."

Eddie that night flipped to the *Today's Bride* apparel guide and examined his own options. I watched him trace an index finger down the column for "semiformal daytime." He squinted at the tiny type then looked up. "Sounds to me like I can just wear my good suit, doesn't it?"

"I'd say," I agreed. I loved how he looked in a suit. I put a check next to "Consult a men's formal wear specialist in your town."

"Next one is plan your wedding and reception music," I reminded him. "How about Peggy Turner for both?"

Eddie began to laugh as hard as he had that day in church. I had a little thrill bringing up a memory that we shared. I thought about how our sitting here at the table with my magazine and a notebook and a couple of cups of tea also would be a recollection that we could bring up anytime in the future, and we would say wasn't that fun, back then, planning all that? And we would answer that question with a yes, because all of it had been coming together as easily and simply as the embossed lines edging the Palatino type on the plain white invitations that already, two months earlier than they needed to be, were stuffed and sealed and addressed and rubber banded by zip code in a shoe box on my mother's buffet. We kept saying that this is so easy, that we should have done this a long time ago.

THE DOORBELL SOUNDED AND INTERRUPTED MY READING THE DEscription of a new line of chemicals Mr. Herrman was considering purchasing for my machine. According to the pamphlet, the mixtures were popular for enhancement of color values and for their being gentler on the environment. The descriptions were illustrated by a drawing of a smiling and healthy cartoon dolphin that was jumping from a wave and, with an agile right fin, was snapping a photograph of a passing sailboat.

I tossed the paper onto the chair and went to the door. Flipping on the porch light, I pushed aside the curtain and made out a scene I had seen light-years before: Andy Ligawiec. On my porch. In one of those green air force jackets with the fake fur around the hood edge.

He opened his mouth in a big smile that displayed a set of perfectly formed corrective dental work. Then I heard "Small world! Got a ring for sale? I'm in the market."

I considered just moving the curtain back into place and

snapping off the light. I hadn't spoken to Andy since the last time he had been in my living room, hadn't been near him since I watched him and my mother that night in front of church, hadn't thought of him since she that time pointed out how he had taken up with a Protestant, and, before that, not for ages.

But there he was, becoming number sixty-two as I opened the door and watched him walk over to the couch and flop onto it. He unzipped his jacket and swung his arms over the backrest. He looked very content.

"Hi," he said.

"Hi."

"Wild, huh?"

"Yeah. Wild."

"I mean, who'd think something like this? Me coming here, for a ring. Wild."

"Wild." I took my seat across from him.

"What's a matter? Hey? You look nervous. It's me! Andy!"

"Did you call?" I asked. I was very aware that I did not look as pleased as he appeared. "I had no idea you were coming here."

"Nah. I'm in the market, as I said, and somebody suggested I try to get a bargain. You know, look for something somebody was trying to get rid of. I read your ad. It jumped right out at me."

"But you didn't call . . ."

Andy laughed a little "heh heh heh" and said quietly, like it was a secret: "Reverse directory."

I made a confused face.

"You know," he said. "Where they have the phone numbers in order, numerically, then the names of whose they are right after them. We have 'em in the office at the plant. I looked the number up, just to see who I'd be dealing with. Damned if it wasn't you!"

"Damned," I said, noting that was pretty much how I was feeling here, alone, with Andy Ligawiec.

"I heard, you know," he offered with a serious face. "I heard you had problems."

"That was a while ago," I told him. "Things are fine now. How about you?"

"Just peachy," Andy answered. "I'm still working at the plant—ten years now. They just moved me up again, to the pulping machine. They pay you plenty to be in charge of that thing, because it has all these huge blades—if you fall in there, you're fucked. I mean it."

"Wow," I said, genuinely—somewhat because of the machine, mostly because I never had heard any variation of that word spoken in my home. Not even on a holiday. I was glad my parents had seen Buzz Muraska's commercial about the can-can sale at the Stop & Shop, and that right now they were hurriedly pushing their carts in the search for deals on cases of string beans and creamed corn.

"It's true," Andy said with feeling. "Guy before me reached in there at the wrong point and we were picking hunks of his hand out of the egg cartons for weeks."

I shuddered.

"They kept one of 'em for him—a box, not a hand," Andy continued. "Had a perfect whole thumbnail right on the lid, right on the place where there's that egg printed on the carton. You couldn't have done a better job if you chopped it off and pasted it on there on purpose. You still at the photo place?"

Right then, I was in the dairy aisle, steering clear of the egg display. "Yes."

"Heard you were. You must be good at pictures."

"I don't have a camera."

"Huh," Andy exhaled. "We're getting a video camera before the wedding. Those things are unbelievable."

"When is it—the wedding?"

Andy fooled with the zippered pocket on his elbow, which had been patched with a fabric of similar shiny weave and color. I found myself noticing something, then saying it: "You have the same coat."

He flashed the teeth again and held out his arms, petting one with the other. "You remembered!" He beamed, appearing greatly touched. "I love this thing. Plenty of good times in this baby. The old lady has to patch it once in a while, but it's good as new, really."

"How is your mother?"

Andy looked surprised. He breathed in, then said in a serious voice, "Not too good. I mean she's OK—I don't know. I don't see her that much anymore."

"But she sews for you—that's nice."

Andy looked at me with confusion that I shared.

"Want to see the ring? I'll go and get it."

Andy was watching me as I walked back down the stairs. "Here it is," I said, and put the box on the coffee table. "Go ahead. Look at it."

He shifted himself to the edge of his seat and bent close to the table as he opened the container. I noticed a second and part of a third chin forming, and a circle of scalp shining through his thinning hair. He suddenly whistled loudly, the kind I am sure he many times has sent in the direction of a passing female. Then he raised his head and his eyes were wide.

"Jeez," he said. "This is miles away from what I gave you. Remember that thing? What an ugly piece of shit that was!"

I had to agree with him, but I also recalled how wonderful he had thought it to be at the time. So I reminded him.

"Yeah, yeah," he singsonged. "But if I could have come up with something like this . . ."

I waited for him to finish his sentence, but he didn't. So I asked "What?"

Andy got a funny look on his face and said, "With something like this, maybe, maybe we would have, you know—gone out for real. At least for a little while."

I was the one giving the little "heh heh heh" then. "You could have spent a fortune," I told him. "It wouldn't have mattered—I wasn't supposed to go out with anybody for four more years. Those were the rules."

"Sez who?"

"My parents . . . my mother."

"And you always listened to them—to her, didn't you?" He said this rather kindly.

I thought about the question, though I really didn't have to. Then I said, "Well, yeah."

"You still do, don't you?"

I felt myself getting defensive. "I've always tried to be the kind of person they wanted me to be."

"What kind is that?" Andy asked, and he seemed truly like he wanted to know.

I thought again, and no particular answer came to my mind, other than someone who was good, good, and good. "A good person, I guess. I don't know," I told him, because I knew that was the first goal. It was not that I should follow these rules and someday become a physician or a bank president or walk on the moon. It was that I be good—no matter the cost, no matter if it made me a good person who didn't always feel so good about herself.

"Well I think you were a nice girl," Andy said. "You still seem like—like a nice girl—woman . . . you know . . ."

I told Andy that I knew, and I thanked him. He was right. I was nice. That's about all that could be said of me. The room was silent, then the radiators clanged to life with a few metallic knocks.

"It's funny," I told Andy, though maybe funny wasn't the correct word. "Your ring, I really didn't want, and somebody stepped in and made me give it back. His, I really wanted but I ended up being the one making myself get rid of it. I don't know what one has to do with the other, but that just came to me."

Andy tilted his head and looked like he was going to try

to make some sense of it. He had the ring box in his hand and was leaning back in a comfortable position.

"Maybe," he said to me, not taking his eyes off the ring, "in both cases, it was supposed to happen like it happened. At least you saw, twice, that somebody cared a whole lot. Even if one of the times wasn't as big a deal as the other, that's two times more than most people see something like that."

I looked at him in the same way I remember looking at Anna's three-year-old cousin when he one day looked up at me from working his Etch-A-Sketch and said to me, "It is really something to live." Some things you just don't expect to come out of some people.

Andy obviously was not caught up in his wisdom. He continued on without missing a beat: "Plus, if you'd stuck with me, you'd probably be the mother of my kid."

"Your kid? You have a kid?"

Andy grabbed for his wallet and flipped to the photograph section with the speed of a detective producing his badge. A goofy-looking grade-schooler—ten maybe (I'm not good at ages)—sent out from a wallet-size school portrait a distinctively Andy-ish grin. Whoever Andy had done this with had contributed an abrupt upturn to the end of the boy's side-angled nose, and a natural wave to his shaggy blond hair. But there was no mistaking this boy was of Andy.

"Sam," Andy said in one quick and proud syllable. "Coulda been yours."

"I never knew."

"Most people don't. Happened in West Springfield, at the rink. Almost eleven years ago. After a hockey game. In the corner. Behind the Zamboni. Ten minutes of fun with a stuck-up little cheerleader from a school that always had a field day beating the shit out of us. I thought I was doing something great for the team, touching one of the untouchables, you know. One night a couple months later her old man is at my door with a baseball bat."

Sam was never allowed to know Andy, and Andy was never allowed to see the cheerleader—two agreements reached that night. Twice since then he has received in the mail a photograph of the boy. "No words ever with it," he told me. "Except for on the back of the first one: Sam, age one."

Andy looked over at me, but his eyes were somewhere else. "I can't even say he's a good kid, because I don't know. But he looks it."

"He does," I said, because there was no reason to think otherwise.

"It's hot in here," Andy said, and he shook off his coat. Swathed in a yellow and black plaid flannel shirt, a small bowling ball of a belly obscured his belt buckle. "Got any beer?"

In the refrigerator, behind a Cool Whip tub of leftover *golombki,* were my father's Millers. He drinks one a day, each afternoon after work, after coming in the back door, after washing his hands in the kitchen sink, after taking his seat at the kitchen table and saying to me or my mother, whoever is closest: "Get me a beer. I'm dyin' of tirst."

I reached for a bottle for Andy. And, just as I was about to close the refrigerator door, I put my hand in for another one. For me.

I brought them both into the living room and opened each with a lobster claw-shaped souvenir of Hampton Beach. No one I know had ever been there, and I never before stopped to think how this opener had ended up in our home, though I had seen it each weekday afternoon of my life.

Andy accepted his bottle gratefully and enjoyed a few long swigs.

I put mine to my mouth and poured some in, tilting my

head back. I caught sight of the ceiling just then: no jagged cracks were ripping open above me, no voice was condemning me for drinking in my own home. So I swallowed and took in some more.

I studied the label, with its fat and angled script. This was the fourth beer of my life, a grand total that had begun its slow ticking off in my senior year of high school, when, in one of the spontaneous acts of my life that just about equalled that number of beers, I told Anna we should take Stevie Przyyla up on his offer to go up to the shack in the woods near the hospital, where he and some other members of the cross country team would be hanging around. I reminded her that we were high school seniors—adults, practically. I reminded her that, in four years, no one had ever asked us to go anywhere. I reminded her that we had known Stevie Przyyla since the first grade.

She now often reminds me that I do better when I listen to her, who that day had protested, then had relented, then had ended up, after smoking a cigar and drinking an entire sixteen-ounce bottle of Carling Black Label, throwing up at the bottom of a wooded ravine behind the emergency room parking lot.

Then I remind her that I had been unaffected by my dose, and that day even had been offered an extra few sips by Ignacy Masztal, who in the four years since graduating from parochial school had blended so well into secular life that he, suddenly "Iggy," had been voted most popular boy in the senior class.

I had two beers at the tail end of Steffia's wedding reception. They were free, and helped me onto the floor for the bouquet toss, in which the bride pitched with such power that the flowers rocketed over the bunch of us and landed with a boom into the band's bass drum. "Sorry, I'm taken!" quipped the drummer, and Steffia got another chance. Her release was slower the second time, and, though I wasn't trying, I did put one hand up, and felt a stephanotis glide from the bottom of my palm right over to and off the tip of my ring finger. I turned to see Helen desperately clutching the flowers to her chest with two crossed arms, like the bouquet was a child who had just leaped onto her from the third story of a burning apartment block.

"No thanks," I say at the family picnic, when Rudyka wants to throw me a Bud. "Don't care for it," I have said at Mr. Herrman's Christmas party. But I would like to say give me one. Got another? Maybe two? Do they come in larger sizes?

"Got another?" Andy swirled his bottle, creating a whirlpool in the last inch.

I raised mine and took a long drink. It tasted of grains and earth and heaviness and Ignacy. "Sure," I said, aware of a light kind of feeling. I fished two more bottles from the refrigerator, brought four replacements up from the bottom shelf, and set the *golombki* back in their place.

Andy told me her name was Cindy. When he said it, his face lit and he had to scratch at his head like there was an energy he felt forced to expend all of a sudden.

She was beautiful in appearance, he told me. "Not the kind," he pointed out, "you'd think you'd see me with."

They had met in line at the bank. "It was the first of the month, and all the old people were cashing their checks. We were about the only people under a hundred in there. They were talking about all kind of gross stuff—what color their phlegm was this morning, how their suppositories don't work. And I'm standing next to this beautiful girl and I'm getting kind of embarrassed. I mean they have music playing, but it's not too loud and all you can hear is how they're going to have to open somebody up because there's an intestinal blockage."

I looked down into the neck of my bottle. "It can't be easy to get old—they probably have to complain," I said. I realized that kind of sounded like Eddie and his making allowances for people's shortcomings, and I took a swallow to wash him away.

"Yeah, well shoot me if I ever sound like that," Andy said disgustedly. "Do they have to advertise it? At the top of their lungs? You don't see us young people standing there yelling about something that's wrong with us—what a bitch it is that I sprained an ankle in softball or that I like partied so much over the weekend I had to call in sick both Monday and Tuesday just to get some sleep? So, to get to my story, they're saying all this and I look at her—at Cindy, whose name I don't know yet—and I go 'Getting enough fiber these days?' She doesn't do anything at first, so I think she's thinking what kind of an asshole is this? But then she starts to laugh, and when she stops, she says something like would I like to see pictures of her grandchildren. We start a conversation like that, because nobody is noticing. They're all deaf as that wall over there—maybe that's why they were yelling. Anyway, I finally get to the window, and then I go outside and put the money in my wallet, slow, so I can bump into her when she comes through the door. She comes out and we have a few laughs about how next time we're going to use the drive-up window. We stand there and talk for about an hour. Next thing you know, we can't stand to be away from each other. Pretty good, ha?"

Andy told me about how Cindy for a long time has had a steady job as an office administrator at the university, how she earns good wages and knows how to save her money and is a good influence on him in that respect and more. She does like to go out, but is just as happy most of the time to work in her garden next to the mobile home she owns, and where both she and Andy now live.

"You know, I'm getting into it—planting, weeding," he beamed. "If anybody told me someday I'd be picking flowers, I would've said they were all nuts. But that's how it is. The wedding's this fall."

"Sounds perfect," I said, because, to me, it sounded nearly so.

"Yeah," Andy agreed. "There's still a little problem with my family. Cindy's divorced, OK? That alone had them crazy. But she's a Methodist, too. Know what that is?"

I smiled. "Not one of us, right?"

"Right," he said, pointing at me. "And you can imagine how that went over."

I looked at Andy. He was standing out clearer to me than if I were looking at him through a magnifying glass. I drew a deep, deep breath. My lungs felt like they went all the way down into my feet.

"What they think about her bothers you?"

"I guess so," Andy said. "I want to say to them that this all is going so good now. Cindy's great—they'd love her if they took the chance. I'd tell them that yeah I've screwed up in the past, but I think really that I'm different. I'm not my brothers or my sisters. That stuff's not for me, being in the church. But that doesn't make me bad. I make money. I don't party too much these days. I'm pretty good to people. I'd tell them that, but they wouldn't listen. They won't even talk to me. How's that for family?"

"Actually," I said, "that doesn't sound too unusual to me."

There was some silence, and I added, "I think they're the ones who are missing out on something."

Andy smiled and downed the rest of his beer. He snapped the ring box and told me he liked it but that he was still looking. He had three weeks to shop before Valentine's Day. Could he call me about it?

"Sure—I'm in the reverse directory," I pointed out.

Andy stopped and looked at me for a few seconds, then apparently got the joke. He laughed at it as he put on his coat.

"It was really nice talking with you," I said. "And seeing

you. Take care with that machine. And, in case I don't see you, have a wonderful wedding. Marriage."

"Thanks," Andy said. "You take care, too." Then he came over and enveloped me in the green air force jacket. The hug was soft and sincere. I got this feeling that, by now, he really knew how to kiss.

He put his head to mine, but only to say something: "The guy was nuts to leave—even for God."

I pulled away. "Thanks, Andy."

He hiked the zipper on his coat and removed a pair of gloves from his pockets. "I'll see ya," he said and opened the door.

"Andy—one question," I said, feeling whenever would I get a chance to find this out? "Did you ever buy yourself something nice?"

He got a fuzzy look: "Huh?"

"With the money from the ring you gave me—did you get your money back? Like my mother told you to?"

Andy was squinting as he tried to figure out what I was referring to. Then something clicked for him and he gave a little Andy-Sam grin.

"How could I get my money back," he asked, "when I stole the thing in the first place?"

Had my mother been behind the kitchen door during all of this, she would now be pointing out how here, in her own home, had been a cursing, beer-drinking, factory-working unknown father who once—once that we know of, that is—was a thief.

I had been there, and all I saw was somebody who somebody else was lucky to be getting.

I went over to the couch and sat where Andy had been. I fluffed the pillows on either side of me and thought of him going home to the trailer, where Cindy might be cooking in the tiny kitchen, singing some Methodist song, setting the little table for two, wondering where Andy was and hoping he'd come home soon so she could tell him about her day as an administrative assistant, and maybe of the seed catalog she found that carries *Nicotiana sylvestris,* the white variety she'd been looking everywhere for.

I thought about how that could have been me. The songs might be different, if I dared to sing aloud, and I would have to start with more pronounceable flowers, but I could see myself with Andy now, the new Andy, the still-rough but less-rough Andy, who knew what he wanted and stuck to that. But after my mother returned the ring, my embarrassment was such that I couldn't even look his way. And now, what had he turned into but a real possibility. A possibility, however, that already was taken. I shook my head and scowled. It was all my mother's fault. I cursed her. Actually, I really didn't say a curse, I just looked over at the small black-and-white photograph of her staring blankly into the camera on the day of her wedding, a length of lace draped around her face, and over the top of the plain white Sunday dress she had to wear because she wasn't lucky enough, of course, to afford a gown, and I said, "I curse you."

The doorbell rang. She had heard me and had come to the front door formally to remind me I was now doomed to hell for that act.

"Ma?" I asked as I moved the curtain and flipped off the light that I'd forgotten to turn off when Andy left. I snapped it back on.

"It's Randy," said the person, who, in the white shirt, skinny black tie, and the quilted Quick Stop jacket he wears when he must assist motorists who have trouble operating the gasoline pumps, was indeed Randy.

"Randy?" I asked, just to be absolutely sure.

"Randy," he said.

I opened the door.

"Hope you don't mind, but I saw the light on and your car here. Thought I'd stop in . . . to say I haven't gotten my father pinned down yet."

"Yeah, yeah," I said sarcastically. I don't know why, but Randy likes to visit and talk, and he always has to start off with the same excuse. I have not heard that Roseanne, who long ago figured out Randy was going to propose, minds him talking to me, so why should I care?

Randy did not move from his place on the porch. "What have you been doing?" he asked with suspicion. He arched only one eyebrow at me and I wondered how he was able to do that.

"It was the weirdest thing," I said. "A guy I used to know stopped to look at the ring."

"Well, it's a small town," Randy noted and he walked inside.

"Yes, but it's that he gave me a ring back when I was fourteen," I said, closing the door behind him. "There was a big scene, and I had to give it back to him. It was so long ago, it's like something I made up. But here he is, still living in the same town and now he needs a ring and he comes to me."

"That is weird," Randy agreed, sitting down. Then he looked at me again, from under that eyebrow. "You've had a drink."

I felt my face redden, more than it probably was already, and acknowledged that I had, and that it had been good. A good drink.

"In your own house!" Randy said this with great exaggeration—he had come to know how some things are with me.

"In my own house," I said, proudly, and reached next to my chair for a bottle that still was partially full. I took a few gulps, then offered him some.

"No thanks—that's all your mother needs to see: me, here, with you, both drinking beer. She hates me as it is."

"Join the club," I sniffed. "She really doesn't like anybody. Don't take it personally. And with you, she goes nuts wondering why you come here so much if you have a fiancée to spend time with."

Randy didn't say anything, just started pulling a little piece of yellow string from the hem of his jacket.

I felt the grains and the earth and saw Iggy egging me on. So I asked Randy what I'd long been meaning to: "Why do you come here—if you have a fiancée?"

He continued with the string, then stopped. Without looking up, he said: "To keep you posted. I keep promising to bring my father—"

"Randy!" I shouted this and he gave a little jump.

"OK. OK." He stopped and put his hands in his pockets in case what he had to say was conveniently written on a piece of paper he kept in there. "It's a few things. For one, I really like the ring. And, no, I can't get my father to come here or do anything. When I want him to see it, he's got a meeting or is away or he can't be bothered. And, as long as I've been waiting around to buy it, time has gone by. In that time, I don't know . . . Roseanne, she's been kind of getting to me."

Randy stopped here and started with the string again. "She says if I had a better job and made more of a paycheck I wouldn't have to take his money and I just could come here and buy it myself. So she's on me about that all the time. Then there's all the arrangements. She asks my opinion, then, when I tell her what I like or what I think or which thing I'd prefer, she says how stupid it is and how men don't know anything. Why does she ask me? She's also starting to bug me about where we're going to live, what we can afford, how does it look to have my father paying for the ring—"

"Randy!" These were the exact same things he would tell me every time we talked. Usually I would ask how things were going and he would tell me all of this sort of thing, then, when it seems like that was out of the way, we would go into things that have nothing to do with any of that, not with marriage or plans or relatives or expectations. We would talk about what we knew of the world, or something that might be happening in town, or about a funny incident that took place at work. But what I wanted to know from him was why? "Why, Randy—why do you come here?" I sounded demanding. I was powerful, suddenly.

"I was just telling you," he said.

"No, you weren't. I can tell."

I drank the end of the beer. Randy wound the thread around his thumb. He had not expected this from me tonight—or maybe ever. I got up and gathered the bottles, went over to the canvas bag I bring to work and I put them deep into the bottom of it, for disposal in the Dumpster we share with the bread store. I sat down again and awaited an answer.

Randy picked up his head finally and said: "You. I just like you."

"Fine. Was that so hard? I like you, too."

"But I shouldn't," Randy said. "I'm supposed to be getting married."

"So? You can be married and have friends who are not married," I told him, driving right over one of my mother's favorite theories. I heard it squish under the steel-belted radials of my words, and I enjoyed the sound.

"Not with Roseanne I can't—not a female friend," Randy said, shaking his head. "She's so jealous it's almost a joke."

"Well you'll be too busy for talking anyway," I said. "All that moving and decorating she wants you to do. You won't have a spare moment."

"I don't really care for that sort of thing," Randy said, looking sad. He broke the thread off the jacket and watched as the tip of his wrapped thumb turned ruby red. "Come to think of it, I don't really care for much of what she wants to do. I mean I like the part about living with somebody and having kids and making a home. And she might be somebody you could do that with: she can cook, she can sew, she can keep a house. We've gone out for three years. You'd think that would mean she was happy with me. But it's like she wants somebody else. I want to own a little store someday—that's my goal. I know convenience stores are big business, but I think people around here like things more old-fashioned. I want to have a little place that's personal, old-time—like Lega's, only not just meat. I'd have fresh flowers. Magazines. Some prepared food you could bring home—good stuff, homemade. And all the things you'd need if you were going to make it yourself. There'd be a tin ceiling. A bench outside where the old men could sit. A barrel of pickles I'd give out for free just for your coming in. I know it's the kind of place I'd like to stop into. I think it would work. She says that would be embarrassing. That's the word she uses. *Embarrassing.* She wants me to become a lawyer or a financial planner or some public figure—somebody that people at a party would take notice of, she says. I don't know if any of this makes any sense to you. Sometimes I just wake up in the middle of the night and my head is pounding."

He sat forward and rubbed his temples, as if that was happening to him right then. This went on for a long while, so long that I almost was embarrassed for him. Then he stopped and looked up at me and said the words delicately, like they were coming out his mouth covered with spikes: "I'm coming to think she's not the one for all this."

Out of nowhere, I felt something in my heart splitting all over again. I brought my hands to my chest because I just felt I had to. "Oh, Randy—I'm very sorry."

He didn't say anything. I saw his bottom lip quiver a little and he made a small sigh, as much of a sigh as most men I've known can produce in a conversation, short and low.

"You OK? Do you want anything?"

Randy just put his hand up, then whispered, "I'll be fine. It's just the realizing it."

"It must be awful," I said, because I could imagine, having been on the other end of it.

He nodded yes.

"I have to tell her," he said, looking up at me with the second saddest pair of eyes I had ever seen.

I could hear the engines warming as the attack on the Pearl Harbor of Roseanne's life was being prepared. Out of the blue would come the news, sinking into the deep every shred of what she thought would be her new life. I didn't care how unworthy of a nice guy like Randy Roseanne sounded to be, I still felt sorry for her, for what she would be hearing, how she would see him looking so strange, coming in the door and telling her that he didn't know exactly how to put this. Just like Eddie hadn't known, but went ahead anyway.

And I say to Eddie go ahead—say it. You are worrying me. Doesn't your cousin want to do the reading? Is your mother having second thoughts about making the cake? We are at the 1 TO 2 MONTHS AHEAD point on the checklist, and several things are left to be done, though we are in good shape: I have mailed the invitations, following the suggestion to use special postage stamps that read LOVE USA; I have recorded each gift as received and have written a thank-you note promptly; I have delivered my dress for the final alteration, which actually is one more layer of lace over the neckline. At the 2 WEEKS AHEAD point, we will send our wedding announcement to the newspaper, will organize a seating plan for the reception, and I will tend to the two lines I have been waiting to check off: arrange name changes on Social Security, driver's license, credit cards, bank accounts, etc.; and arrange to move all belongings to the new home.

"The wedding bands—I know we should get on those," I say.

"That's not it," Eddie tells me. He wants me to sit down, and he pushes me by the shoulders gently down into a seat on the couch, next to him.

"I've just been to church," he says.

"Aw, Eddie—we were supposed to go at three—couldn't you have waited?" It is Good Friday. We had planned to attend the short service that starts at the exact hour when Our Lord, hanging on the cross, cried out to God why had he forsaken him, then surrendered his spirit.

"Do you remember me telling you about my Uncle Francis?" Eddie asks me this and I notice a little sheen of sweat on his face, which is a little paler than normal.

"Take off your vest," I tell him. "You don't look so good."

He just asks me if I remember.

"The guy who saw the statue move," I say right off, because ever since Eddie told me the story about him, I have spent most of my time in church going cross-eyed staring at Saint Mary.

Eddie's Uncle Francis had wanted to live in Alaska ever since it had been made a state, and he watched a lengthy television documentary about the land and its people. He held a great desire to move there, but he had his wife and three daughters to think of and provide for. Think of them—you all can't just up and leave for the wilderness, said his friends. How'll that look if you move from here—like there's something wrong with your hometown, his relatives clucked. Francis stopped telling people about his dream, but kept it inside his head for a long time. Twenty-one years later, he is sitting in our church one Sunday, and it comes over him to ask Mary if he should move to Alaska. So he looks up at the statue, and, in his heart, poses the question. He watches and then and there the statue gives a gentle nod. Then another, slow and definite, right at him, right into his eyes and down to his heart. He says there is nothing he can do but believe. Uncle Francis grabs Cioci Nellie by the hand—in the middle of the mass—and drags her to the exit. She of course thinks he is having some kind of attack. They get outside and he tells her they are moving. The next month they were gone. They haven't been back.

"Is your Uncle Francis dead?" I ask, assuming that is why Eddie looks so bad.

"No," he says in a whisper. Then, just a little louder, he says, "I asked a question. I got an answer."

None of this makes any sense to me, and I tell him that.

Eddie takes my hands. His are freezing. He sees his ring and he goes to move the band so the stone sparkles. "Do you remember my candle—the Saint Jude?"

I tell him I do.

"How I was praying for what I should be doing—really be doing?"

I tell him I remember that.

"Well," says Eddie, and he takes a deep breath, "I got an answer."

I wait for him to tell me what it was. He doesn't. "Well? Are you going to tell me? What is it? Are we going to have to move? Is it something you already know how to do?"

"I love you, you know."

"I know," I say. "Tell me what it is!"

"Before I loved you, I never really knew what I was going to do with myself for the rest of my life. There was a great desire in me to help people, on a greater scale."

"That's a nice thing to want to do," I say, proud of him. This is a fine person. I rub his hands to warm them, but it seems to do no good.

"It got so confusing for me, trying to figure out my life, that I came back here. You know that—this was all meant to be time to rethink things. I never dreamed I'd fall in love and be getting married."

"You never know," I say, trying to sound cheerful. Eddie just keeps the same serious expression.

"I once had thoughts about becoming a priest," he tells me. "I even sent for literature for a place near Boston—a seminary for older men who want to join the priesthood."

"Are there lots of them?"

"Enough," says Eddie. "I know because last week—remember when I went to Worcester to get some shoes? Well I kept driving and I took a tour of the place. It's been in my head ever since. I went to church this morning and I prayed to the Blessed Virgin. I asked her if I should become a priest. About a minute later, she nods. Twice. Just like for Uncle Francis."

"You're kidding me, right?" I ask this, even though I know Eddie is not given to extensive jokes.

He holds my hands tightly. "No," he says. His eyes are wide and stare into me desperately. "I'm not kidding. It actually happened. It was a miracle."

I am getting a sick feeling, but I am not exactly sure why. "So what does that mean to you?"

"It means I am going to become a priest."

Eddie's words hang there. I wait for my mother to snap up my window shades and yell that I am late for church. I want to be asleep so I can wake from this. But reality is slapping me in the face, and seems to be doing so with great joy: Who did you think you were even looking at somebody like this, never mind falling in love with him and planning a marriage and a life you could run by yourself? See what happens?

Eddie looks gray. "If I ever knew that this issue wasn't resolved, I never would have gone near you—believe me," he is saying. "I looked into it long ago. I didn't think about it since I moved here, only when they'd send me the pamphlets—they got my change of address and would invite me to open houses or garden parties or retreats. I never went to any of them. I felt I had thought it out completely, and that it was not for me."

I feel stunned, and most of what I hold in my heart quickly empties and only my blood pounds around in there, free to move wherever it wants, without having to watch out for all that messy, sloppy, love and emotion I had been cultivating in there for Eddie Balicki.

Then I feel so mad—the angriest I have ever been, I am sure. "You can't do this! You love me. You want to marry me. You were going to give me a new life. You said all that. Right here. Not four months ago. The wedding is next month. You can't do this!"

I see the shine is gone from Eddie's eyes. Looking in there is like looking into a hole in the ground. I can see that whatever we have had is breathing its last.

From my finger I wrench the ring and pitch it at him so hard it sticks with a *thock* right into the cloth of his green down vest.

"I want you to have it, it's yours," he mumbles hollowly, picking the thing from his vest very carefully, like it is a shard of glass in a wound.

I see some small pieces of feathers escape from a slit the point of the stone has made. One bit sticks beneath a prong in the setting and he extracts it with a shaking hand, rolls it between his fingers then gently places the ring on the stack of *People*s.

Saying he will pray for me, he goes to the front door and lets himself out.

From somewhere outside, I hear the tolling of three church bells. I fall against the back of the couch.

Eddie has forsaken me.

I give up my spirit and I die right there.

That is another thing that seems so long ago I easily could think I invented it, were it not for the stone-and-metal reality shining in its box on the coffee table, were it not for Randy, once someone who might remove it from my life, sitting across from me.

I looked down at the knees of my jeans and I set my hands flat on top of each of them. My fingers long, pink, and white, unadorned.

Randy shifted on the couch and I heard him breathe in and out, once, slowly. "When he told you, that was it?"

"That was it."

"You never saw him again?"

"I never saw him again. Well not in person, and it wasn't really him. It was a picture of him. Somebody who knew him had gone to some ceremony—a pre-priest kind of thing—and took pictures and dropped the film off at work. The roll started off with somebody's ceramics class—all these pictures of ladies posing with their cookie jars. Pigs in chef's hats, the Pillsbury dough boy, a mushroom you just lift the cap off of to get to what's inside, that kind of stuff. They must have had a party when they finished the project, because they were all filling their jars with cookies. They looked like they were having such a good time. Then, all of a sudden, there was a crowd of people on a long lawn, next to some stone building. Everybody was dressed up. There were nuns in habits, and even they looked fancy for the occasion. And then there he was, in this long white robe thing, with a very ornate scarf hanging around his neck. He was holding a huge Bible. Smiling. Looking like he was having a life."

"That must have stunk," said Randy.

I nodded that it had.

"I don't want to hurt Roseanne," he said out of nowhere. She and her impending doom right now seemed ancient history, but I realized her fate had been sealed in the past half hour, right here, in my living room, on my couch—the place for such thing, it seemed.

I thought about that. "I think you have to hurt her," I decided. "Living somebody else's idea of a life, how is that?"

I heard the kitchen door swing open and a yell: "Where are you?"

"I'll be right back," I told Randy and I went to the kitchen.

"Hi. I have a guest. We'll be in the living room," I said quickly into the kitchen and from the doorway, where any beer could not be detected on me.

"Wonderful sale. You should have gone," my mother said. "We picked out what we thought you'd like, but if it's not the right things, you have only yourself to blame for not coming along."

"Fine. Thanks. See you later."

"Go. Go sit with someone else's fiancé," she muttered, not bothering to look up from her work of emptying a paper bag full of can after can of generic-brand cream of mushroom soup.

Randy was at the edge of the couch, his hands folded in an all-too-familiar praying posture. He had opened the ring box and was staring into it.

"Come on," I said lightly. "You'll be like me, looking at that thing like that."

Randy gave me a little smile and sat back. "There's just something about it. Kind of draws you in. Where'd he get it?"

"I don't know. I never asked, he never told me. At the time I figured it didn't matter."

"It's so beautiful. She really, really would have liked it," he said, making it sound like Roseanne was dead, which, in a way, she kind of was.

"When are you going to talk to her?"

"I don't know. Maybe tomorrow morning," Randy said. "I don't work until the afternoon. Best to get it over with. Tonight she's at some bridal fair—all these exhibits on invitations and caterers and limousines. A good opportunity to win things, too. She's done more research on this . . ."

"I have to admit, there was something fun about some of those things," I said to nobody in particular.

"I feel, kind of, I don't know—better?" Randy said.

"You'll feel worse before you feel lots better," I told him, "but at least you've made a decision."

Randy got up and reached for his coat. "I want to thank you for listening to me," he said and he held out his hand. I took it in mine and in that split-second of contact, my mother came into the hall to go upstairs. I saw her look at us and get a disgusted look on her face. I told Randy to take care of himself. And I gave him one piece of advice: "Tell her that you're sorry, OK?"

"I will," he said, nodding quickly. "I really am."

After I closed the door, I realized Randy had no more excuses to call me or visit me. There was something sad about that.

I went back to the spot on the couch I had taken after Andy left and before Randy arrived. I took the afghan off the back and lay down on the couch and tried to think about nothing in particular. When I had Eddie in my life, I used to think of him even when I got up at two or three in the morning. I would think how, over on the other side of town, he was sleeping right at that moment, on the handmade bed that I knew I would be sharing with him soon, covered by his blue and yellow quilt I was going to know the warmth of, under his glow-in-the-dark crucifix that was so bright, he had told me, that you could find your way at night to the bathroom without having to turn on the light. I thought how, now, I no longer had any idea of any of Eddie—where he was or how he looked or anything. We had gotten so far away from each other, the way you do when your paths fly off on two separate and opposite courses. He had become my Sam. I could have nothing to do with him. I did not know him, but I continued to wonder.

# 20

◆◆◆

SOMEBODY HAD GONE TO EUROPE, I GUESSED IT TO BE, AND had visited an ice cave. They had taken photos of the cave, which was more like a building than a hole in the ground. Rooms and the items they contained all had been carved out of the ice, and the people on this vacation didn't just take pictures of each room, they got into them and pretended they were living there.

In the kitchen room, which held an ice stove, ice sink and ice counter, ice kitchen tables, and something that couldn't be called anything other than an ice box, these people, wearing big yellow ski jackets I figured they had to rent at the entrance, posed like they were using the sink and setting the table. You kind of had to imagine they were, since there were no utensils or anything, just these milky white appliances and furniture.

The husband, a pale guy with closely cropped red hair and skin as white as that row of cabinets behind him, looked to be in his late fifties. He sat at the table and held his hands in fists like he was banging his knife and fork on the surface. Give me my food. Now. He had a stern look on his face, and actually was pretty good at cocking his head, scowling and lifting his dark red eyebrows. The wife, who appeared to be about his same age, was smiling at him from a heart-shaped face framed by an aqua plastic rain bonnet she must have thought would keep her head warm in there. At the same time as she was smiling, she was motioning like she was just about to test a spoonful of soup from a pot she'd just taken from the stove.

She snapped him snoozing in the ice bed, and I could just see him clicking off the ice lamp carved on top of the ice night table.

He photographed her smiling coyly as she peeked from behind the ice shower curtain in the ice bathtub.

Somebody photographed the both of them dropping their hankies into the ice washer and dryer set in a small ice utility room.

I stopped making exposures for a minute and wondered if they had held up the whole tour group while doing this, or was this ice cave not such a great attraction and they had the entire place to themselves, except maybe for some old guard who didn't speak English but who had learned over the years just how to operate a wide variety of visitors' cameras.

All in all, they had taken a full thirty-six-frame roll in there. The other two rolls in their batch were of beautiful flower gardens, and of hedges that had been shaved into the shapes of animals. There were shots of each of the two posing under quaintly carved business signs on skinny cobblestone streets. Wooden cheese wheels, bowlers and cutlery hung over them as they smiled and pointed upward so the viewer would be sure not to miss the highlight of the picture.

Toward the end of the roll, there was a photo of the two of them, looking kind of glassy-eyed and happy, hoisting huge beer steins as a guy in tight lederhosen, an embroidered shirt, knee socks, and a tuba stood next to them and puffed out his cheeks like he was blasting some song. Then there was one of a rainy tarmack, with lots of green woods in the distance, just over an airplane's wing. And then there was one of the man, lounging on a rocker and staring blankly into a TV while a football game played. He had on a bowling shirt stitched with the name ALBIN, and also wore blue and white gym shorts that contrasted sharply with his very white and bony legs. He held a salad bowl full of orangey cheese snacks set on his lap. Behind his head you could see the top of a big beer stein.

I was sorry the trip had ended. The ice cave and the bushes and the signs had been a nice diversion, and gave me something other than Randy's difficulties to think about. I figured by now he had met with Roseanne and he probably was back home getting ready to go to the Quick Stop. All that while I had been sitting at work, in my own world. I got the same feeling I do when I know there's a funeral going on at the church. I can lounge in my living room with the TV on and a magazine in my lap and everything's fine, and know this same hour is the worst one of someone else's life.

I headed home, wanting to do just those kind of lazy things, but I saw as I drove up to the house that we had company. I realized with a chill that it was a police car that was parked out front. My heart started to beat so furiously my whole body was feeling it. I didn't think I could breathe. Somehow, I pulled into the driveway, where both my father's truck and my mother's car were straight in their usual places.

I didn't even put my car in park. I just shut off the engine, pushed open the door, and ran to the house. I tore into the living room and there was my mother, sitting on the edge of the couch, one hand on her forehead, the other busy swabbing her nose with a Kleenex. My head moved like it was on a motor, short jerks left to right to left and then I saw him—my father was in the doorway, writing something on a notepad. The inventory was complete. We were all still alive and we were all in our home. But there was a pudgy cop leaning back in my father's La-Z-Boy, finishing a glass of cola.

"What's going on? Are you OK?" I almost yelled this.

"Oh, oh, oh," my mother wailed, hefting herself from the couch and over toward me, arms out, landing in a hug. It was brief. She shoved herself away from me, ran the back of her hands across her reddened eyes and screamed, "You left it out!"

"What? What are you talking about?" I looked to my father for help, but he turned and headed into the kitchen.

"I told you this would happen. I just told you," my mother reminded me. "Didn't I say go to Friendly's? No, I don't want to be seen, you said. Well now look what's happened."

When she said the part that was supposed to be me, she used a whiny voice.

"What?" I put each hand up in the air. I looked to the cop, who was picking something from the lip of his glass. "Will somebody explain this? Please?"

"A larceny, miss," said the cop, who stood up rather quickly and left the chair rocking wildly.

"I don't . . . larceny?" Then I remembered "Dragnet." They were always talking about larcenies. Something had been stolen. But our house was here, the truck was here . . .

My mother sobbed something that sounded like a long *ahhoooo* then shakily made out the words:

"They took your r-i-i-i-ing . . ."

I cocked my head. I didn't wear a ring. But then it hit me: I did own one.

"Oh my God," I said slowly, then I reached for the arm of the armchair and sat myself in a long motion.

My mother quickly blessed herself and shot me a look. She did not like to hear that phrase other than in a church song. I remember when she called me at work to tell me my godfather had died suddenly, while raking the leaves in front of the house. He just fell into the pile and wasn't discovered until somebody in his family complained how he hadn't finished the job and then went out to scoop the heap of leaves into an old bedsheet.

"Oh my God," I had murmured when she told me about that.

Usually, because it is not worth angering her, I say oh my gosh. But I was startled to hear about the death. I was shocked. I was sad.

So I said oh my God.

"Do you have to say that? Do you know how bad that sounds?" she asked me from the other end of the line.

My godfather was dead was all I was thinking.

And now, all I was thinking was that my mother's prophecy had come true. Someone had come here and had taken the ring. It was gone. Just like that.

"How do you know? I hide it—"

She cut me off: "Yeah you hide it all right, right here on the coffee table. I came down this morning and was folding the afghan you left here. I saw the box, open, right here on the *People*s."

She took her forefinger and tapped it several times, for emphasis, into the face of the president's wife, whose thyroid problem—a malady she shared with the White House dog—was being examined in a cover story titled ONE GLAND LADY.

I remembered. The ring had sat on the head of the president's wife last night, as it glowed in the dark, the last thing I had seen before I had closed my eyes.

"You're right. It was there—but I had been putting it away every night. Only last night, I didn't go upstairs. And I was in a rush this morning. I forgot."

"Well it's too late now," said my mother. "See what happened? I told you. I said bring it to the restaurant. I said meet them there. Or tell them you keep it at a bank. Anything. But leaving it out in the open when so many people have been in and out in and out in and out looking at this thing. Night and day somebody always looking. I tell you 'Make a decision! Get on with your life!' You say no. It has to be the right person. Well what do you care? There have been lots of right persons—the ones who want to buy it. Just sell it. Get it over with. This is enough nonsense. And now look. For the first time, a police officer is in our house. What will people think? Parked right out front, no less."

My father came back into the room and my mother began her sobbing again. He had a glass of something for her. I think it was brandy. She wrapped the Kleenex around it and took a sip.

I looked at the cop. I wondered how much of this sort of thing he must see every day.

But he wasn't looking just then. He was making some sort of notes. The radio clipped to his belt let out a fuzzy spurting sound every once in a while. I saw a wooden-handled gun. That was probably the first time there ever had been a gun in our house. This was all too much.

Then I realized I had seen this cop before. I knew he wasn't a real policeman, only a helper, because I had read a story about him a while ago, how he had nabbed a teenage prisoner who was being transported on the turnpike by some authorities. This kid had on handcuffs and the people who were delivering him somewhere didn't think he was so dangerous, so they put him in the backseat all by himself. At one point, the point in which the car had been passing through our area, he put his handcuffed hands around the neck of the driver and yelled that he was going to kill him. The guy driving stopped the car, of course, and the kid jumped out and spent the night roaming through the woods. The next day he stumbles out of the thicket onto a stretch of road where this cop was making a little money directing traffic at the site of a sewer repair job. He was sitting on the tailgate of a water department truck, eating a Fluffernutter, when the kid came thrashing his way out of the brush right there in front of him. Well I don't know what kind of a night he had experienced, but the prisoner knelt down in front of the cop right there and told him he surrendered. The cop put down his sandwich and took out his gun and pointed it at the kid. With the other hand he loosened the radio from his belt and called in a backup unit. He received a commendation from the police chief and his photograph was printed in the *Penny Saver*. And here he was, was sitting in my living room a couple weeks later, not doing too much of anything, it seemed.

"What does he say?" I asked my mother, motioning to the La-Z-Boy. "When did you call him—how did you know it was gone?"

My mother sniffled. "Like I said, I saw it there this morning, when I was folding the afghan. I was just about to take it—the ring—and hide it somewhere for you—I don't know, under the bed maybe—when the phone rang. It was old Tczup. His car wouldn't start and he needed a ride to the hospital for an appointment. So I just took my coat and went to his house."

She looked at the stack of magazines and blew her nose. "I was only gone about an hour, and when I came home, at first I thought your father already was home, because the back door was unlocked. I put my coat away and called for him. 'Stash! Stashu!' No Stashu. I got worried, like maybe he had fallen and couldn't hear me. So I ran around into this room and the next one and when I saw he wasn't anywhere, I started to get worried. There could be somebody in the house waiting to grab me, since the door was unlocked. I ran down the stairs. Then I saw the coffee table—the magazines, they were not like I left them, and the ring, it was gone."

She looked straight into my eyes. "That's when I called the police."

My mother said she then had run onto the driveway and stood out there until the police car arrived, just in case somebody was still in the house. The policeman checked each floor and room, including the little closet in the basement where the water pump is, and came back out to tell her it was OK.

She said it had been embarrassing for her to be standing outside her own home while people were riding by and seeing as plain as day, she mentioned again, that a police car had been called there.

I shook my head.

"But don't you worry," she told me. "They know who did this."

"Who? Did they catch somebody?"

"No, miss," said the guy in the chair. "Thanks to shrewd thinking on the part of your mother, we are questioning a suspect right now, down at the station. I'm just here to get some last details." I looked at my mother, who had half a fake smile clamped onto her lips and who was nodding yes with little motions.

"What did you do? Did you see something?"

"You bet I did," she answered. "Right here. In my own home. That guy who was here last night. The guy who is always here. The one who never wears normal clothes. Always in something with writing on it, like a little boy in play uniform."

"Randy," I said, then realized what had happened. "You can't think it's Randy!"

"Not only do I think," she rebounded quickly, "but I know. He was here just last night. Late into the night."

I squinted my eyes at her in a very dirty look.

"He was here and he knew where you had it," she told

me. "He obviously came back today and took it. He's no fool."

I was sitting at the edge of my chair, looking into the cut-and-loop pile in case any clarity had fallen somewhere in there, just waiting for me to scoop it up.

I spotted some.

"You mean Randy is down at the police station?"

"Your mother knew where to find him," the cop said with some pride in my mother, obviously oblivious to my unhappiness with her conclusion.

"Randy's being questioned?"

My father was looking at me like I could read his mind—which I kind of could but right now was too frazzled to try. I could tell he wanted me to stay, to sit close on the couch with my mother and to tell her things like the neighbors wouldn't remember in a week that a police car had been in front of the house. But we all knew that it would be remembered far into the future, perhaps even at the point eons into the next century when police will be able to beam themselves into your living room when you have a crisis such as this one.

I looked at both my parents, and at the cop, who said he would be returning to the station.

"I'm going, too," I said, then left for my car without looking back.

"Go," I heard my mother yell, just before the storm door slammed. "Go and be with that crook. The one who has a fiancée. See how that looks."

"Randy is not a crook," I said aloud to myself as I turned the car key I had left hanging in the ignition. Not Randy. I leaned back into the headrest for a second, then heard a knock on my window. My father was there, making a motion to roll it down.

"Do you want me to go with you?"

I realized this was quite a sacrifice. She wanted him here. She needed him here, she would say. I reminded him: "She'll want you here. No sense in getting in trouble. I'll be OK—it's very nice of you, though."

He put his hand in the car, onto my shoulder. "You're the best gal, remember." Then he didn't say anything for a few seconds. When he looked like he was ready to add something, he just gave me a few pats and shook his head and smiled.

The police station was only about a mile away, located in the small brick building that mostly is the town hall, stuffed in a few rooms in the back. I jerked my car to a stop next to the stone marking the Bicentennial time capsule and ran inside the building and past the glass windows of the town clerk's office, where the large Armenian man who had been elected our town clerk was sitting and signing some papers beneath a huge rug hooked into a scene of dogs playing a poker game. Before he won the job, a huge and faded map of the town had hung there. When he replaced it with the rug, the news was on the front page of the *Penny Saver*. People were upset. That had been our town up there. The clerk pointed out you could no longer make out any of the lines on the map, which was true. And he noted that at least on this rug you could tell what was going on, which also was the truth.

The town clerk looked up and waved at me as I passed his windows. I smiled, though I knew he knew I wasn't there to buy anything from him. I was going right through the door marked POLICE, and was entering a small corridor with bulletin boards covered by photos and information on criminals, all staring at me even when they were looking to the side. There was an old gray water bubbler and a worn bench with initials scratched deep into the front edge. None of the doors had any titles on them, so I just guessed and picked the one at the end of the hall.

I found the dispatcher, a bony woman with a length of red hair pulled back into a bun she speared with a number 2 pencil. She had on jeans and a smock top and pinned to it was a button with her name. It read I'M HOLLY, like this was a steakhouse and she was going to take my order.

"Yes, honey? What can I do for you, doll?" she asked, eyeing me up and down. I took note that for people who regularly deal with filth and bad news, the officials I had met so far that day were very easily affectionate, with *misses* and *honeys* and such.

"Er, I'm—do you have, well let me tell you," I stammered. "I'm looking for a guy they brought in. They think, my mother thinks, well he's here because it looks like he stole something. Only he didn't."

Holly sucked hard on what was left of her cigarette, ground it into a dingy green plastic ashtray, then pursed her lips to the left to send a long stream of smoke out of the way of my breathing path.

"In there," she said, pointing with a long finger ending in a very short, almost not-even-there nail. "But you can't go in. He's being questioned. You can wait out here."

I thanked her and sat down at a seat placed sideways against the front of her desk. She worked on a pretty messy surface, with wire bins holding stacks of official-looking stuff, and piles of other papers impaled on a big metal pin. She had written notes all over what was visible of her blotter, a calendar from January of last year. I wondered why she never thought to flip it for a clean surface, then realized it didn't matter.

There were a couple of big, beige telephones, and on a round stand, there was a bulky microphone like you see in old movies about the days of radio shows.

Every once in a while, from a small black box next to the microphone, came the same sounds I had heard coming out of the walkie-talkie the cop in my living room had been wearing. When that noise occurred, Holly flew to her chair and hit a button on the big microphone and said into it, "Base," and then we would both wait for something to happen. Nothing did.

"You a sister?" Holly asked me.

"No. I develop photographs."

She narrowed her eyebrows. "Good. But how are you related?"

I felt stupid. "I thought you meant sister, like a nun, like because there are nuns today who wear normal clothes and not the habits that they all used to wear so it's really hard to tell who is a nun and who isn't—I know sometimes I look at somebody myself and I wonder if she's a nun."

I was breathing quickly. I was nervous about being in a police station, about having to face Randy, who my mother probably single-handedly had already sent to some big house somewhere.

Holly looked at me, bringing her face a little closer to mine, like I was some writing she was trying to decipher.

"Jeeezus," was all she said.

The speaker made its sound.

"Base. Over," Holly spoke, exhaling so smoke clouded the microphone. I expected to hear coughing from whoever was on the other end.

"Five to base, over," somebody said through some crackling.

"I read you, fiver, over."

"Holly, babe, what's with the suspect?"

"Still being interrogated. Over."

"Do you think they'll keep him? Will they need someone to watch the jail tonight? I could use the extra bucks, ya know. Over."

Holly looked at me, then at the microphone.

"Don't get your hopes up, fiver, over," she said.

"Shit. Over—I'm sorry, I mean wait—how'm I ever gonna pay for the honeymoon? We're gonna end up at the Motel 6, I can tell. Over."

Holly stuck another cigarette into her mouth and flicked a small plastic lighter with the words I ♥ BINGO printed up the side.

"We have company, lover, over and out." With each word, the cigarette bounced.

Holly winked at me. So she was engaged to the accidental hero. Slowly I moved my eyes to her left hand. There was a skinny little silver band with a sad punctuation of a diamond sticking up on four short prongs. I think she saw me check it out because she suddenly began to finger it from beneath, with her thumb. The stone was gray and dead, with no sign of a flicker.

"Pretty, ha?"

I smiled. "Yes."

I was getting sick of waiting. "When will they be done with him?"

"Let me check, hon," Holly said, and she pushed a button on the phone. Cradling the handset between her ear and shoulder, she began to pick at her cuticles.

"Hey—you done? Somebody here wants to see him."

She waited for an answer, and rolled her eyes at me, as if I knew the kind of people she had to put up with here.

"I don't know. Some developer," she said into the phone.

"Tell them I'm the person who owns the ring," I said, and Holly repeated that.

"G'wan in. Good luck," she said to me a moment after hanging up the phone.

I thanked her and walked to the door she was pointing at. It opened just as I put my hand on the knob. A tiny little policeman was sitting next to it, and he reached to fling it open all the way. At a table long enough to fit a large family for holiday dinner sat another policeman—older and with many folds of loose skin overflowing his shirt collar. He stood halfway up when I entered. Next to him, in his work shirt and tie, his collar unbuttoned and loosened like you might think it would be in such a situation, Randy sat next to him. He shot me a look just like I felt I deserved.

"It was my mother! She called. I had nothing to do with this."

Randy glared. Then he started to yell. "How could you, how could she have done this? To have me picked up at work like I killed somebody! I need that job! I didn't take anything! You know me—don't you?"

I told him I did, because I felt like I did. I knew that Randy would never do such a thing, even for the simple fact that his taking it would have been too obvious—something my mother had not taken into consideration.

Both policemen had been sitting there silently. Then the one with the neck folds spoke: "You'll be happy to know that he was at the shop all day."

"Then why do you still have him here? Why don't you let him go, and tell his boss it was a mistake?"

"We're considering that there might have been an accomplice," he answered. "You know—somebody he might have hired to go and perform the deed?"

"That's ridiculous," I told him. "Please just let him go. It was my ring. I say it's OK."

The two cops looked at each other. I put my bag on the table so I could find a pen and a piece of paper. I pulled out the envelope my paycheck had come in and flipped it over. "Here," I said to the policemen. "I am going to give you a written thing that will say it was OK to let him go and that I have nothing, no charges, to file, or whatever, against him."

And I began to write just that, bending down to begin it. The policeman at the door slid a chair over to me, and I sat down and finished. Then I signed and dated the paper—I even put my Social Security number on the bottom—and slid it across the table to the older officer, who looked to be the more official of the two.

He took it in two hands, moved his eyes down the length of the envelope, then cleared his throat.

"Identification, please?"

I reached into my wallet for my driver's license, on which I appear waiflike, I think.

The policeman studied the license, then my face. "I would say this is sufficient," he concluded, but then began to shake a finger at me. "I must tell you there's no changing your mind. You're saying here he had nothing to do with it."

"I didn't make my mind in the first place," I said defensively. "I said it was my mother. Randy was at the house last night, so she figured he came back the next day. She was wrong. That's the truth."

"No matter. Just go," said the policeman. "We've spent enough time on this already."

Randy stood up and collected the contents of his pockets, which had been piled in a heap on the table. There was a skinny, worn black leather wallet, a large set of official-looking keys, a couple scraps of folded paper, and a ticket stub of green cardboard. It was overturned, so you could not see the show he had attended. But on the back, there was my phone number, in black felt tip.

He scooped all that stuff into his pocket, then turned to the older cop. "This isn't going to give me a record or anything, is it?"

"No," he said. Then added, like he had seen in a movie probably last night, "Just keep your nose clean."

I did not thank the officers. I just turned for the door.

"Miss," one of them said, "do you want us to continue the investigation?"

"Sure. But look for someone else."

I liked the way I had sounded no-nonsense. But once we were into the hall, the door to the room shut behind us, I lost that tone. "Randy, I'm so very sorry. My mother is crazy. I can't believe she did this."

"I know, I know," he said, then looked over at Holly, who was looking over at us and working at opening a sack of Doritos. Randy touched my elbow. "Let's just get out of here."

"Bye, kids," she called. "Hope everything works out."

Holly sounded like she meant that. She waved with a hand that held a freshly lit cigarette, and a little S of smoke rose in the air.

Randy had been brought to the station in a cruiser, so he had no way back to work. I volunteered to drive him, and offered to buy him a meal or something. As I told him, it was the least I could do.

"I could use a cup of coffee," he said. "And not one from work."

I suggested Friendly's, the place I suddenly remembered as being the one at which my mother had suggested I conduct my business in the first place.

Randy said that would be fine, and I showed him to my car. He was taking his jacket off. One sleeve got hooked on his watch, and he struggled with it and made angry motions as he did. He was mad. I knew it.

"You have every right to be upset," I told him.

"Look. It's not you. I've had a hell of a day. Even before all this."

"Roseanne," I said, realizing all of a sudden exactly what day this was.

"Roseanne," he said. "I saw her the first thing this morning. She came at me with all these pamphlets she picked up last night—honeymoon packages and china patterns. There was even a brochure from some photographer who'll shoot your wedding then will give you a coupon for a free baby portrait—but you have to redeem it within a year after your wedding. She was really excited about that one."

I went around to Randy's side of the car and unlocked the door. I saw that he was sweating, even though it was far from hot out, and I remembered the first time I had seen him, in the store parking lot, with the long ends of his hair sticking to his neck.

"You feel all right?" I asked him.

"Yeah. Coffee."

"Right," I said, and went over and got in the other door.

Randy was working at rolling back the sleeves of his shirt. I looked at his forearm, which was somewhat muscled and had one of those huge veins crossing the top, sticking up like it had been added on in the last minute and there hadn't been enough room for it down deep with all the others.

"I feel terrible about this," I said.

"No harm done, I guess," Randy told me, sounding somewhat resigned. "It's just shook me up. My father always told me he'd kill me if I ever got arrested. Here I am, thirty, and I'm still worrying about that. It's funny—once you're somebody's kid, you're always somebody's kid. There seems to be no way around that."

What he said was true. "I know about that one," I said, and even chuckled a little.

"What about you?" Randy asked. "You lost your ring. What are you going to do?"

That was a very good question. I had come home to such a scene, then had rushed myself to the police station, and now, for the first time, once he mentioned it, I realized that this was going to have an effect on me. Not on my mother or on Randy or even on the honeymoon account of Holly and her fiancé.

Eddie's ring—my ring—was gone. The final piece of my thing with him was now in somebody's pocket, headed who knew where.

I let out a breath, then tapped my upper lip with my finger. I didn't want to cry in front of Randy.

When we got to Friendly's, we found a booth, then I excused myself for the ladies room. It was a one-person setup, with a toilet and a sink in a space so small you could hardly turn around. I ran the water cold and pushed my face into handfuls of it. For towels they had one of those boxes with a length of linen coming out of it. I dragged a long pull of that over to the mirror, where I blotted my face and stared at myself at the same time.

For months after Eddie left, I used to spend a lot of time in the bathroom, sitting on the counter, resting my back against the wall alongside it and staring so closely into the mirror my eyes almost crossed. I never before had looked at myself in such a way. I examined every bit of my face—every inch of skin, every hair, every pore, every fleck in the color of my eyes. I looked at the lines in my lips, how my nose—without warning—jutted from the rest of my flat face and round head suddenly and with purpose. This was me, what people knew of me. I looked and looked to see, in the first place, what somebody—what Eddie—would have seen in me. Then I looked further, to see what had not been there for him.

Now, in Friendly's, in the mirror with the sticker that reminded employees to wash their hands, I looked again, to see what I was now. I made a note that at all the times I had done this, I had looked very much the same. So the defect had to be something invisible.

"You sick?" Randy asked me when I came back to the booth after what must have been a long time. He was pouring a plastic thimble of cream into his coffee. I watched the white swirl into the black. Though I do not like coffee, I like pouring the milk or cream into other people's cups. Once the contrast stops and the whole thing turns beige, they can have it back.

"I'm fine," I said, and thanked Randy for his concern. "How about you?"

"OK. Like I said. It's today, it's a lot of old stuff. I could hear my father: 'Land in jail and you can rot there for all I care.' And he'd let me, too. There's no doubt."

I looked at Randy. I did not mean this in any other way than it sounded: "I would come and get you out."

NO. THERE IS NO RING. IT'S NOT BEEN SOLD. NO. THERE JUST is no ring. Good-bye."

My mother slammed the phone down so hard that the little bell inside let out a ting.

"How long will this go on?" she asked me.

"You mean the calls?"

"I mean the calls. You know I do. Didn't you cancel the ad?"

"I canceled the ad. These people probably meant to call a while ago but are just getting around to it."

"Are you sure you canceled it?"

"I'm sure."

I was positive. I recall with great detail, two months ago calling the *Penny Saver* on the day after the robbery and asking for the classifieds.

"Account number?"

"Excuse me?"

"I need your account number, ma'am."

"I have no idea what it is," I said. "But I know it was seventeen months ago that I ordered it. I have to cancel now. Could you do that for me? It was one of your guaranteed ones. I didn't know then how long it would take."

"Guaranteed? And you want to cancel? It worked, ha? Aren't they great? A real deal? You know what? We're doing this little promotion thing where if you have a successful guaranteed ad we'll make a commercial thing out of you—we'll take your picture, of you and the person who bought your merchandise, and we'll run a story next to it. We have one this week—did you see it? The man who sold the Kharmann Ghia he had since college? His wife had triplets and they have to all of a sudden buy one of those ugly van things. Can you imagine? Giving up a cool car like that? That's why I'm not having kids. Look in the paper—there's this picture of him handing over his keys to the new owner—this real gorgeous woman. You can tell she doesn't have triplets. . . . Well he's there with the keys in one hand and a stack of diapers in the other. He looks grossed out by what's happening to him, losing his car, but he's kind of laughing. You gotta see it."

I was waiting for him to go on, but he had stopped, I was pretty sure. "I'll take a look," I said.

"Make sure you do. Now about you, let's see here. What category?"

"Jewelry and Gems."

"Jewelry and Gems, number 509 . . ." I could hear him charging across the keyboard of some kind of computer. A few taps later he'd found the correct column.

"Jewelry and Gems, number 509. Here we go. Guaranteeds: RUBY TUESDAY?"

"Excuse me?"

"Does it go RUBY TUESDAY—or Wednesday or Thursday—any day's fine for this ruby and diamond?"

"No."

"CAN YOU KNIT—How about a purl? Pearl pendant, that is . . . Hey—that's a good one. Is it yours?"

"No." I took a deep breath. "Mine is the lite of heaven."

"No."

"Yes."

"Nooo."

"Yes. It is. I can look up the receipt, but I'll have to call you back."

"Oh, I'm sure it's yours, it's the ad. I've been seeing it for so long." He stopped and made a little squeaking sound. "This is such a trip. You're the lite of heaven! Wow!"

"So can I cancel?"

"Sure. You have to forgive me. We just look at these things every week, take the expired ones out, put new ones in. And it's like you look at something for so long, you feel like you know it. You know?"

"I guess," I said, feeling I could say that truthfully.

"So it went, ha?"

"You could say that."

He whistled. "Five thousand bucks. Cool. What are you gonna do with it?"

"Cancel the ad, will you?"

"Sure. Doing that right now." He shut up, and I heard a few little bangs of a key, and the sound of something being snuffed.

Then there was nothing.

"That should do it," he told me. "Well, OK, let's see, what else? All paid? That's it! Have a nice day, now!"

The following Thursday I got a copy of the *Penny Saver* at the day-old bread shop and brought it into work. I sat down at my machine and looked at the classifieds, at Jewelry and Gems, number 509. There was a canary diamond that you could SING FOR JOY over, a faux emerald pendant over which THEY'LL BE GREEN WITH ENVY, and a diamond solitaire that would guarantee YOU'LL NEVER BE ALONE.

The lite was gone.

I remember I folded the paper and stuck it into my tote bag. Then, hastily, I sent through the first roll of film.

That was two months ago. Other than Anna, or a chance call from someone who is reading an old *Penny Saver,* the phone does not ring for me. I get up, I go to work, I come home. I eat each night with my parents, usually something that has cabbage in it. I watch television. I knit. I go to sleep under the yellow and orange bedspread. There are no dreams.

Life is very much as it was before I ever looked across the church and saw a statue ask a couple of old ladies to move over. "See. No more craziness around here," my mother points out often, and sometimes she pats me on the back when she says this.

After Eddie left the house that Good Friday, my father had come up to my room to tell me "I am veddy soddy." He stood there looking at me after he said that, and I got up off the bed where I'd been moping and hugged him. I had to move his slack arms around the back of me, and we just stood there. In a little while, I don't know how long, I felt him draw me closer, on his own.

My mother never offered any sympathy over the death of my new life. She initially said I must have had done something wrong—"really wrong if it was enough to send him off to the seminary"—then she said whatever I had done had been a good thing—he really hadn't seemed like the right one for me.

"I have my girl back," was how she tearfully prefaced the phone calls to let relatives know the ring had been stolen and the attempts to sell it would be no more. She since has tried to cook more of my favorite meals and desserts. And, when all those things are heaped on our plates and those plates are set on the table, she tells both of us that "It's good to be a family again." I really didn't think I had gone anywhere, or had torn us apart, but my mother sees a change in our dynamic, and it makes her very, very happy that I am where I am, that we are where we are—which is right back where we used to be. Where the three of us probably always will be.

So when Randy calls out of the blue one day, she tells him I am not home. He calls again another day, she tells him the same thing. He catches on and tries me at work.

"Telephone," Mr. Herrman says. I know it will be my mother, so I don't rush. I am in San Francisco. I see the Golden Gate, which I notice really is orange. I see Fishermen's Wharf, where a little girl whose front teeth are missing is holding a huge boiled crab in each of her hands. I see a gate at Chinatown, and a display of coolie hats.

"For you," Mr. Herrman reminds me.

I leave the machine and go to the phone. "What?" I ask my mother, who I know wants to fill me in about the triple coupon sale at the Fruit Fair. Last time, she was able to get a case of cream soda, a loaf of rye bread, two jars of spaghetti sauce, and some Efferdent for $2.59, once all the discounts were tripled. She went on about that one for about a week.

"It's Randy."

My eyes were on the parking lot, where a moving van with a *Mayflower* ship on the side of it had docked, its driver puzzling over a map. "Randy? Randy?" I asked, not knowing why I did so twice. "How are you?"

"I'm doing OK, I tried to call you at home. Did you get the messages?"

"No."

"I didn't think you would. I got your mother."

"Oh."

There is some silence. Then Randy asks would I like to meet him for a coffee—or a tea. He has news, he tells me, and he sounds pleased.

"I'm kind of busy," I say, because I feel I have to. I have not heard from him since the ring was stolen. If he and Roseanne have made up, I don't want to know about it.

"Maybe another time," I offer in a not-too-encouraging tone. I couldn't help it. Randy, for me, was some kind of history.

"You sure?"

"I am. Today's no good," I tell him, and I realize I have an excuse: "Good Friday. I'm fasting."

"Oh," says Randy, sounding a little confused. "I'll call another time."

I hang up.

Back in San Francisco, there is an estuary. Large yellow rubber boats and people in scuba gear are circling something large and black and alive that barely breaks the surface of the water. Crowds stand in the reeds on the shore, waving and calling words that can't be deciphered on a photograph. Some of the people hold signs: WE LOVE YOU. One has a big arrow and reads THIS WAY OUT. The thing in the water has a large, sad and unblinking eye that stares out at me. It is lost in the city and it is not asking for help. People have offered it, but whether or not it is accepted I don't know. The roll ends. I decide to go home early.

It is a warm late-winter day. Marek Cholewa, who has been old ever since I can remember, is in his front yard, one hand on his walker and the other working the pair of pruning shears with which he is clipping bits of growth from some kind of a bush. He has no free hands to wave at me, so he just motions his head in my direction when I honk my car horn at him.

I can see way from the Cholewa's house that we have company. The sedan at our curb is long and boxy and blue, and, I see when I drive closer to it, has the word POLICE across its trunk. I screech into the driveway and fly into the house. My parents stand in the living room with the Fluffernutter cop, who is holding something small in his hand and who is telling a story that is making them stare in amazement. "His fiancée—ex-fiancée now, I assume—came right into the station last night. Mad as heck. Figure how you'd feel if you knew your guy stole the engagement ring he gave you?"

"What happened?" I yell. My parents turn. My father has his usual neutral face on. My mother's has hardened to rock. "The ring," she growled. "It's been found."

The policeman extends his arm and opened his hand. From inside a twist-tied Baggie, looking no worse for the wear, the ring beams its light.

There it is. Back in my house. Back in my life.

"Funniest thing," the cop starts up again. "Guy who stole it told his girl he paid thousands for it. They were at a party in the trailer park last night and the guy throwing the party recognized the ring—I guess he came here once and saw it? Well, he said something about hearing on the scanner that it had been stolen. The girl questions her guy, who's by now a little drunk, and he says yeah so what if I didn't pay for it? I saved a lot of money. Well she's real mad about that, and when they go to leave, he's a lot more than half in the bag, so she drives, and she goes right to the police station and throws the ring on the counter, then leads an officer out to her car to arrest the guy. He comes into the station, still thinking he's at a party, and we ask him if he did it. He boasts how he did—how he just came in here—into your house—and took it off the coffee table. Piece of cake, he said."

I look at the ring again. It is a tough ring. It has been through a lot.

"Who is it?"

"His name is Ronald J. Wilkins," he says. "Know him?"

"No," I say after thinking a little bit. "Wilkins sounds familiar . . ." In my mind I see a little van idling outside the home of a sick person. "Does he have a brother Dick—Richard?"

"That's who bailed him out!" the cop exclaims, answering me dramatically, like we are on a game show. "Boy, that guy was flipping out, yelling at him about what this would do to their business. I guess he—Ronald—does dumb things all the time."

He moves the ring closer to me, offering it. "Go ahead, take it," he says. "Wilkins's trial will be coming up. Since he confessed, I guess we don't need this. If we need you, we'll call."

I still don't take the thing. Even touching the bag it's in means something. A new connection.

My mother can't stand it. She snatches the bag from him. "Thank you, officer," she says and shows him to the door. He puts on his cap and tips it at her.

My father goes to his chair. My mother rushes over to me, grabs my hand and plants the bag in my palm. I feel the point of the stone jab into my lifeline. "Tomorrow morning," she says angrily. "Bright and early. We get in the car and go to Springfield. We go to a jeweler like we should have in the first place. We get rid of the thing. Once and for all." Then she stalks off for the kitchen.

I look at the clock. It is 3:25 P.M. Somewhere in all the commotion, God had died. I needed to go and see him.

By the time I got there, the line reached to the back of the church. There were people in business suits and boys in baseball uniforms and nuns in habits, all taking time from their day, waiting for their chance to pay homage at a small replica of the cross, then pray at the grave. Halfway down the aisle everyone followed the custom of dropping to their knees and making their way like that to the cross, where they gave a kiss to each of Christ's wounds. A solemn-looking altar boy held out the cross, and used a piece of paper towel to rub off germs and lipstick marks between venerations.

I caught a wave of garlic and turned to see Mr. Lega. He had his white butcher's outfit on, and a green zip-front sweatshirt over that. He smiled at me and whispered, "I smell, right?"

"Well, a little," I lied.

"People want their homemade kielbasi for the holiday," he whispered louder, and I also could smell that he had already begun toasting Easter. "What can I do?"

I knew he would be starting to ask about my parents, and about my uncles and about my aunts, and he probably would do so all the way down the aisle and up to the cross. So I told Mr. Lega the line was too long for me and that I was just going to sit for a while. Some who had the time were kneeling here and there in the pews, staring at the unadorned altar, at its statues and crucifixes wrapped in purple fabric since Holy Thursday. I knelt to say a prayer. Good Friday always had been a sad day for me, even before Eddie. I prayed that day what I usually prayed on that day—that I was sorry Jesus had to die for people's sins. I thought that was terrible. What had he ever done to deserve that? Then I sat back in the seat and looked up. In front of me was the statue of Saint Mary.

She was up on her own altar, to the left of the main one, dressed all in flowing blue robes, spreading her arms out and over the racks of votive candles that glowed at her feet. I looked at her face. Well, to be honest, I gave it a little dirty look. I knew she is the mother of God, the spiritual mother of everybody, but she was the one who had told Eddie to leave me, and, being a good kid, he had obeyed her. I glared at her again. She looked back at me from beneath her blue hood. She was wearing a loving expression.

I unzipped my coat and took the bag with the ring from my front pants pocket, where it had been digging into my thigh. To my right, the procession of kneelers continued. One woman was reprimanding a kid who, while on his knees, had found a dime and was loudly announcing that.

I looked back up at the statue. I stared into its blue eyes as I had so many times since hearing the story about Uncle Francis. Was it in this same pew that Eddie had sat this day two years ago? Could it have been his eyesight? Could it just have been the light from this angle? Tell me, I screamed from inside my head, right at the statue. Did you really do it or was he seeing things? Did he use you as an excuse to leave? Why did you do that? Tell me!

Wanting to put her on the spot, I stared and stared and stared some more. But it wasn't working. She just stood there, looking like she loved me, pointing at the candles that represented so many more people begging something from her. Then I heard it: "To give you a new life."

I shot forward onto my knees, grabbing the seat in front of me to keep from collapsing. I had heard a miracle. With my own eyes. I swung around. To my right, Mr. Koss was saying his rosary, his eyes intent on Mary. He looked like he had heard nothing out of the ordinary. Beyond him, in the center aisle, Mr. Lega was kneeling his way to the crucifix, holding his stained apron out so he didn't run over it. There was a big gap between him and the next person in line. No one over there looked the least bit distracted. It hit me that this is how these things go. The kids who saw Mary in Fatima were the only ones to do so. I had heard of her appearing daily in Medjugore to some students, and they converse and pray with her and nobody else sees and hears what they see and hear. A handful of people in Portugal and in what used to be Yugoslavia, and Uncle Francis and Eddie and I. All in on this.

I was breathing heavily, like I had run a race. "To give you a new life." I said that quietly to myself. I had heard it before.

"Confusing, isn't it?"

My mouth dropped open and I looked up at the statue. But the voice had come from behind me, as, I realized, had the one before it. I turned around and saw Maria Dusza kneeling just to my left in the seat right behind me.

"Doesn't really make sense," she whispered. "Does it?"

"What? What are you talking about?"

"How you're supposed to take what you hear," she said,

fingering the crystal rosary that was hanging from her hands.

"What do you mean?" I didn't want to give anything away. I only knew her to be odd, and somebody I had hoped I wouldn't see again.

"The messages you get. How you can talk with somebody for a minute or for an hour or for a day and sometimes one little thing they say sticks in your mind. Or how somebody can only say a few words and that's all you think about. You're lucky. How many people get it spelled out for them?"

I looked to the aisle and saw the Fluffernutter cop drop to his knees.

"I see you have it," she said, and motioned with her folded hands to the ring I held in my right hand. In my religious experience, I had grabbed it so tight it had broken through the Baggie. It glowed and glinted light into her rosary beads, illuminating them up like they'd been plugged in. "I'll be home."

Maria Dusza crossed herself, genuflected and left. I looked up at Mary. She hadn't stopped staring at me.

# 22

◆◆◆

THE EDGES OF THE STREET ARE JAMMED WITH CARS. I PARK WAY at the corner and start walking, past the piano tuner's house, past the empty lot where he used to graze his palomino. Past the Romboletti's Colonial, with Teofil's homemade baseball backstop now marking one corner of his mother's vegetable garden, blue lake pole beans soon to be covering it. Past the rectory, which I long ago thought was the house in which the priest and his sons, the altar boys, all lived together. I have walked this path so many times I know where I am even though I keep my head down and count my steps: two per square of sidewalk, no stepping on the cracks, staring down at the toes of the same patent leather flats in which I took that first long walk to Eddie's house.

I see the sign outside church. I see that on the mass schedule someone has hand-lettered and stuck with electrical tape a cardboard insert that reads EASTER SUNDAY! 9 A.M. SERMON BY OUR OWN SEMINARIAN, EDWARD M. BALICKI. I am at the walk now, going up the stairs, pulling open the heavy door and letting myself in. I step into the vestibule, which is crowded with many men who like to say they go to church but who really don't go all the way in.

I heard the Gospel being read. The voice is familiar. Soft, like of somebody who has a cold. The voice is saying, with the same great feeling and emotion I used to hear whispered with warm breath into my ear, "This is the word of the Lord." The people respond, "Praise to you, Lord Jesus Christ." Then they take their seats.

I excuse myself through the men, through their woolen coats and elbows and folded Sunday papers, and then I am looking right down the aisle, at the lectern, at Eddie—Eddie of the pew on the right. Eddie of Friendly's. Eddie of the blanket at the lake. Eddie of my ride to heaven. Eddie of the tea and the vermicelli and the rust-colored couch. Eddie of the belief that I was something to behold. Eddie of my love at first sight. Eddie of my new life.

He is now Eddie of the long white robe cinched at the waist with a length of white cording. Eddie of Christ the Shepherd Seminary. Eddie of God. Eddie of no connection to me.

He is starting to preach and is trying to do so without looking at the paper he holds, but each time he looks up to make eye contact with the parishioners, he returns to what he has written only to scan desperately for his place.

"On this Easter day, we must remember," he reads, then looks up at his audience. His dark eyes sweep down the aisle, to the back of the church and happen to land right on my face, which, he probably thinks, is something he is hallucinating. He says nothing, only looks. I look back. The church is quiet, but my heartbeat is booming off the walls, rolling across the Stations of the Cross, bouncing up into the choir loft and disappearing down an organ pipe. A couple of people cough and a few shift in their pews. Some of them, I imagine, think this pause is for dramatic effect. But it grows too long for that. I look straight at Eddie and he looks straight at me.

For the year I had him in my life, I had dreamed many nights and days about walking slowly down the aisle toward him, looking lovingly right at him, holding at waist level a fresh bunch of flowers. Today I hold a small plastic Lega's bag at my waist. And for another reason entirely, I want to take that first step in his direction. Then another, and another. The only thing that would be missing, other than my Lace Memories and a promise from Eddie, would be my mother wailing in the front pew and my father gently holding my hand, as I like to think he would.

Eddie suddenly goes, "Ahem," just like he used to. Then he looks down at his paper and those eyes dart all over it.

"We must ask Almighty God for guidance . . . um . . . Jesus' goal was to save man. Uh, and woman," he looks up again and again. "We must ask God, for our goal . . . what is our true goal in life."

I don't wonder where I have heard this before. I get an image of a poor stub of a candle barely lighting a prayer to someone who comes through when no one else can.

A little kid to my left crawls beneath her pew, her bloomers disappearing behind her mother's legs. Past her, at the end of the row, I see the huge crucifix, actually large enough to nail someone to, and someone—a plaster Jesus—actually is hanging there, surrounded by a forest of Easter lilies. At the base of the cross is a padlocked wooden box. Written on its lid are the words FOR THE POOR.

I look to my right, to the front of me, to the left. Nothing is stopping me from my plan, which is to walk to the crucifix, to reach into the plastic bag and remove the clump of bills, to try to stop my hands from shaking as I jam them all into the small slot. Green, numbers, one, five, lots of zeroes I will cram through the opening, where they will unfold and pop to the bottom of the box. I don't know how long it will take me to empty the bag, but, when I am done, I will have laid $4,9991.75 at the feet of Jesus.

I will have returned to Eddie, to the poor, the estimated cost of his ring, minus the guaranteed ad. It is the right thing to do. It is the good thing to do. And I am good at that, at being good. It is what I told my mother I was going to do when she snapped up the window shade yesterday morning, dressed and ready to drive to the city, to a jeweler, to his cash register, to the end of what she long ago said had gone on too long. I thought she would like the idea, but she had snarled then that I was crazy. She had snarled the same thing when Maria Dusza, two hours later after I called her, delivered $5,000 to me in twenty-dollar bills and a couple of rolls of quarters, handing the money to me in the living room, where she slowly placed the ring onto her right hand and then shook mine and asked if she could say one more thing and then I wouldn't have to listen to her again. I told her to go ahead. "To be awake is to be alive," she said. She gave my hand a squeeze, then whispered: "Thoreau."

I closed the door, and pushed to make sure the catch clicked into place.

Eddie of the pulpit is shaking as he adjusts his microphone. "Finding our true goal," he goes on. "Not just what we think we should be doing, not what someone else tells us what we should be doing."

He stops here, on purpose this time. He looks out at me. I hold the bag tighter. Something in me suggests I take his advice. So I listen to what is in my head. The only thing I hear from within there is "What are you doing here?"

I don't have an answer, but I know I should leave. I look at Eddie, who is struggling to connect some sentences. Though he is stumbling, he will make it: as sure as his mother supposedly predicted on the day of his birth, he has gone back to God. I will leave him there.

I excuse myself through the men, their woolen coats,

their elbows, their papers. I bless myself at the holy water font, above which hangs a copy of the weekly bulletin. A name—two actually—catches my eye under the heading for upcoming marriages: Roseanne Malachowski—Roseanne Malachowski and Tadeusz "Buzz" Muraska.

I get into my car and drive in the direction it is pointed. I roll down a window. I turn on the radio. The "Polka Explosion" has been pre-empted by a live broadcast from church. "That was the sermon by our very own seminarian, Edward R. Balicki," Freddie Brozek whispers into the microphone like somebody who's covering a golf tournament. "His message was slow at first, but interesting, I guess, once you thought about it. I know I'll be thinking about it. And we'll all be praying for Seminarian Balicki. I'd say he has a wonderful future serving God."

I flip off the radio and enjoy the sound of nothing. Once in a while, the Lega's bag ruffles a little with the breeze coming through the window I've opened a little.

LOOK OUT! reads the sign decorated with a painting of a rabbit in an aviator's cap, tossing decorated eggs from a single-engine plane. LOW FLYING PLANES!

As if on cue, a red and white wing swoops over my windshield and I see the plane set down onto Soja's field. I drive closer and see another sign: SEE THE WORLD: EASTER PLANE RIDES $20.

Pulling off the road, I watch the plane roll to a stop. I see its propeller slow to where you can count the blades. I admire how the pilot hops lightly from the cockpit, which is open like in the old movies.

I never have flown. "You would have wings if you were supposed to fly," my mother likes to say, especially after seeing news footage of plane wreckage. "I'm staying here on the ground."

That fact, I think, is the reason I grab the Lega's bag and cut through the brush at the edge of the field and walk over to the pilot and a heavy, bearded man, both of whom are standing near the plane, looking at a clipboard.

"When can I go up?"

"How about now?" asks the man I assume to be the plane's owner. "Twenty bucks for a half hour—including a free photo of you up there, in the sky."

I stick my hand into the bag and take out one of the many twenties. The man can see all the money I have and he gives my face a quick look. I know he has to be wondering what I am all about. I like that.

"Sign here, please," the man says, extending the clipboard. "If anything happens to you, we're not liable—OK?"

I want to tell him I'm hoping for something to happen to me, but then think he might take that the wrong way.

He leads me over to the plane and dresses me in the same type of leather cap and goggles worn by the pilot, a slight blond woman who already is in the driver's seat. Then the man gives me his leather coat.

With a push from behind, I climb into the front compartment. Then I am strapped in. The red propeller, only a couple of feet in front of me, coughs and whirs.

We begin to move, bumping over the field, at a slow pace. A few cars have pulled along the field and the people are getting out of their cars. They yell, "Good luck!" "Safe trip!" I give a little wave and they do the same.

Without warning, the plane jolts forward at increased speed and the bumps are more frequent and harder. We head straight for the edge of the woods, then we are going into the tops of the trees, then into the blue, blue sky. I am off the ground. Without wings.

I dare to look down. I see the woods and the river below. I see the road I took to get here. It is exhilarating to be in the open, hit by the wind, and I grab onto a metal bar at my side to keep myself from flying out onto the clouds. We go higher and it becomes scarier to peek over the side to the all of a sudden small world, but I say to myself look down there. There, on those black roads and those brown squares of land and that purple river, is where it all happened, where it all came together, where it came back apart again, where it got to where it is now. As we circle Soja's field, I can see a bare outline of new grass coming up in an old and long skidmark that cuts very close to the riverbank. We go over another field and then a wide stretch of woods. With no leaves obstructing them, I can see the backs of deer. Then there are houses—only a few at first, then more and more, closer and closer together. There are people getting in and out of cars, kids playing ball in front yards. In their finery, families are posing for portraits on their front steps.

At my house, Rudy is easing from his truck. Rudyka leans into the bed and takes out containers of something she's cooked. My mother goes out to help her, and, I know, tells Rudyka that I have gone off. She is right.

We fly over the church and there is Eddie, standing outside in his white robe, shaking hands of people who stand in a long line. I see him shade his eyes and look at the plane. We pass right over him as if he was as small an issue in all this as he looks from here.

There are many cars at the drugstore, but nowhere else on Main Street. Except for two in front of Koziol the Cobbler, where a man and a woman are standing near the FOR SALE sign that has been stuck into the front lawn there since last November, when Bolac Koziol and the children suddenly up and went "to work out our grief" at an oceanfront condo in Boca Raton. I know the truck. Even from how many hundreds or thousands of feet up, I know the man: Randy. Looking at his dream. I watch as he and the woman walk over to her car, which, like the FOR SALE sign, has a gold key painted on the side. It occurs to me while I am up here how many little things go on all at the same time. Some big, some small, all connected, even though most seem not to be. From inside my helmet, I hear the muffled sound of the propeller. Something else is working its way through—Bolac reminding me that life is not easy. Anna's cousin reminding me it is something to be alive. And the voice of whoever it was who spoke to me on Good Friday.

There is something I do not hear, but wish I would: an excuse—my mother telling me that there is nothing but potatoes here. That I will have no life with her. But she does not tell me to go and forget about her. She does not put me onto a cart that takes me to a train that takes me to a boat that takes me somewhere better. I see I must do that myself.

That moment, with the wind in my face and feet way, far off the world, I see my new country in the form of not just meat, but fresh flowers. Magazines. Some prepared food you could bring home—good stuff, homemade. And all the things you'd need if you were going to make it yourself. A tin ceiling. A bench. A barrel of pickles. The kind of place I'd like to stop into. I think it would work.

The pilot swings around at the end of Main Street, which must be the fifteen-minute mark. I let go of the metal bar and take a pen from the leather coat. I write on the Lega's bag, in big letters, and tie it tightly.

We are lower on this pass and the earth below is larger and more vivid. We fly over Anna's house and I see her helping her mother tie a huge purple inflatable egg to a tree in the side yard.

At Eden Street, a young couple with a baby in a carrier and a little boy dragging a tricycle come out of the front door of the apartment house. In the back of the building, where Eddie had a small yard for his flower bed and bird-feeder, there is a wooden swing set and, on its side in the mud, a plastic playhouse. Down the street, the Creviers are two small figures in matching pink coats and cloches, arms linked as they walk to Saint Yvonne's.

As we approach Koziol the Cobbler, Randy is leaning

against his truck. Having no experience with this, I don't know if I've timed it right, but I pitch the bag from the plane. I see it fall steadily straight and land solidly on the sidewalk. And I see Randy look up, then walk to it. I see him pick it up and I know what is visible through the plastic. I watch him stretch the wrap to make out the words "You must do this." I see him look back up as we fly away. His mouth is hanging open.

I lean back. I feel very light and very pleased. We fly over the Common. I feel a tap on my shoulder and I turn to see the pilot aiming an instant camera at me. I go to protest, wanting instead to look down at two dogs tussling next to the jungle gym, and a circle of kids dressed in white blurring in a circle on the merry-go-round. But I change my mind and I turn around as much as the straps will allow and I give a face that says, yes, I can sit here on this metal chair many, many feet over the backyard where Harriet Bukowski is tossing some leavings onto her compost pile, and can say that something is happening.

I see the flash. "You think it will come out well?" I shout this to the pilot, over the parking lot of the Fruit Fair, over the engine and the wind and the nothing, even though I know I cannot be heard.

I see her blue scarf fly wildly. I see her blue eyes look right into me and down to my heart. I watch, and then and there, her hands leave the controls and angle out to each side, pointing down at the earth. She then gives one gentle nod. Then another, slowly and certainly.

I know we can see what we want to see, but I also know that is not what has happened here. So I nod back. Once. Definitely. For I find myself unable to do anything but believe.